DIRTY DOGS

DIRTY DOGS

Stephen Parkes

Matador
9 Priory Business Park,
Wistow Road, Kibworth Beauchamp,
Leicestershire. LE8 0RX
Tel: 0116 279 2299
Email: books@troubador.co.uk
Web: www.troubador.co.uk/matador
Twitter: @matadorbooks

ISBN 978 1800463 776

British Library Cataloguing in Publication Data.
A catalogue record for this book is available from the British Library.

Printed and bound in Great Britain by 4edge Limited
Typeset in 11pt Adobe Garamond Pro by Troubador Publishing Ltd, Leicester, UK

Matador is an imprint of Troubador Publishing Ltd

For animal lovers everywhere

1

"DIVE! DIVE! DIVE!" The alarm on Terry's phone jars him out of deep sleep. He can afford to hit the snooze button once; he turns towards Rebecca, sliding a heavy arm over the duvet across her. She is awake.

"Well done Pet, what time did you finally get back in?"

"About half two; she didn't come out for another twenty minutes after I got there. Wouldn't answer her bloody phone. I hate that place, it's such a shithole."

Easing his way gently out of bed, Terry pads naked down the landing with the urgency always required for an early morning pee. He shoots an apprehensive look out of the window.

There it is – shit on the fucking car *again*! A perfect contrast right in the middle of the sunroof of the Range Rover. Even from here you could tell it was shit, another carefully placed turd, third time this week. Fuckers. Nice start to the day!

Same thing yesterday. He had hosed it off, but the jet of water hitting it just served to spread it out, breaking it up into a spray of "shit confetti" flowing down the sides of his beautiful white car. He had hosed it down the street until it felt sufficiently far away to be able to breathe in without it invading your lungs.

Feels like driving around in a badly cleaned toilet, the scene of a midnight accident. NOT in a fifty-grand car! Tinted windows, go-faster stripes and a turd on the roof, what's the fucking point?!

Terry's chest tightens, someone would have to pay. He is pretty sure who it was, his daughter's arse-piece of a boyfriend. It had been going on ever since Terry told him what he really thought of him, the unpleasant little tosser, but he did need an element of proof before he actually taught him a lesson.

But not now, not today. He will quietly clean it off and get on, because today is special: he is going on holiday.

***

Terry looks down at Rebecca, his Rebecca. She has nodded off again, her mouth hanging slightly open, snoring gently. God, she is beautiful! It makes him tearful just looking at her. He has no idea why she ever let him near her; let alone occasionally allow him to jump all over her…he draws breath.

Time to dress and get going, got to drop little Chloe back to the flat (assuming Mercedes is actually conscious after last night), drop off the cat, drive to Heathrow, glass of champagne in the BA lounge, next stop Paris! Everything nicely planned.

Nothing to chance. Their fifteenth anniversary, fabulous hotel, a load of treatments – Becca loves her treatments. While it cost an arm and a leg it would surely be a wall-to-wall naughty-fest for four days. Almost definitely. Fantastic!

Showered and dressed, Terry skips, as much as a seventeen-stone man can skip, down the stairs. A shape at the foot of the stairs makes him pause; something slightly wrong, out of place.

It's Tiger – but Tiger doesn't look quite right, in fact, not right at all. He is an awkward, unnatural shape, and as Terry takes another step the truth dawns. Terry knows what a dead cat looks like; it looks like Tiger does now.

No…Please, no…No! It's our anniversary, a week of massive naughtiness, maybe even the elusive blowjob, and the fucking cat has to die on the way! She's going to cry all week now; it will all be going up in smoke!

Terry sits halfway down the stairs trying to think. Tiger lies slightly twisted on the floor below him.

He hears movement from the bedroom. "Cup of tea Pet?" he calls, gathering himself.

Terry dashes into the kitchen, flicks the kettle on, cupboard open, black bin bag torn off the roll, waits for the kettle noise to use as a shield, back into the hall, listens carefully. Glancing up to the landing, he bends, gently takes hold of Tiger's tail and slides him towards him.

Now at speed, less need for silence, into the bag; he's pretty stiff. Quick knot in the top, and out the back door onto the doorstep. Door shut. Kettle boiling. Step two complete.

Tea, biscuits and newspaper delivered, Terry slips back down the stairs. Tiger's food bowl lays untouched on the

3

kitchen floor, so he empties it quickly down the waste disposal.

No stone left unturned. He hates the smell of cat food, in fact he has never really liked Tiger, touchy little bastard. He puts on his coat, opens the back door, retrieves the Tiger-parcel and shoves it into the carry case left by the door, and heads for the car, Tiger safely onto the passenger seat…and safe.

Relax, breathe…

Back upstairs, Becca is just leaning over Chloe's cot cooing her goodbyes: "Say hello to Mummy for me." She is wearing Terry's favourite, a short, silky black nightie that he would usually stop to interfere with a little, but not this morning. "Don't forget to take your key Tel, Mercedes probably won't be awake to let you in."

She certainly won't be awake after the skin-full she had last night.

***

The last month had been pretty painful with Mercedes: first he had had to explain to her why the baby-listening device didn't work from the pub half a mile down the road, and ever since then he had become her personal chauffeur from anywhere she decided to pass out pissed.

He had started to dread the text messages she sent him – they always spelled bad news – and the fucking klaxon noise she had put on his phone, which he had no idea how to remove, made him physically jump every time it went off, and usually with good reason.

She had found him asleep in front of the TV watching *Das Boot* – and God only knows where she had downloaded it from, but now his alarm and half his texts came in with *Das Boot* sound effects. He knew how to use his new iPhone, but had no idea how to *use* it.

Last night had been typical. He and Becca had climbed into bed around eleven – and at twelve thirty the Klaxon had gone off. Jolted awake, Terry struggled to read:

Cn u gt me – at Bnka – M

Which loosely translated as Mercedes needing to be picked up from The Bunker, the grimmest nightclub in Peckham. It was indeed in an old World War II bunker, and it hadn't taken much work to turn it into a complete shithole.

He had sat outside in the Rangey for twenty minutes – being sized up by the locals. It was funny how his daughter managed to *send* texts from down there, but never actually answer the phone, claiming there was no signal. When she had eventually appeared, she could barely walk, feet stuffed into four-inch heels, skirt barely doing its job. Terry had driven all the way home with the seat belt warning beeping furiously because she was too pissed to even *try* to do it up.

***

Still plenty of time. Flight at 2pm; got to be at Heathrow a couple of hours early and it is now only eight forty-five. Terry picks up the carry cot, Chloe is freshly changed and peaceful.

"Won't be long Pet, will drop Chloe off first, then take Tiger on to Pussy's."

He pecks Becca on the cheek and heads down the stairs.

Pussy Galore, where Tiger was booked in for the week: the only decent cattery in Peckham. He would just have to think of the right tale to spin Becca when they got back about how poor Tiger had "died on the job", surrounded by his catty harem – not fool proof, but better than crying all the way to Paris!

He lets himself into the little ground-floor flat, sets Chloe's carry cot down on the sofa – Mercedes is snoring loudly next door. Terry steps into the bedroom; Mercedes has not moved from where he shovelled her onto the bed last night – and apart from some red-wine dribble on the pillow, everything was pretty much as he had left it, still in her party gear, which in total was materially smaller than the average nightie. She stirs and he leans over and kisses her cheek. He calls slowly and clearly:

"CHLOE IS NEXT DOOR, LOVE – SHE'S HAD HER BREAKFAST."

Terry is rewarded with a grunt as Mercedes rolls herself over in the bed and pulls at the covers. She IS quite a big girl; she always carried her puppy fat a little, but since the baby she had put on a bit more. Ridiculous; bloody eighteen and a mother already. No time for all that though. Terry bends down, gently touches her hair and heads out.

Driving aimlessly, Terry feels a trickle of perspiration making its way from his shaven head, round his ear, down his neck.

Where to go? Need a better plan than just driving around Peckham. Can hardly deliver Tiger to Pussy Galore now. They are likely to notice he's a bit dead.

The thought of asking them to freeze him for a few days passes through Terry's mind, but how do you explain that one? "Freeze him, please, thaw him out when we get back, and I will tell the missus you killed him."

6

Not a lot in it for Pussy's. Got to do something with him though. But what…what?

As Terry drives past Sainsbury's, a mixture of stress, adrenaline and testosterone, usually only found on the field of battle, courses through his veins.

He sees the bins: big metal charity bins.

Why not?

***

The Rangey is up close to the Oxfam bin: CLOTHES AND SHOES ONLY – PLEASE BAG GARMENTS. Well, Tiger certainly *is* "bagged" – a furtive look around, it is still only nine thirty and no one around. The car door is open, and in one swift movement the bag is quickly popped into the metal swing door and tipped back into the bin itself.

Job done!

***

Got away with it! Tel, you are a fucking genius mate! Cool under pressure.

Terry drives carefully down Peckham High Street and slowly the elation subsides, the adrenaline departs, and in its place a gentle wave of nausea.

***

Pulling into the lay-by, engine running, he grips the wheel and rocks slowly back and forth.

Why?! Why had it seemed a good thing to throw Tiger into the fucking Oxfam bin? It was *such* a bad idea.

A world of awful possibilities course through Terry's now acute mind and he begins to sweat again. A dawning thought worming its way into his consciousness: Tiger has an address tag round his neck. With his address on it. Now Mr Oxfam is about to get a decomposing cat in his next delivery with Tiger's and, more importantly, Becca's address round his neck! Shit! Shit, shit, shit!

***

The car engine rumbles gently beside the Oxfam bin; still no one around. Terry sits and looks at the bright-green bin, its drum-style entrance grinning at him, chest height, like a huge open mouth. The mechanism was one-way. Contents into the drum, tip the drum backwards and the contents fall inside; impossible to get anything *out*!

It had not made much noise when Tiger dropped in, so it must be fairly full. Looking around, Terry finds a plastic crate to stand on. Tipping the drum halfway back, squeezing his arm over the top of the drum and feeling around inside…

Plastic against fingertips, but out of reach, barely brushing. Up onto tiptoes, tight shirt-buttons straining, finger just catching on a bag – *must be Tiger* – straining, reaching…

Got it!

As Terry's fingers close around the bag, the crate he is balancing on tips over, and as he drops, the mouth of the bin closes, trapping his arm against the top of the metal container, leaving him dangling in mid-air, his feet scrabbling just four inches above the ground. He roars in pain and feels his shoulder tear; in panic his other hand flaps for something to hold onto, finding nothing. The crate is just a few inches out of reach as he stretches out his legs to reach it, the pain in his arm taking his breath away, his shoe just catching the edge. Just another inch…fuck…*fuck*…just another inch.

2

BECCA OPENS THE door. Terry has been fiddling with the key in the lock for nearly a minute. There he is, on the doorstep: white as a sheet, with a horrible, horrible leer etched into his face, his teeth fixed in a permanent grin. He is straining as if terminally constipated, or worse – but his arm!

"Terry! What happened…? My God Terry!"

He stumbles through the door, arm in a makeshift bin-bag sling. The sleeve of his coat is in shreds, there is dark baked-on blood on his sleeve and hand. He is panting for breath, saturated, sweating, the buttons of his white shirt popped open, shivering uncontrollably.

Through the door and into the hallway, Terry manages to reach the stairs and sits down, his healthy left arm holding his mangled right. He tries to say something: "Becca" comes out as if he has been sucking on a helium balloon. He waits, as Becca stares at him, and his breathing slows a little and he manages to speak.

"Hit by a pussy."

Becca just looks at him, aghast.

"No…hit by a bike – at Pussy's."

Becca moves him into the kitchen, sits him on a stool and unravels the tattered, knotted bin bag from his arm. He manages to explain, eventually, that he was hit by a motorbike as he was coming out of Pussy's after dropping Tiger off. He is obviously in shock; Terry's attempt at normality is just to keep grinning, teeth clamped together, lips apart.

"Just drove off – bastard!"

He can barely make a sound, but keeps grinning, drawing back his lips over his teeth now in an attempt to smile. Becca starts to cry.

***

Finally, driving to the airport, Becca behind the wheel, Terry beside her, quietly trying to control his breathing, air whistling gently with each breath through his teeth.

"We should have gone to the hospital. It's SO stupid! You think you can just push a dislocated shoulder back into the socket and forget it ever happened? I KNOW it is something to do with the shit on our car. You've done something stupid; I know you have! You don't look like you've been fighting again, but I KNOW it's the shit business Terry! You are SO bloody stubborn!"

Becca takes a small bump in the road at speed, just a gentle bounce, but Terry cannot suppress an agonised groan.

***

11

Heaving the bags out of the back of the Range Rover, Becca wrestles them onto the trolley.

"It's alright Lamb, I can manage," she puffs.

Terry stands leaning against the car. There is a chill in the Heathrow air, but he is sweating, jaw fixed, brow furrowed. There is a sweat-ring around one armpit of his shiny charcoal "going away" suit. The bin-bag sling has been replaced by white crepe bandage tied in a knot at the back of his neck.

It's going to be fine, just fine – oh fuck, it hurts – just hold on, Tel, it will be fine.

Becca checks them both in. The BA stewardess examines the Executive Club Gold card that Terry had paid a fortune for, as a bit of "show" from a bloke at work; same sort of bling as the Range Rover. Holding their passports, sizing up each of them in turn, she pauses, looking at Terry.

"Are you all right sir, can we assist you at all?"

"Himekay," he tries in a squeak, then deeper, slower, "No, I am OK…thank you."

The stewardess stares at Terry, glances at Becca and her face says: *He is clearly NOT OK!*

"Sir, you have a seat in the emergency exit row, so you would need to be able to open the door in case of an emergency, and I am not sure you could do that with your arm. I think we will have to find you alternative seating, and the flight is very full, and you *are* quite late sir."

***

Terry can smell his own perspiration. The worst bit was when Becca had to take his shoes and belt off for him at security, then put them back on him the other side of the

X-ray machine. It had taken forever. Why had he worn the bloody tight Prada slip-ons? He had kept trying to bend down, but couldn't make it, Becca sticking her finger in them, pulling the heel back, but he just couldn't squeeze his foot into them.

"Push now Lamb."

But every time he did, she just pulled her finger out! Now Terry is gingerly waddling towards the "B Gates" sign, with the heels of his Pradas folded down like a pair of badly fitting wooden slippers.

"Try to hurry Lamb."

He is trying to walk on tiptoe to stop the Prada red leather tag digging into the fleshy underside of his heels. It was all right when he started, but they have been walking for bloody miles. The pain in his shoulder is throbbing to his heartbeat.

Finally in the departure lounge, gate B 48 – the longest walk available in Terminal 2. Becca has managed to pull one of the Pradas on when they call for boarding.

"Passengers with young children, Club Europe and Executive Club Gold and Silver may board now."

Terry is quickly up, one Prada on properly, the other with his foot still painfully balanced on the flattened back of the shoe – limping slightly on tiptoe, wiping the sweat from his brow with a now-saturated handkerchief. He eases his way forward like a wounded war hero, pushing in front of a couple with two young children, and finally along the gang-walk down to the plane.

Into their seats, either side of the aisle.

Bloody anniversary and they still couldn't sit us together – fucking BA, fucking Gold Card. They can all just fuck off.

Terry eases down into his seat, and finally kicks off his shoes – *bloody ridiculous things* – and shuts his eyes.

"Excuse me, buddy?"

Terry's eyes jerk open. 'Super-Size Me' Homer Simpson is standing in the aisle beside him, waiting to get into his seat by the window. Terry tries to stand, but the seat in front is too close for him to achieve the angle required to get up without using his arms. He tries unsuccessfully to push himself up with one arm, so starts slowly rocking back and forth attempting to get to his feet. As he reaches escape velocity, his head just bumps into the seat in front. Terry performs this rocking-puppet act for several seconds; the aisle is backed up now with anxious passengers all eager to seize their share of the overhead lockers. Super-Size looks terrified that he is going to have to sit beside this mentally ill Brit for the entire journey. Terry finally manages to lurch out of his seat, into the aisle, by wrapping his good arm round the headrest in front, painfully trapping the hair of the shrieking female passenger in the seat. The pain in his arm is excruciating. Super-Size eases his way across to his seat like a whale out of water as Terry profusely apologises to the hair-victim.

"Thanks, buddy."

Terry lowers himself back into his seat. As the chain of fretting passengers scavenging for seats surges past, a wave of nausea hits him.

Oh God – Oh GOD! – going to be sick, must make it to the bathroom...

Much faster now he has mastered the getting up technique, he repeats the movement in a blind panic and stumbles into the aisle, oblivious to the cries of the woman in front as he whacks the side of her head as he drags himself upright. The bathroom is only four rows ahead, but the aisle is full of bodies, backpacks, wheelie bags. Terry thrusts his way forward, shoulder bumping against people, seat-backs, rucksacks – "Owtheway! OWTHEWAY!" Each touch on his shoulder shoots blinding pain into his head. Terry finally reaches the bathroom, shoves the door open, swallowing hard to keep from throwing up. He tries to pull the door shut, but then there is no room to kneel in front of the toilet pan. Pre-vomit saliva floods his mouth as he shoves the door back open; falls to his knees, head in the toilet pan, feet sticking back out of the open door, retching, heaving, and he hurls everything he has ever eaten in his life into the metal pan. As his body spasms, the white-hot pain in his shoulder finally overwhelms him and Terry slumps unconscious into the toilet, his good shoulder wedged down one side, his cheek jammed against the seat. Passengers and stewardesses jostle for position to watch, horrified, through the toilet door.

"Is there a doctor on board?"

3

THE NURSES IN *the hospital are absolute crackers…*

Terry sits up in bed, the painkillers making him feel pretty good about life. He has no memory of arriving. By the time he wakes, he has been undressed, cleaned up, put in a decent sling and filled with morphine. There is Becca, sitting beside him in the chair; she looks fabulous, like she was dressed up to go on holiday.

As memory slowly returns, Terry is loosely aware that he is not where he is meant to be, but the morphine takes the edge off the whole "big old thing" and Terry just settles back on his pillow and smiles.

The nurses are absolute crackers – and Becca looks fantastic.
Sleep comes again.

***

"So how *did* they get me out of the toilet?" Terry asks, as Becca drives.

"It was the big American sitting beside you who actually lifted you out, and the stewardesses were brilliant, said they had seen it all before."

Terry shifts in his seat, not quite the fairy-tale anniversary "shag-fest" he had been hoping for, but he was still alive, which had been in doubt for a while, and they should get the money back on insurance. Still time for an alternative "romantic interlude" once his arm had recovered a bit. Dislocation and tendon damage they said, probably three months till good as new. The black eye and bruised cheek didn't look so good where his face had wedged beside the toilet pan, but Terry knew he would be able to spin a great streetfighter's yarn about that one.

"Shall we pick up Tiger? Or would you rather just get home Lamb?"

Tiger! Fucking Tiger! How could I have forgotten...?

"I think we should just get ourselves home; Tiger loves it at Pussy's – they treat him like a king – and I'm starting to feel a bit groggy Pet."

Terry feels the butterflies returning to his stomach. Tiger...he will need to think very hard about Tiger. It was a miracle he had managed to keep hold of the Tigerbag. It had been a nightmare untying it, and managing to get Tiger's ID tag off him with only one arm working was now only a hazy memory, and it hadn't done much for Tiger's looks by the end of it. Finally, Tiger was neatly back in the bag, minus his identification, and nestled into the "General Waste" bin outside Tesco's. The world had gone bloody mad with all this recycling stuff; he'd probably end up in Belmarsh for not composting the fucking cat.

"I'll pick Tiger up tomorrow Becca."

Terry is sitting down in his favourite chair in front of the TV, a repeat of last night's *Match of the Day*, feet up on a stool and a nice cup of tea on the side table. Becca has gone into protection mode, looking after him. Paris would have been brilliant, but maybe she might wear some of that new lingerie anyway, once he could actually move without wincing. Maybe even give him a bit of a treat, with his crocked arm! He knew Becca quite liked to be in control sometimes.

Becca clatters around the kitchen, preparing lunch. Terry opens the post while Crystal Palace lose to Brighton.

His hand works perfectly well as long as his arm is still. The usual junk mail, and the last one – *always leave the dodgy-looking one till last* – from Her Majesty. Probably a new tax code or some bollocks; always in those cheap, nasty brown envelopes, so you would know it was bad news. He had never opened one without a slight sense of butterflies in the tummy before reading about some other imaginative ways the fucking government, didn't matter what flavour, was going to pick his pocket yet again.

It was unusual to receive an actual letter from the taxman, they usually just had numbers and the words *Remit Now* somewhere towards the end – but this one was actually quite long, and the words *Criminal Offence* and his mother's name seemed to stand out from the page. The second page was more normal, but the total number, £149,543.18, and the paying-in slip indicated that they must have made some sort of mistake.

It had been nearly two years since his mother, Lilian, had died, and the Will had been read and monies distributed.

Terry had not been an executor, his brother Jonny had taken care of all that, and the money had been very handy indeed – in fact he and Becca were living in it. Their four-hundred grand inheritance, getting them out of Peckham and into a nice almost-detached house in Denmark Hill, just down the road really, but not Peckham. Terry read the letter; then read it again, and then again, just in case it had changed since the first or second readings…and it had not.

***

Terry sits patiently in the car, on a double-yellow on Peckham High Street, across the road from the police station. It is a damp, miserable Sunday morning, a week after reading the taxman's letter.

Jonny comes down the steps, long black leather trench coat, hands thrust deep into the pockets, he looks furtive, not wanting to be seen, like a nervous rodent. Jonny has always looked a bit "ratty", and now especially so. He looks across the road to the car, crosses, looks around as if under surveillance, and climbs up into the Range Rover.

"Thanks Tel, they're not being terribly understanding about it…"

Terry starts the engine, moves off, his shoulder making him wince as the Range Rover goes over a small pothole. He probably shouldn't be driving with one hand, but the indicator is right by the steering wheel where his good hand rests. As long as he doesn't need the wipers he will be fine; plenty of painkillers and a quick vodka and he felt pretty safe.

Jonny sits beside him, his hands worrying at each other like a pair of impatient ferrets.

"How did they find out Tel?"

"What do you mean 'HOW DID THEY FIND OUT?!' She's fucking dead. It wasn't a secret, except to the bank, and the taxman! It might even have something to do with the bloody eulogy you put in the *Daily Mail*, JonJon! It might have something to do with hundreds of thousands turning up in our bloody bank accounts unannounced! I don't know how they found out, and it doesn't fucking matter – the fact is, THEY DID!"

They drove along in silence for a minute, Peckham's early morning detritus passing damply by the window, soggy rubbish strewn liberally across pavement and road; Saturday evening was always a lively, messy affair here.

"I just can't believe it JonJon. What do you mean 'Fuck probate'? You can't just fucking ignore it and pass out the money, Jonny! Bruv! You never told anyone, not the bank, not the taxman; fucking no one, apart from the funeral director, that she was dead?! You have to apply for probate – the taxman tells you what you owe, you pay the tax and then hand the rest out. Instead you told bloody no one, completely ignored the forms for the taxman, and you didn't fucking tell US – your family?"

"DON'T JUST KEEP SAYING FUCKING SORRY! Sorry isn't going to pay the bill *or* keep you out of fucking Wandsworth!"

Terry's hand clutches the wheel tighter, narrow rivulets of sweat work their way down the sides of his head, forming a small tributary around his ears and shaven sideburns, before soaking into his collar. He is shaking – part anger, part fear, part pain from his shoulder. The veins standing out from his temples, the pink and the blue.

"It's not going to come to that Tel, it's all just overblown. I thought if we just swerved it a little we wouldn't have to pay the tax we would get stuffed for if we filled it all in properly – I thought no one would care! We can just tell them we were slow in applying for probate, and that we're sorry."

"WE are going to tell them nothing JonJon. You might be my little brother, but YOU are going to tell them exactly what you did, you fucking dickhead! How are you going to convince them you are sorry when you just wrote us all cheques emptying Mum's bank account while her pension is still being paid into it two years later Jonny. The bank doesn't know she is bloody dead even now?!"

Terry can feel an asthmatic tightening of his chest as his anger starts to form a tangible cloud in the bubble of space they occupy in the car. He could kill him; fucking kill him, the little shit.

"I can do a runner if it gets too heavy Tel…"

Too much. Too fucking much!

Terry swerves the Rangey over to the bus stop outside McDonald's, bumps at an angle as one front wheel goes up the kerb, wincing, foot on brake. He grabs Jonny with his good left hand: shirt, throat and tufts of chest hair, jamming him against the window and screams, out of control, into Jonny's face.

"DO A RUNNER! DO A FUCKING RUNNER! YOU WILL NOT BE DOING A RUNNER YOU MORON – YOU WILL STAY AND FUCKING MAN UP!"

Terry is facing Jonny full on now, rage filling him as he squeezes the handful of brother ever tighter. His foot comes up off the brake pedal, the car, still in *Drive*, moves gently forwards at an angle onto the pavement and into the metal bin, already overflowing with McDonald's empties, like a giant walrus mounting a timid female seal – and comes to a halt.

***

They had all sat there in Jonny's front room. Terry and his sister, Tasmin, all dressed up in Sunday best, suited and booted, scrubbed up for Mum; their other halves and the older kids seated around the kitchen table; Jonny, in his best, and probably only, suit standing in front of them, thinning black hair slicked back carefully over his white damp pate, announcing what Mum had left everyone. There were two years between each of them, Terry the eldest, then Tasmin, and finally Jonny, proving the rule about "free spirit" third children. JonJon took a deep breath, cleared his throat unpleasantly, and started to talk in his best Michael Caine voice, pausing frequently for effect to emphasise the gravity of his message.

It was a very decent sum, she had never spent anything, and since dad died the ISAs and investments had just gently rolled up: five hundred grand, and with the house they had bought off the council she was a bloody millionaire, and he and Tas never even knew! Jonny had taken over mum's finances, so Terry had never really needed to be involved at all. She had given Jonny power of attorney years ago. Mum had never liked dealing with finances. After she died it had all gone very smoothly, with Jonny handling all the paperwork and formalities; or, more to the point, totally ignoring the paperwork and formalities. No wonder it hadn't taken long.

And now they were fucked. *Or more precisely, I am fucked.*

He had taken his share, a little more than his siblings as he had produced an "heir", though he found it hard to think of Mercedes as an "heiress", nearly four-hundred grand. After a little upgrade of the car, he had ploughed it all into a new house; really stretched the mortgage to the hilt as well. The only problem was that it shouldn't have been four hundred, he should have paid about a hundred and twenty grand in inheritance tax, and now he was sitting on a letter from the taxman demanding a hundred and fifty grand – not just the tax itself, but a bunch of penalty fines *and* interest too!

Bloody taxman, charges you 7% interest on what you owe him when you can't get 1% on your savings! Who did they think they were? Worse than NatFuckingWest!

All that was assuming Jonny managed to convince the coppers that he had done this all himself, which was true of course, and that Terry and Tasmin had no idea what was going on.

They would have to sell the house, couldn't get any more on the mortgage. It was already too much to afford, and work hadn't been going so brilliantly lately. What could he possibly tell Becca? He could try, "Sorry Becca, your cat's dead, I fucked up the holiday when I threw it in a bin. Now we have to sell the house because my brother is a half-wit criminal."

All likely to go down pretty well I should think...

***

Eventually, Terry forces himself to breathe, rage subsiding, and slowly relaxes his grip on Jonny in the car and becomes

23

aware of his surroundings. He has attracted quite an audience as he carefully reverses the car, the metal grinding and scraping beneath him. Terry winces as he hears his number plate crunching as he finally pulls free of the McDonald's bin.

Back in the road, Terry stares out of the window at the dozen or so faces peering at the pimped-up Range Rover. Deliberately opening the blacked-out passenger-side window, Terry leans across Jonny:

"WHY DON'T YOU ALL JUST FUCK OFF AND DO SOMETHING USEFUL?"

He pulls away from the kerb and heads for home.

Why had Jonny done it? How could anyone think they would get away with something that obvious? He just said it had seemed a good idea at the time.

***

When mum had become ill, he moved her into the rented flat in the old-folk community, helped her sell the house, and then Jonny had started converting the various investments, endowment policies, ISAs, shares, premium bonds, everything, into cash parked in National Savings deposit accounts, all of which he had access to.

Needless to say, the taxman wasn't told about any of this at all. After she died, Jonny had just taken the doctor's certificate to the funeral director, and that was it!

Now Jonny could end up doing time, and the rest of them had to find a boat-load of cash. It made telling Becca about poor Tiger, and how he had "died on the job" at the local cattery, seem like a doddle.

4

"**HE'S HAD HIS** willy cut off, Tel! How could he 'die on the job'? What stupid sort of job was that then?"

"Becca, he'd just been 'snipped', not had his dick cut off. It just means he can't have baby pussycats, it's like a vasectomy. In fact, it IS a vasectomy. That's why they thought it was safe for him to play with the girls there, they didn't know it would be too much for him!"

"So, less than twenty-four hours after you drop him there, the staff at Pussy's, a respectable animal-boarding service, decide it would be a good idea to let OUR CAT loose on all the ladies and he dies trying to shag them all. Then YOU get run over by a motorbike outside as you leave. I don't think so Terry, I don't bloody think so!"

Finally, Terry had been forced to tell the truth, or at least a different truth: that he had been run over on the way *in* to Pussy's, carrying Tiger in his carry case. Tiger had not survived, but Terry had *so* wanted Becca to have a wonderful holiday he had not told her. Pussy's had very kindly agreed to dispose of Tiger, and he was *so* sorry to have deceived Becca – it had been wrong, and he deeply regretted it. He had loved Tiger…good old Tiger.

There were tears and shouting, but eventually Becca had consoled him; poor lamb.

"Can we at least have his ashes Terry?"

"Of course Becca, of course we can."

***

Terry knocks on the door of Tasmin's little terraced house. The cracked, multi-coloured crazy paving between the low wall and the front door was almost obscured by overflowing black bin bags, a large pile of builders' rubbish and scattered parts of rusting bike frames that would clearly never terrorise motorists or pedestrians again.

Terry had been dreading telling Tas about the taxman. He had texted to check if she had received the same letter, but she clearly had no idea what he was talking about. Her text back to him was full of the usual incomprehensible bollocks, but nothing to indicate she had a clue what was heading her way!

In fact, Terry really just dreaded having to communicate with his sister at all, she was just so fucking weird, and SO fucking irritating. Someone had to do it though, and he didn't trust Jonny to actually tell her the truth. So here he was.

Tasmin answered the door, her long, greying, straggly mop of hair, framing what could have been a pretty face except for the boxer's nose, a gift from the family DNA shop that all the siblings shared. She was wearing her best "serene smile" to show Terry he was welcome in her sanctuary, stepping back from the door and wordlessly performing an elaborate arm-waving gesture to beckon him in.

"Hello Sis." Terry moved to kiss her on the cheek, and Tas turned her head so far to the side as she air-kissed nothing in particular, that Terry just got a faceful of hair and his sister's ear. He dutifully kissed the ear, assuming ear-kissing was the latest "New Age" ritual his sister had adopted. He followed her down the hallway, stepping over the pieces of dirty, screwed-up bedding that were littering the hall floor. He just hated it here.

Karma was sitting at the flap-down kitchen table, peeling a gnarled brown root over a water-filled saucepan with a small knife. How could you take someone seriously when they had a name that was so obviously made up – *Karma Al Hambra*? She had found him on a package holiday to Tunisia, one of the swimming pool attendants. She had her wicked way with him for a week and married him in a tiny back-street Catholic Church in Tunis. She had him baptised and married on the same day after slipping the local priest $100. Tunisia wasn't so big on Christianity, and nor was Tas, but it was the piece of paper that mattered!

She managed to bring him through customs, waving her marriage certificate around like a fucking flag – and now he served as her ever-ready willy-machine.

Just horrible, fucking horrible.

Karma flashes him a perfect, white-toothed, grin and bows his head down almost into the saucepan. Karma was wearing boxer shorts and a T-shirt, sitting with his legs wide apart, a dark tangle just visible through the gape of his fly-buttons.

I want to be anywhere else, fucking anywhere else.

Terry nods and smiles at his brother-in-law. Waste of time talking to him, he still didn't speak or understand anything other than the few words Tasmin had taught him in the six months he had been here, and most of those were expletives shrieked as she rode him round the house.

You couldn't move in the place for fear of sitting, leaning or stepping on something entirely unsavoury. All horribly cheap "alternative" paraphernalia.

About five years ago, Tas had decided she had a "gift" after a stoned session with a mate's Ouija board, and ever since she had been training with almost demented intensity to become a medium. She did tarot readings, palm readings and pretended with orgasmic frenzy to be in contact with the "Other Side". Even when her "customer" had only come to have an ego stroked with *"You have a long life line"*, he would also get *"You will have a long and active sex life."* Tasmin managed to bring sex into just about everything. The walls were plastered with posters of séances, demons, angels, the most awful masks, and pieces of fabric and hair that had clearly been recently glued together in some awful parody of pagan art. Well-worn magazines littered the floor from such august bodies as the Spiritualist Association of Great Britain, The British Psychic and Medium Association and the UK Association of Psychics.

Where did all these fucking nutters come from? We can't have imported all of it from the Americans…surely?

"Tea Terry. I'm making tea." More of a statement than a question.

"Lovely."

Terry sits gingerly on a tatty, overstuffed sofa, avoiding

what appeared to be a scabby, hairy, badly skinned goat draped across the back of the seat like a throw. He perches on the edge, only for the seat to be so soft he is immediately sucked deep into the sofa's clutches. He would need to be pulled out again. The hairs from the "goat throw" nestling against his cheek, the deep "meaty" smell of it assaulting his nostrils.

Terry starts to feel sick.

"Karma is teaching me Muslim, Terry. I can't tell you the peace it's given me. The connection. It's truly extraordinary what Allah has to offer us. It's helping SO much with the Other Side. I'm just coming on in leaps and bounds. I'm going to convert… to become a Sunny Muslim. I know that's why you are here, but you are just wasting your time. Karma and me, we have something special, and that special something is Allah: when we come together, we can feel God there in the room with us Terry. Everyone coming…"

Tasmin looks beatifically upwards, her face illuminated by the grubby round paper lampshade suspended from the ceiling.

Terry doesn't know much about Islam, but he is pretty sure it doesn't have that much to do with sex; and he is equally sure that getting in touch with the Other Side via a Ouija board wasn't in the Koran, but he needs to stick to his mission.

"Actually Tas, that wasn't really what I was here for. I am SO pleased you and Karma are making a go of it, and I am sure you will be very—"

Tas cuts across him. "He's a HEALER Tel. Would you believe it, a healer! It's so exciting; he lays his hands on me everywhere…and it just tingles! A healer! We are such a good partnership Tel. And the bedroom Terry, I just can't tell you—"

"No Sis – don't tell me about the bedroom, not now Sis, because I DO have to talk to you about a little problem we have. Something Jonny seems to have done wrong…"

Terry is distracted by a noise from the kitchen. He looks over to see Karma crooning over the saucepan as he slices small pieces off the now-peeled vegetable: it is yellow and slightly bendy, clearly not something grown in a field in Essex. As he and Tasmin stop talking, the crooning seems to louden and intensify, Karma oblivious to his audience.

"What the fuck's he doing Tas?"

"He's blessing it Tel…or healing it…it's just fantastic isn't it?"

Terry realises he needs to deliver the news fast and get out of there – he is actually slightly scared of his completely loopy sister; she has not a chance in the world of reaching the "Other Side", but she tries. She tries with a fervour that Terry has only seen on the Millwall terraces and a little something in the back of his mind is hoping very hard that she never "breaks through". Millwall hooligans meeting the spirit-world didn't sound like a healthy combination.

She is SO off her trolley, and now we have shit-for-brains healing bloody vegetables for fuck's sake!

Terry preferred to steer well clear of Tasmin's house, everything about it gave him a sense of unease the second he reached the door. You didn't want to touch anything, sit on anything, and a constant need to look up in case something unpleasant dropped on you from above.

As succinctly as he can, Terry explains the problem with the taxman, what Jonny had done, and his sister just smiles and simpers through it all.

"Don't worry Terry – I haven't spent mine anyway, at

least not much, just what Karma needs to live. I've still got the rest because mum hasn't told me what to do with it. I ask her almost every day, and *now* I know why she hasn't answered me Terry! She has been taking care of me; and *now* she has spoken."

Terry is about to ask her what she has actually done with the money when Tasmin rises gently up from the sofa, leans her head back and begins to sing the chorus of 'Karma Chameleon' in a most unnerving falsetto. It is time to go.

***

Outside, Terry dusts himself down for anything that might have stuck to him from the sofa. Even the tea had tasted really strange, but Tas destroying one of his beloved Culture Club favourites was the last straw – why had she started singing anything anyway? She was just beyond bonkers. He has done the job though and now it is time for a stiff drink.

5

A WEEK LATER, life has calmed down a little. The new cat, Scooter, named after the manner in which Tiger had met his extraordinary death, is being litter trained as if he were a small human: cooing and gentle cajoling as he pees his way around the house. Terry knew they should have got a proper cat, but they did such a great selling job on their "special needs" refugee pets down at the pet sanctuary it was impossible to say no.

"He's a little traumatised – but he'll settle down if you show him love."

Becca had lapped it up and now the scraggy little shit was dragging his arse in one long slow-motion wipe across the carpet at every opportunity, but Becca seemed happy.

Terry flops down on the sofa – the journey back from the City had been pure pleasure as always, standing up all the way, wedged up against a chap in his running gear, sweating profusely. He had clearly been running away from someone unsuccessfully trying to spray him with deodorant. You can't really say anything, can you? Just stand there, attempting to use the *Evening Standard* as some sort of shield!

Scooter inches his way past Terry, dragging his little arsehole along the cream shag-pile carpet as if trying to dislodge a flea; his hind legs stretching forward, with front legs doing all the dragging.

He doesn't seem to actually leave a trail of anything, probably just some imaginary cat clinker.

Terry sighs and gets up, wearily pouring himself a too-large whisky, slumping back into the sofa as Scooter eventually reaches the wall and also sinks back, exhausted, in a mirror image of his new master, unsure what to do now he has reached the end of the runway.

***

"You *said* you would get Tiger's ashes Terry; it seems wrong to just start to transfer our love to Scooter without a proper goodbye to Tiger. What did they do with his body? It's not right that he is just 'gone' – just like that. We should have a little service or something, he was part of this family for seven years. They *must* have the ashes, surely, and you would have thought they would offer them to us."

Terry ponders this for a while, calculating whether to wait for Becca to develop her train of thought, and potentially watch it form into something either impossible to deliver, or worse, actually lead to the truth – *or* he could step in with some form of diversionary plan. He isn't entirely sure about transferring "love" to Scooter, in fact he definitely hadn't "loved" Tiger really, and finds Scooter positively distasteful, with all that arse business.

"I think they sent me an email about it at work Becca. Let me check it tomorrow when I'm in the office and I will give them a call."

"Sonia had her horse turned into a necklace, you know, the one that they had to have put down when it broke its leg."

This was news to Terry. He remembered *big* Sonia and that poor fucking horse, but that sounded like a bit of a stretch that she could get it round her neck.

"I don't think you can turn a horse into a necklace Becca, maybe they plaited some hairs into one or something?"

"No…it was its DNA – you know its "life juice", that thing they discovered about everything. You take a bit of whatever pet you want to make a necklace out of, they get out its DNA and put it into a pendant thing, hanging from a chain – like they did in *Jurassic Park*."

This *really* could get out of hand now. He had heard Sonia's poor husband, Alan, talking down the pub about his wife walking around with a vial of horse piss round her neck, and this must be what he was talking about, but how would you know whether it was piss or DNA in some piss-coloured liquid? And what did DNA look like anyway? Alan had said he thought all the horse's legs had broken simultaneously under his wife's weight, which *was* an unkind thing to say, but they were all struggling to picture how she could actually get on the poor thing's back anyway without tipping it over.

"Could we get Tiger's DNA out of the ashes do you think?"

"No Becca, I'm pretty sure it has to be alive, or like a fluid or something. I'll just arrange to get his ashes tomorrow."

"I don't think that's right, you know; the dinosaur couldn't have been alive could it? And they still managed to grow another one from the DNA. We could try mixing the ashes with water to see if we get any DNA out of it – *or* we could see if he left any hairs on his cushion and see if they have any DNA."

Eventually Terry managed to divert the plan away from the awful DNA idea, telling Becca that Alan genuinely believed his wife had been duped by the company, *Forever Together*, and that the stuff in the little test tube round her neck, which she even wore to bed, actually *was* piss.

"Alan really struggles when Sonia tells him it's 'cuddle time'. She's not entirely unattractive, but the piss is a real turn-off for him. Even if it isn't piss – he *thinks* it is, which has the same effect on him. I don't think there is much 'going on there' nowadays Becca…and I think it's the piss."

***

The small urn Amazon delivered to work the next day had little paw prints on the lid, which looked more dog than cat to Terry. So the only problem now is to find ash, or something very like ash. Finally getting home, he shows the urn to Becca.

"Here he is, poor little fella – they *had* been keeping him safe until we picked him up, just a little amount."

He goes to pass the urn to Becca, who instinctively pulls away, squeamish.

"I don't think I can actually touch him pet, just give me a little glimpse at a distance, then we'll put him away somewhere safe."

They are standing in the kitchen, so, from a distance of about four feet, Terry just lifts the lid a little so Becca can see the top of the ashes.

"They are very dark aren't they…I was expecting more sort of grey."

"That's the cremation process Becca – very very hot, so all the dust just burns up leaving this gritty sort of stuff. You can just see the little flecks of white, I think that's all that's left of Tiger's bones."

"Oh, that's horrible Terry. Shut him away now Lamb, he's at peace now, we should respect that, he can live up on the top shelf of the bookshelf with the other bits and pieces."

Terry shuts Tiger away carefully. The faint smell of Oreos just catches his nostrils.

***

"I think you should come upstairs Terry."

Terry sits forward, instantly alert. *Bake Off* had been about to start. Tea, custard creams and *Bake Off* was a pretty powerful combination, but he knows that tone: a touch deeper than normal, with that wonderfully lush, provocative lilt. He can feel an instant blood rush.

"That sounds like it might just be worth my while Becca…"

"Maybe it is, maybe it isn't. You will have to come and see, maybe bring a couple of glasses up."

Frisky and alert, Terry speed-forages around the kitchen. Glasses and a bottle of wine in hand, he mounts the stairs, stopping to tuck in the front of his shirt, which has escaped the confines of his trousers. He scurries along the landing to peer round the bedroom door.

"Becca…Oh Becca, they are *very* sexy!"

"Thought you might like them. They *were* very expensive. You get what you pay for with Lingerie though, don't you Tel? I think I might need help getting out of them."

Terry stands with the wine bottle in one hand, glasses in the other, as Becca slowly pirouettes, her stilettos catching slightly in the carpet. His eyes can't stay in one place. It's like trying to decide where to start on a thousand-dollar buffet; he knows he is goggling in a quite uncontrollable way and his throat has tightened as he puts the glasses down and attempts to pour the wine.

"Tel, it's going everywhere, you need to look as you pour I think Pet."

Terry is indeed attempting to pour two glasses of wine without looking at either the bottle *or* the glasses. Blood careering round his body. Like lying in bed as a child, Christmas Eve, wide awake at 4am, *knowing* that all those wonderful shapes in the dark at the foot of the bed are presents, but having to stay in bed, every fibre desperate to leap at them and rip off the careful wrapping.

He notices at the top of the tiny black triangle of silk, a shape, the dark blue feathers of a small arrow, stark against the whiteness of her skin; he drops to his knees in front of the altar as she peels the silk slowly downwards with her painted thumbnails.

Terry can't speak, in fact he is struggling to keep control of any part of his body. He makes the effort to stop holding his breath.

"I knew you would like it Terry, it's for you: I thought about what to have for a long time, it's a *real* one, not just one of those painted-on ones."

"Goddd…Becca…it's beautiful, and sooo sexy."

"I had it done properly, by a real artist. I have been keeping her covered up for you until she had settled down. I think she might need a kiss now, Tel…"

"Who did it for you, Pet?"

"It was an artist. She does need kissing now Tel…"

The only place Terry knows locally where you could get that done is Tats R Us, he tries desperately, but vainly, not to think about it. Tats R Us, just off the scruffier end of the high street, run by Scotch Barry who he sees down the pub most weeks.

Unable to simply accept a gift from heaven, Terry *has* to ask whether it was Barry who was the artist in question.

"It might have been Lamb. It was very professional; not even that painful."

On his knees, inches from that thousand-dollar buffet, Terry finds himself swarming with conflicting thoughts, feelings, and he just can't help it.

"So, Scotch Barry did this Becca. Greasy fucking Scotch Barry! Crawling all over your…your…with a bag of needles, and a hard-on!"

"Noooo, Tel, he never had a hard-on. I would have noticed."

"But Becca – greasy fucking Barry crawled all over your…your…for hours. And I see him down the pub every Friday. It's just not right Becca, not fucking right!"

"He didn't Lamb. I covered it up with masking tape so he wouldn't see it all. Tel, you're spoiling it!"

"Fuck's sake Becca, you're telling me that greasy Scotch tosser stuck the smallest bit of masking tape you have ever seen over your fanny, 'cos Becca, the fucking arrow runs through pretty much all of it, so he couldn't have covered up a lot could he?! And then you reckon he NEVER gets a hard-on and never actually touches it Becca?!"

"He NEVER got a hard-on, Lamb; I would have known. And he NEVER touched me like that. And anyway, it just bloody hurt with all those pins. It's for you Tel. It fucking hurt…and it's just for you!"

Terry realises he is in danger of a complete meltdown. Becca has lost all her swagger, on the edge of tears, and it clearly *was* for him.

"Becca, Pet, don't cry, it's lovely, it really is. And they're needles, not pins Pet, and if he didn't get a hard-on he must be gay. Come here Becca. It's gorgeous. YOU are gorgeous."

A gently familiar childhood smell reaches Terry's nose.

"You've had to use quite a bit of TCP Becca…"

6

FRIDAY NIGHT. FIVE pints down.

Got to get away. Fucking Barry, grinning at me, leering at me, letting me fucking know. I'll kill him, little shit.

Terry leaves the pub in a cloud of red mist – an anger that has nowhere to go. Leather bomber-jacket and too-tight jeans failing to hold out the pouring rain and bitingly cold wind, but he doesn't feel it. He has no idea where he is going, or why, he just knew he had to get out. He finds himself in a scruffy kebab shop about half a mile from the pub, staring up at the back-lit plastic menu behind the counter – there are no other customers. There are three jumbo sausages in batter lying behind the glass of the warming tray. Terry orders all three.

"Don't wrap them, just in a bag with some salt please mate."

Walking down the road again in the rain, Terry tries to eat himself back to normality – the batter of the sausages is tough and rubbery, while the inside has the texture of barely warm paté. He chews his way through all three of them, the grease running down his hands onto his sleeves, almost forcing himself to swallow. It doesn't help his mood. He just feels quite sick and bloated now, shaky cold and desperate for a piss.

What DO you do when a bloke has spent two hours sticking pins in your missus' fanny and then the tosser laughs at you in front of your mates? Fucking sat there staring at me, with his finger working around the insides of a bag of pork scratchings – pork fucking scratchings – leaning across the table and offering me the bag, just leering at me as he did it.

Terry still doesn't know where he's going. Washing the sausages down with half a kebab doesn't help, the chilli sauce burning his lips. He drops the remaining half into the road, and as the mess of grey flaps of meat, soggy pitta and lettuce burst on impact he feels a strange sense of guilt.

You are not meant to throw shit in the road – that was his upbringing. *You are in London, the most beautiful city in the world – you are fucking lucky...so DON'T throw shit in the road!* He steps off the kerb and starts to push the scattered kebab into a slightly neater pile with his sodden shoe. Pathetic. His stomach really hurts now, and he badly needs a piss.

As usual, at times of need, an inane song springs into his head, courtesy of his subconscious attempting to divert him from his plight, and refuses to leave:

"Stand and deliverrr…"

Fucking stupid song. Fucking Adam Ant. Over and over. Fucking ridiculous.

"Stand and deliverrr…"

God's teeth! It's not right; it's just not fucking right. What was she thinking of? I really need a piss!

"And deliverrr…"

Stop that stupid song for fuck's sake Terry!

He is walking down Mandible Road, hands tucked deep in his jacket pockets, bald head freezing in the rain.

"Stand and deliverrr…"

Kicking at a black plastic bin bag, sagging wet on the pavement, it spills its turgid contents over his shoe.

He knows he needs to get away, if he goes back it can *only* get worse, much worse, he needs to go home.

Terry looks up, and finds he is back outside The Badger's Arms.

Fucking stupid name for a pub.

He can make out Barry's whining little fuck-pig voice above the babble; he pushes the door, almost certain he is going to kill him, but not before he has had a piss though. Adam Ant has been drowned out for a moment by the noise of the bar.

Cold and wet from the rain, Terry faces the urinal, his freezing hands struggling with the zip, the fat from the sausages melting as his fingers finally tease out warm dick. Head back and eyes shut, the relief spreads through him. The door opens and Terry hears footsteps and feels the presence of another beside him. "Alright Tel?" in a light Scots lilt. A small bomb goes off in his head.

***

Lying on his back on the floor of the gents, Terry's shoulder is screaming at him. He is sweating, lungs heaving, and bleeding. Scotch Barry lies beside him, clothes torn, sweating, panting for breath, bleeding. They are both filthy from a mixture of their own sweat, blood and snot; as well as the stains of dirt and piss picked up from the floor as they writhed around clawing at each other. One of the urinals is smashed. A sharp, unwholesome explosion of jagged, yellowing porcelain everywhere. The urinal flush goes off and the water sprays onto the floor, flowing around them.

Neither really lands a blow, apart from Terry's initial backhand forearm. Just a frantic scratching, swinging, wrestling match as they grunt and heave their way back and forth around the toilet, locked together in a parody of mating/fighting.

Terry slowly realises he hadn't even tucked himself away after his piss, his shrivelled cock still peeking out as he lies there. "Fuck…oh fuck."

Tonto, the giant, hard-as-nails, South London publican and his Neanderthal cellar-man appear and drag both Terry and Scotch to their feet.

"Put your cock away Tel. And Barry, will you fuckin' put yours away too man! There'll be a fuckin' bill for this lot heading your way boys. Now fuck off out of my pub and sort yourselves out! If you weren't 'regulars' I'd break both of you in half. Look at the state of this fucking place."

The gladiators are escorted out of the door. The entire pub has gone quiet, everyone backing away as the urine-soaked posse march through the Snug and out the front door.

"Both had their fucking cocks out!" Tonto grumbles as he turns back to the audience of Friday-night drinkers.

"Listen up people! You'll all have to use the Ladies' for a bit – the Gents' is out of action!"

The room settles down. Two regulars, good mates really, just having a bit of a barney, with their cocks out, covered in blood, dirt and piss, nothing to worry about, no harm done, nothing unusual for a Friday night.

***

In the alley beside the pub, Tel and Barry are still panting, half leaning, half sitting against the wall, checking their faces gingerly for wounds.

"I niver touched her, Tel, ah swear. I was only havin' a laugh in there. I was bang out of order man, ahm sorry. Most of the tattoo was done by Meng – ah just drew it on, Tel. She had half a roll a fucken' masking tape over it all. Meng's a girl, Tel. She loves doing the fannies!"

"I know who fucking Ming is, Barry. I'm sorry mate. You really fucked me up."

"Ah thought you were gonta to kell me. I've pessed all over ma'sell, and all over you…ah think ma nose is broke!"

Terry and Scotch limp the 300 yards to Terry's front door. It is 11.30pm, the lights are off and he lets them both in. They strip out of torn, soiled clothes – Barry in the downstairs cloakroom, Terry in the kitchen. Terry fetches an armful of trousers and T-shirts from his wardrobe in the spare room, the first-aid box from the garage, and slowly the blood is wiped away. Generous blobs of antiseptic cream ooze out from plasters roughly stuck over cuts and scratches mainly from broken pieces of the filthy urinal. Tonto didn't believe anyone would be eating out of the urinals, so considered anything more than a cursory wipe to be overkill.

Bloodstained towels alongside bloody wet handfuls

of kitchen roll on the floor; piles of filthy clothes stinking of sweat and piss all shoved into a fetid pile in the corner of the bathroom. Finally finished, they make their way to the living room and, groaning, gingerly lower themselves into voluminous armchairs. One small table lamp lifts the darkness.

Terry retrieves a bottle from the drinks cabinet, and they sit there in semi-dark, each with a tumbler half full of Famous Grouse. Scotch has a plug of red-stained kitchen roll extending from one nostril, and they talk.

In fact, Terry talks. It just all seems to gush out: the tax bill, the house, the shit on the car, Tiger, all of it, nothing spared. A level of trust spawning between combatants, warriors, honours even – a bond. Two men who had their hands on the same pussy; the same bag of pork scratchings.

"I love her you know Scotch, always loved her, even when she was in JonJon's class at school, only eleven years old. She had a crush on me, the older kid. I was fifteen, used to have to look after JonJon, save him from getting the odd kicking – he was such a little shit even then. She set her sights on me way back then…and I've loved her ever since Scotch."

An awful boozy melancholy sets in and Terry just sits there, staring into the corner, full of *Bambi-is-dead* overblown emotion.

***

Terry never knew how they got from there on to the slightly bizarre subject of dogfighting. Reminiscing; it had been Scotch talking about his "Daa". The whisky was long gone, as was the half bottle of Napoleon that had followed it. Terry recalled hazily that Scotch seemed to know an awful lot about this stuff: where the big money fights were, who ran them, how you got an invite, and much more.

Quite a lot for a bloke who runs a back-street tattoo and forgery shop.

"Ye would'nae believe the stuff ah hear, Tel. The bondage boys for their piercings, they trust me like yer granny trusts her hairdresser; I had to tattoo a 'sun' round this bloke's arsehole, Tel; s'incredible, he wanted zips tattooed down the length of his cock, and his helmet an angry fucken' RED! Fucken' RED! What's he gonna be doing with that bad boy? It's not his missus he expects to be scarin' with that fucker!"

"Ye want tae make good money fast, get a good dog Tel – a good dog and take hem on the road."

It was 3am before Scotch had finally staggered out the front door – ill-fitting black joggers hanging round his ankles, brown brogues and a Millwall footy shirt five sizes too big, with "Vinny Jones" emblazoned across the back. Terry remembers them both laughing till tears flowed, a lot of leg slapping, and agreeing something about a Pit Bull and money – it all seemed terribly funny.

Terry's head sagged back against the top of the armchair, the whisky dulling the throbbing that seemed to envelop his entire body, his face, his hands.

Dogfighting. Took him back to his old dad. Those were great days, fond memories: his dad taking him to race whippets, and then the bloodthirsty thrill of the dogfighting in the "derelicts" behind the allotments. He had never been allowed in to actually see anything, his dad never wanting him to be too upset, but the shouts and baying of the men, waving notes, bellowing, the guttural snarls of the dogs: brilliant, shocking.

Head tipped back, eyes closed, mouth open, Terry snores at the moon.

7

WEDNESDAY NIGHT, STANDING in the chippy.

"And a bag of batterpiss me old mate."

Dimmi the Greek, labouring over the steaming vats of oil.

Batterppiss was a particular delicacy: all the excess bits of burnt batter that escaped from the fish, scooped up and served in their own little bag – cholesterol magic. Couldn't get them anywhere else nowadays, some people called them batter "bits", others "scraps", but "batterpiss" had stuck in The Greek Plaice. They sold far less doner now that everyone seemed to be on a health kick.

Scotch had followed Tel into the chippy, long greasy hair framing a face full of plasters and bruises. Terry knew he looked the same, but with more fat and less hair; not a pretty sight. Becca was at her mum's with Mercedes and Chloe, so when Scotch said he needed to talk, Terry had suggested they go back to his with their fish and chips. Scotch orders chips and batterpiss, both equally drowned in salt and an endless spray of vinegar.

"It'll just go soggy Scotch."

"Ah noo Tel, thas how ah like et."

"TAKE THAT FAG OUTTA MY FUCKING CHIP SHOP! You wanna me lose my licence? People here no fucking respect, no fucking common sense!" Dimmi shouted.

Scotch carefully stubs out his half-smoked cigarette on the sole of his shoe and slides it back into the packet for later. His mouth says "Sorry", but his expression says "Fuck you".

***

Sitting round the kitchen table, eating off the paper with their fingers, Scotch tells Terry about his latest tattoo design and a couple of his more bizarre piercings.

"That's fucking horrible Scotch; I'm trying to eat!"

Scotch rambling about their scrap in the pub and his subsequent wounds: "Never even realised ah still had ma dick oot."

Scotch asks politely after Becca, Mercedes and little Chloe. Then Terry listens patiently to a five-minute meander about the dogfighting scene up in Glasgow, Scotch's exploits as a lad, how his Da had been a bookie for every illegal game in town, from poker games to bare knuckle, and the dogfights.

"Great days, Tel, great days…"

"But Scotch, what did you actually want to talk to me about?"

"That's just it, Tel, those great days: they are still going, still happening. It's a big scene, big money. That's what we talked about the night we had the scrap, Tel. You need cash fast, and this just might be the way to get your hands on some…and maybe a lot! What a crack, Tel, *what* a crack! All we need is a dog or two, a *good* dog or two, take them on the road…get into the money game!"

***

Why the fuck had he let Scotch talk him into this? Money, the chance of some easy money, the chance of getting the taxman off his back without Becca ever knowing, without having to sell the house – that's why!

They had hired an unmarked white van, thirty quid for the day, and driven all the way across London for two hours to Garston, north Watford, to a tiny industrial estate. A huge faded sign, *Business Units to Let*, hung at the entrance of the white-painted single-storey building, split into half a dozen separate units with cheap metal doors, surrounded by cracked, pitted tarmac parking bays.

"It's the only one used Tel. No security, no cameras, no nuthen. Why would you need anythen? No fucker in their right minds would ever break in here."

"That's probably right Scotch."

***

So here we are, breaking into a police station in the arse-end of Watford.

More accurately, the building the police use to hold animals waiting for an extermination order from the courts.

Some things you search for on Google, others can take a more circuitous route. Scotch had taken a professional interest in the labia-bleaching treatment on a solid, rather butch North London goth who was the latest victim of Shazza, his piercing assistant. Labia bleaching had developed a bad name since a couple of celebrity accidents, and Scotch's was one of the few places you could still get it done. The goth had a part-time job with her local council's animal welfare department, looking after what she described as "fucked up" animals.

"We just feed 'em, walk 'em and piss off 'ome; pretend we spend the day there. Good money though. 'Doggy Death Row' we call it. Fuckin' sad really – we get all sorts of weird shit in there."

****

Scotch picks his way through a gigantic bunch of keys: selecting one, trying it in the lock, then another, and after a minute of jiggling, finds the one that springs the door. And they are in.

Not many residents are home. It's smelly, a mix of disinfectant and mould, but strangely quiet; three rooms off the corridor, the first with some big fish tanks, only one dimly lit and occupied by a very large, motionless snake.

The next room is empty, barring a single cage on a table at the far end with a badger in it. Terry pulls the door shut.

What in God's name are they doing with a badger in there?

Finally, the third room. This is what they were looking for: along the base of the wall a row of dog pens sit side by side, with three Pit Bulls curled up on the floors of their cages, and a fourth cage with a small off-white poodle, standing alert.

"What the fuck has the poodle done Scotch? I understand the others, but a dangerous fucking poodle?"

The poodle just stands observing Scotch and Terry approach the Pit Bull cages, the slumbering dogs barely acknowledging them.

Scotch pulls on his thick leather builders' gloves and picks up the sturdy three-foot pole hanging on the wall, a strong metal one-way opening loop, operated by a thick nylon cord attached to the end. He inserts it through the slot above the door of the first metal cage and clips it to one of the thick metal rings attached to the dog's collar.

Job done, Scotch slides the bolts back and opens the cage door. Led by the pole, Dog One, ginger-brown, sluggishly gets to his feet and obediently walks across the linoleum floor and towards the row of three cages that Terry and Scotch have brought in from the van. Doors open, awaiting the dogs. Dog One is manoeuvred into the cage. Scotch jiggles the release cord of the pole, Dog One is unclipped and Terry snaps the door shut as the pole is withdrawn. Dog One settles, curled into a sleeping position. Together they lift the cage, walk it back to the van, and push it to the back; a perfectly executed military exercise.

Dog Two, a dark molasses brown, follows, almost to the step, gently going along with the programme.

Terry is relaxing a little, still whispering.

"This is less of a disaster than I thought it would be Scotch; they are bloody docile. Makes you wonder what they did that was so bad they need putting down."

"This isn't 'normal' Tel. The girls put shet in their food,

keeps 'em quiet, easier tae handle; don't thenk they're meant to, but et stops them getting too fresky or barken' the place down all the time. Pitties are quite placid dogs, easy tae train. Love children and all thet. They are jest a bet of a handful when you set 'em on other doggies! Piece ae cake Tel, I told you it would be!"

Dog Three, a patchwork of golden and dark brown, is more alert than its friends, standing in his cage, and he seems particularly interested in Terry as he stands watching over Scotch's shoulder as the pole is attached. He doesn't need manoeuvring towards the van as the others had, leading the way rather than being pushed along, trotting, squat and upright.

Dog Three has no intention of wandering happily into another cage though. He has been in a cage for quite long enough, and these two masters seemed pretty docile, so there has to be a chance for a dash to freedom...

Scotch is manoeuvring Dog Three through the cage door with the pole when he stops in his tracks and turns side-on to the door; his centre of gravity seems to drop, which gives less leverage with the pole. Scotch can drag his head to the door, but his body just shifts around again, all the while emitting a slow, deep rumble, not threatening and not really exerting himself. The dance continues for a couple of minutes.

"Fuck's sake Scotch, he's only a *little* bugger, just lead him in there."

"He willnae go, Tel, he's just bein fucken' awkward. Go on Puppy, just get yersell in there for Christ's sake! I think we're gonna have to left hem in."

Terry takes the pole from Scotch, pushing Puppy's head

into the cage opening. Scotch leans over and lifts the dog's rear legs a few inches off the ground and starts to "dry-hump" Puppy in the direction of the cage.

Puppy doesn't really struggle, but just tenses himself into an awkward muscle-bound bundle. Then, very fast, he twists his head and body away from the cage, wrenching at the pole attached to his neck. Terry's shoulder sends a stabbing pain down his arm and he drops the pole and slips to his knees on the lino floor. Scotch, hanging on to Puppy's rear quarters, yells and straightens up, lifting Puppy so that he's dangling off the ground.

Puppy would like to bite Terry, there on the floor, but he has been lifted upside down by the one with the funny accent, so he clamps his teeth onto the nearest soft object, which happens to be Scotch's groin.

Scotch wears his jeans baggy, and, as a skinny Scot, has a well-defined "lunchbox", the entirety of which is now clamped, denim-clad, firmly in Puppy's jaws while Scotch hangs onto his hind legs. Puppy does not rip and tear; he just clamps on, as any self-respecting Pit Bull would do, the low growl now a very different and less benign intensity. Scotch screeches in pain, falls backwards and lets Puppy's legs go. Puppy remains clamped, immovable, his head in Scotch's groin, his rear legs on Scotch's chest in an appalling parody of a "sixty-nine". Stubby docked tail and little arsehole shoved low down, as Scotch's reflex action brings his head up and curls his body forward to protect himself, only to be met by Puppy's arse on his chest.

Terry has the pole in his good hand and is back on his feet.

"GETTITOFF!!! GETTOFFF!!!"

Scotch's hands vainly reach down to Puppy's mouth.

"Don't move Scotch, stay still, fucking STILL…and for fuck's sake keep the noise down!"

He takes Puppy's collar in his good hand, but he has become one with Scotch's groin; any movement in Puppy's head directly translates into more screams of pain from the prone Scotch, tears streaking down his cheeks.

"DON'T TOUCH HEM – DON'T FUCKEN' TOUCH HEM!!!"

It's clear that pulling Puppy from his sixty-nine will end up mutilating Scotch, and while there seems to be some justice in this, explaining it to the police, doctors, and even Becca does not seem an attractive option.

"Try to keep quiet Scotch…please…"

Terry swings one leg astride the canine sex-trap and bends over and starts working his thumbs into the Pit Bull's mouth, one either side in an attempt to prise the jaws apart. Pathetic – apart from getting hands full of slobber, being unable to exert any pressure with his aching right arm makes no impression at all.

Puppy doesn't even change the tone of the low rumble he's emitting; it's stalemate, although the sixty-nine now looks like a threesome, with two grown men appearing to "spit roast" a small dog.

Terry un-straddles the pair and takes a step or two back, panting. Scotch is on his back, in a sweating, trance-like state, his hands gently resting on Puppy's haunches, who relaxes a little and farts steadily but gently – an awful "meaty" fart…

"Tel…TEL…urggghhh…fuck…fuckenfuck… urrrgghhhhh!" Simultaneous castration and gassing complete Scotch's misery and desperation, his head lolling back to escape the smell.

In a rare flash of inspiration, Terry decides on a new approach.

"STOP!" he commands, in his sternest, deepest teacher voice. "STOP!" He is standing in front of the pair and Puppy's eyes are trained firmly on his.

"Stop" clearly isn't going to work, and what does a fucking dog think "Stop" means anyway?

"RELEASE!" commands Terry. Puppy's ears immediately prick up, his full attention on Terry.

Now, louder: "RELEASE!"

Puppy releases his denim mouthful. Scotch emits a groan of relief and anguish.

"COME!" Terry commands, growing in confidence, and Puppy scrambles off of Scotch's chest, finds his feet, and pads towards him.

"SIT!"

Puppy sits, acknowledging a new master.

Scotch is sagging back on the floor, hands cupping his battered groin, groaning.

Terry is getting the knack now, and Puppy marches smartly into the cage on his instruction, circles and lies down on the cage floor, and the door is secured.

***

It takes twenty minutes for the pain to wear off sufficiently for Scotch, his trousers and off-white underpants around his knees, to feel able to start gingerly exploring his swollen, reddened wedding tackle for punctures and lasting damage.

Each touch around his testicles is punctuated by a groan.

Terry can see no sign of blood, and Scotch seems to be slowly recovering.

"Pull your pants up Scotch, there's nothing wrong with you."

After a violent disagreement about the definition of "nothing wrong", Terry, painfully slowly, pulls Scotch onto his feet, legs shaking like jelly, his arms resting on Terry's back. Terry has never pulled a grown man's underpants on before, and vows gently under his breath not to do it again, as the perfume of dog slobber and sweaty unwashed groin wafts around him. Finally, jeans almost pulled up, if not done up, Scotch stands erect, face the colour of his underpants.

Carrying Puppy's cage back to the van, Terry, with one good arm, and Scotch, walking as if he has a red-hot marrow up his arse, finish the job. Scotch, face full of bile, sneers at his caged tormentor.

"He was just afraid Scotch. We all do daft things when we are afraid."

"IT was not fucken' afraid Tel. IT had just decided to bite my fucken' cock off; so excuse me if ah don't feel so good about the little fuck-shite!"

***

Just getting Scotch into the car was a challenge, his knees held wide apart as if holding a basketball between them. Eventually he was in, his legs stretched straight in an attempt to hold himself up off the seat.

"Won't be a sec Scotch, hang on in there."

A couple of minutes later, Terry emerges with the poodle

under his good arm and puts it in the back with the three cages.

"Yer fucken' jokin' Tel. The fucken' poodle! What are we gon tae do wi tha? Feed it to the pitties? Aggghhh!"

Speech is too much of an effort for Scotch and the pain in his groin is sending deep throbbing waves through his lower body. He settles back into the seat to focus on his own discomfort.

"Fucken' idiot"

Terry ignores the jibe and concentrates on driving, barely able to change gears with his debilitated left arm. Scotch still cannot close his legs or sit properly. He is visibly holding back tears throughout the excruciatingly painful, never-ending journey back to the lock-up, which he had sourced for the princely sum of £25 per week from one of his "customers". Both men moan at every tiny bump, a comic marathon that makes them unpleasantly irritable.

As Terry unlocks the garage door, he turns and sees the number plate covered over with masking tape.

"SCOTCH! We've just driven all the way across London *and back*, down the Edgware Road, past more cameras than fucking Kodak, and then through Peckham, the peace capital of the south, with our number plates covered up. It's like an announcement that we are up to no good, you complete dick!"

"Ahm sorry Tel, meant to take them off after we picked up the dogs – takin' care Tel, just takin' care…"

"The cameras can see your face Scotch you fuck-wit. All the way across the congestion zone with about 600 pictures of us in a van with a blacked-out number plate. God's teeth Scotch!"

They painfully drag and bump the cages into the lock-up, the poodle just follows tamely, park the van and, with a last furtive look round and a sigh of relief, shut the garage door.

The gloom is broken by two strip lights running the length of the double garage. The rusting shelves are stacked with cans of dog meat and big bags of biscuits. Bowls for food and water are stacked and at the ready. Scotch had been to the local cash and carry to stock up on everything a dog-lover could need: leads, muzzles, collars and strange bags of dried yellowing sinew wound into parodies of bone.

The dogs do not seem to be fazed by their new surroundings, and stand in their cages quietly, alert, watching the two masters: Scotch bent over a little with his legs wide apart, white as a sheet; Terry has the sweats again as the pain in his arm subsides to a familiar dull throb. The poodle just sits quietly in front of the cages, his pom-pom haircut looking perfectly coiffured – like Marilyn Monroe posing in front of Alcatraz.

***

The van is back outside Denny's hire shop. Scotch has staggered off with half a bottle of brandy and a packet of paracetamol. Terry settles down into the enveloping sofa, a huge grin spreads across his face as he pictures those canine jaws clamped tight…

Tattoo THAT, motherfucker!

He is asleep within seconds.

8

SHAZZA'S SISTER, RAZZA, has been drafted in to feed, water and walk the dogs daily. Razza is a gaunt little thing, full of facial piercings and attitude.

In most families a "Shazza" would just be a nickname for Sharon, but South London's finest happily christened their daughters Shazza and Razza. Quite sweet, but probably not enhancing their employability.

Razza was "good with dogs" according to her sister, and with half a kilo of metal laced through various bits of her face, that was probably a useful addition to her CV. She had fed each of the dogs, passing their bowls through the flap-door in the cage, and then opened up each of the cages in turn, exchanging the prisoner collars with their shiny new cash-and-carry versions, and had taken each out for a twenty-minute walk.

She reported back that they were "OK". Not an extensive report; she had several thick metal rings laced through one side of her lower lip, making speech a slightly muffled and lopsided affair, but Terry had to admit that it seemed Razza was indeed "good with dogs".

***

Two weeks had passed. Terry and Scotch split duties between them, Scotch busy arranging the fight tour, getting back into the scene, with his dad up in Glasgow putting him in touch with the various players on the circuit. A lot of this communication was via instant messaging. Terry only just managed texting, and had never taken the time to work out how WhatsApp and other IMs worked. Scotch also seemed to make a lot of arrangements on what he referred to as the "Dark Web". Terry had only ever heard this mentioned on the news in relation to paedophile rings and terrorism, but Scotch seemed to think that almost anything "slightly murky" was handled this way, to avoid Mr Google and other prying eyes knowing every site you had ever visited.

This surprised Terry, given the quality and quantity of porn he had been able to access on the normal web. He couldn't see why you would need a secret web if you could see that type of shit just using Google – but he did understand that it would be nice *not* to leave an audit trail every time.

Terry's job was to train and condition the dogs, and to arrange the transport. He had bought Cousin Ricardo's ancient caravan for a magnificent £250 and filled his evenings after work converting it into a mobile kennel and dog-repair centre, steadily getting the old crate road-worthy again. The new layout incorporated a small chemical toilet, three dog cages where the bed had been and a small table.

The kitchen area had been gutted, leaving just a small sink and a worktop. The whole thing was a complete rust-bucket; what was left of the grey-tinged white paint was slowly flaking away, and the green mould that spread out from every joint and rim was clearly there to stay. The one thing he was sure about was that no one would ever nick it. The only cosmetic change that he thought worth making was to paint over the word "Wanker" that had been thoughtfully sprayed across the whole side of the caravan. He had used some old white gloss paint for this, which just served to emphasise how filthy the rest of it was. "Wanker" was still visible, if less stark, so the "Wankavan" was born.

Razza was there every day now, taking the dogs for long walks, always separately, feeding them on Scotch's carefully constructed recipes of CSJ, a specialist dog food designed for "working dogs". Scotch would go on and on about "dense energy nutrition", his secret home-made supplements and, less attractively, the stool density of the dogs, which he tested regularly and carefully between thumb and forefinger.

Razza had also given them names now. Instead of "Dogs one to three", they were now named after Razza's favourite rum and rum-based cocktails: *Cuba Libra*, Dog One; the strangely appropriate *Captain Morgan*, Dog Two; and finally, *Mojito*, Dog Three. The poodle had developed a mild twitch, and was not deemed worthy of a name, now just known as "Poodle".

Terry was actually growing fond of the dogs as their personalities were slowly revealed under Razza's watchful eye; their names definitely fitted them, and Mojito was the clear leader of the stubby, strutting pack.

It was becoming harder and harder to keep this all from

Becca. He was out every evening, either with the dogs, with Scotch or sorting out the Wankavan. Not much of a handyman, he would come home with knocks and scrapes from hefting the cages and securing them around the caravan. He had explained this to Becca by saying he was working on an old motorbike he wanted to get roadworthy. Less explainable was the distinct smell of dog, or worse, the slightly sickly smell of Scotch's strange dog-food mixes.

***

The stresses and strains of the last few weeks seemed to have robbed Terry of his normally reliable sex drive. He had unwisely discussed this with Scotch, who followed up by sending him a constant stream of links to various websites where he could buy any manner of useful chemical remedies to assist him in the area of erectile dysfunction, as they so clinically put it.

This being a man's most reliable friend, it had seemed only right to sample different pills from different websites. He now had a drawer full of Viagra, Cialis and the aptly named "Iron Bar" pills. He had scared both Becca *and* himself with the latter; it had seemed bloody good fun at first…and at second…but then the "stalky" didn't subside for another hour, which made it almost impossible to go for a piss. While it looked pretty impressive, the fact that he couldn't actually feel very much, coupled with the problem that it just wouldn't go away, meant that "Iron Bar" was now relegated to the back of the cupboard – but not the bin, just in case.

The websites made it seem pretty simple, but Terry was scared that if they were delivered to his home address Becca might discover what he was up to, so he had them delivered to work.

It had said they would be delivered in unmarked packaging, but the first of the deliveries had clearly been opened by someone in the post-room, and Julie, the office PA he shared with four of his colleagues, appeared with the badly Sellotaped package, contents clearly showing, handing them to him in slow-motion across his desk, with a look of some sympathy, and more than a little distaste.

"I was on the fucking train home Scotch, with the mobile going off. Looks like it was from a bloody UK landline, but some bloke in Delhi or something starts asking me how I'm getting on with my Viagra, and whether I need more yet! Fuck's sake Scotch, I've got a year's worth of the stuff, and three weeks later they are calling me to ask if I need more! I tell them to piss off, but they just keep ringing. I must get twenty emails a week from all over the planet asking me about 'pleasing my beloved' – what if Becca sees them?!"

"Shud ha given them a fake number Tel. Just don't ansa. I don't know why you didnae just use one website; *three* websites, just plain daft man."

***

Determined to find out what was occurring with Terry's evening activities, Becca had taken action.

Rather than going the traditional route of searching his pockets and attempting to identify the variety of odours Terry was wafting around the house, she took the more direct route of actually asking him.

Appearing from his now-regular evening shower to

find Becca sitting astride a chair, Christine Keeler-style, dressed up in Terry's favourite nurse outfit and red heels. Just as he reached the point of unclipping a suspender, Becca coyly slipped out of his grasp, crossed her legs and peered seductively over the rim of her play-glasses.

"Doctor…I think you should tell me what's going on…"

Terry's resistance at the best of times was pretty weak – to be fair, his resistance had been weak where Becca was concerned ever since they had started getting "intimate" twenty-five years ago, him seventeen and she a "knowing" fifteen-year-old, no longer the skinny twelve-year-old in his brother's class at school. But this was frankly unfair.

So out it all came: the Will, Jonny, the tax bill, Scotch, the dogs, the caravan, everything – except the complete Tiger-truth, which didn't really count.

Becca had been shocked, then very angry about being kept in the dark, then worried about the finances, which had never been her strong point, and finally decided:

"We had better go and see these dogs Terry."

He realised the dose of "Maybe I'll get lucky" Viagra was just going to be a discomfort rather than a release, so he had reluctantly agreed.

"Now Terry – NOW!"

At five to midnight on a cold, miserable Tuesday, Terry let himself and Becca into the lock-up and introduced Becca formally to his canine Holy Trinity.

***

Extraordinary!

He would never truly figure out Becca, or any woman

really, but who would have thought she would take to the dogs like this; and even buy into the whole improbable plan. Not just buy into it; Becca had insisted on becoming a full-blown partner in crime. She had almost literally fucked his brains out after they had got back home at 2am from the lock-up; the chemical assistance had not even been required as Terry's libido seemed to return after unburdening himself from his murky secrets. They had collapsed, exhausted, into a sweaty tangle. For the first time in weeks, Terry slept untroubled.

***

So now Becca was helping Razza with the dog exercise and conditioning regime, working with Scotch on the increasingly scientific mixture of supplements that went into the feed. It still made Terry distinctly uncomfortable seeing Becca and Scotch together. He could not quite reconcile his feelings about the tattoo incident, though he had become very fond of the tattoo itself.

Becca had insisted that she would be coming on the fighting forays and had been adding small feminine touches to the Wankavan. The dogs themselves just doted on her! Mojito particularly seemed to have transferred his affection and obedience to Becca, as she was clearly the "alpha" dog of the human pack.

The dogs could all be trusted together now. Scotch and Terry's concern that they would rip each other to pieces if left together was clearly unfounded; in fact, it was hard to see how these muscular little bundles would ever actually fight anything – that is until the moment they saw another dog out walking. You could sense an immediate change in their step, mood, and level of attention. They bristled, and you could feel a tension flooding through them, and a barely audible, guttural rhythm emanated from each of them. They all had it, different, but definitely there on the edge of hearing. The only dog immune to all of this was Poodle, who seemed to have been adopted like a "special needs" brother by the Pit Bulls; he would periodically accompany one of them on a walk, prancing along without a lead, like their ultra-camp minder.

***

Over cappuccinos in Starbucks, Scotch announces that he has lined up the first outing: an industrial estate just on the outskirts of Milton Keynes. Terry and Becca are worried that the dogs so far have given no real indication that they are up for anything terribly ferocious – they make other dog-walkers uneasy, as their own dogs inexplicably shied away from one of the passing Pit Bulls, but that seems an unlikely indication they are fit and ready for real fighting.

Scotch has consistently been upbeat about their ability to "put on a show"; but Terry has never been able to get out of him just why he is so confident. Scotch irritatingly implies that he knew the reason *why* they were all locked up in the police pound and that he and Becca should just relax.

Cocky little bastard. It's not HIS twenty grand that's going to be at risk. The whole idea is to make enough money to get the taxman off our back, but twenty grand stake money is a fucking fortune!

He feels sick at the prospect of falling even further into the money hole.

***

Razza bursts through the Starbucks' door: white as a sheet, out of breath and shaking. The normally placid Captain Morgan had been on his evening stroll and had taken offence at the way a particularly prancing collie had looked at him. He'd yanked the lead out of Razza's hand, and by the time she had dragged him off, the Captain had come close to decapitating his new friend; its front right leg terribly mangled, blood everywhere.

Razza had done a runner, with the Captain proudly trotting along beside her, blood smeared around his mouth, leaving the collie's owner and a couple of passers-by in shock and tending to the Captain's victim, who lay, unable to stand, blood-soaked and whimpering.

"Really fucked it up he did. Nothing I could do. Didn't give any sort of signal. He just leapt at it, got his teeth around its leg and kept twisting about. It was awful, I couldn't get 'im off. And then he just let go and I legged it with 'im! No one followed us I don't reckon. It was like my dad rippin' off a turkey leg at Christmas. 'Orrible…"

At least that was what she seemed to have said, the whole speech delivered at speed, each word filtered through her own little oral steelworks.

They sit Razza down with a cup of tea, clinking against her metalwork as she slowly calms. Scotch looks over to Terry.

"I told ya…I told ya nae ta worry. They'll do the job; they love the game."

Terry sits back, nursing the now cold cappuccino.

Note to self: probably not a good idea to join Razza and her dad for Christmas lunch.

9

IT'S ALWAYS A fiasco when they are both trying to get out of the house fast. This is one of the days they both work, Becca to her job down at King's College Hospital, Denmark Hill's claim to fame. Only three days a week though, but the money is pretty essential. Terry emerges from the spare bathroom, which becomes his on these mornings; his toast popped up a while ago, slightly burned, pretty cold. He pops it back down for a few seconds. He will eat it as he marches along for the 08.15 train.

"I just hate it when they send a new one Terry, you *know* I'm not racist, but I *do* need to be able to communicate with them, and their English is just bloody non-existent."

The agency Becca has been using for the ironing lady, her treat to herself for working just a couple of hours a week, seems to specialise solely in Eastern European girls, and usually with no discernible trace of English.

"It's bloody ridiculous, they seem to send a new one

almost every month. As soon as they start to work out what they are meant to be doing, off they go – and along comes another one and we start all over again!"

"I'm sure this one will be better Pet, it's not rocket-science ironing a few shirts."

Terry kisses Becca goodbye as he heads off to the station.

Never mind the ironing, might not be able to afford anyone soon, might not even have a fucking house for her to iron in anyway…

There is a queue halfway down the road as he reaches the station, trains screwed again, happens at least one day a week just to make work more fun. He'll have to try to sneak in unnoticed again, and he is already cutting it fine.

The train is packed.

He usually has to stand, but with all the delays the trains are completely crammed. Bodies jammed together, trying unsuccessfully not to touch, or breathe too deeply. At least 50% of the passengers are either texting or attempting to watch something on their phones, the seated minority smugly turning pages, while the standing struggle with newspapers squashed up against their fellow commuters' backs, heads, arms, as the train bumps and jolts its way up to the city – Shoreditch High Street for Terry, then a fifteen minute walk down to Aldgate.

A vibration in his pocket, and he fishes to extract his phone. The loud submarine sonar "blips" indicate it is not someone Mercedes has programmed in for a *Das Boot* "special". There is a feeling of belonging as Terry joins the gadget slaves raising his iPhone to his ear.

A ghastly mixture of high-pitched noise and shrill whistling blasts his eardrum; instinctively Terry pulls the phone away from his head. The noise continues and he attempts to listen again. A couple of his nearest neighbours glance and quickly look away. He taps the red phone sign, hanging up the call.

As he slips the phone back into his pocket, the sonar starts again, and he answers to the same noise as before, loud bells and someone shouting. The voice is female, and could have an Eastern European twang.

"Hello, I'm afraid I'm on a train – I can't really hear you," his voice is slightly raised, competing with the racket the other end, eyes fixed on mid-space.

If anything, the shouting just moves up a notch, as the shouter realises she has an audience.

"Sorry, I can't hear you!"

"Katina nummmer arm!"

The bells and shrieking get louder, so the voice also gets louder and more urgent to compensate.

"Sorry, it's a bad line. I still can't hear you." Terry also gets louder and more self-conscious as the carriage "ears" perk up, everyone studiously avoiding eye contact.

"Isskatinaaa…Ifegotttnn nummmmmmeerrr."

What the fuck is going on – this foreign woman on a speeding fire engine is shouting at me down my mobile phone – what have I done to deserve this?

"PLEASE SPEAK MORE SLOWLY – I CAN'T HEAR – WHO ARE YOU – WHAT IS THAT NOISE?"

"ISSSKKKAAAATTTNNNAAAAA – IFE ORGOTT LARM BERRR!"

Oh, God…the penny drops – it has to be the new ironing lady Becca was talking about, the agency has both their mobile numbers because of the crap reception in the hospital. The orchestral plane crash coming down the phone is the burglar alarm – and Miss Ukraine doesn't know the number.

The racket is getting worse, the words competing with heavy breathing as Katrina runs up and down Terry's hall with her phone trying to escape the noise.

"Hi Katrina…The number is…"

"ISS   KAAAAATTTTRRYYNNNAAAAA   –
ALAAARRRRRMMMM NUMMMERR!"

Terry is shouting too now – there is a hush through the packed carriage, and a healthy space has developed around him…people no longer looking away, but rather staring at him as they recognise a good panic when they see one.

"TWOOOO SIXXXX OHHHHH NINE!"

"I FORGET ALLAAARMMMM!"

"Pleeeease stop shouting and LISTEN…TWO SIX OH FUCKING-NINE. Oh God…please, please listen."

"I am sorry, I am sorry, I am—"

"Just put the number in Katrina!"

"I caarrrrnnnn heer yooooo! I do the OHHH now!"

Complete silence. The line goes dead as they dip below ground to pass beneath the Thames.

Fuck! FUCK! Terry stares up at the train map above the door – Surrey Quays. Fucking thing won't come up above ground again till Shadwell – how could anyone look forward to arriving in poxy Shadwell.

Sheepishly looking around at his fellow travellers, sweating and sticky, clutching his phone.

"Cleaner…forgotten the alarm number…sorry about the noise…"

Terry's companions on his journey look at him as if they are trapped in a room with a naked, dribbling psychopath.

A decent number of people get out at Canada Water, all the banker-boys heading to Canary Wharf, and the carriage has emptied a little. No one ever gets in at Canada Water because no one actually lives there…at least he has a bit more room now.

Waiting for the phone to return to life, seven minutes it takes as the train pulls out of Wapping and slowly emerges above ground. One bar on the phone – now two. Terry stabs at the green ring button and waits.

Please God, tell me she put the fucking number in…

"Mr Terry."

Blissful quiet, the sound of a kettle in the background and not much else – major relief. Terry smiles beatifically into the phone and people start moving away again. There is nothing like an over-joyful Londoner on a train to make everyone else feel uncomfortable.

"Iss Katrina heer – I put the nummmer in…OK now…I soree…Gudby."

Silence.

***

"Why does she do this to me Becca? It's just not fucking decent. I mean, WHY would you send your father a text like that? She knows I can't stand the little bastard anyway, and I'm fucking sure it's him leaving the turd parcels on the car."

"I know Tel, but it means she trusts you. She just wants your approval."

"But Becca, how many daughters actually TEXT their fathers to ask them about bloody anal sex – I mean, how many Becca ? It's obvious that she's asking about the little tosser who got her pregnant in the first place! YOU don't even let me do that…so why does she think it's OK to ask me about it? It's just not fucking OK!"

At least she can't get pregnant again like that; though she'll probably be the first woman in the world to give birth to some sort of "poo baby".

"What do I say to her Becca, what do I fucking say?"

"Just tell her you love her Tel. That's all she wants to hear."

"It's NOT what she wants to hear Becca! She's NOT asking me if I love her, she's asking me about arse sex Becca! I will tell her I love her, and tell her NOT to let that little fucker anywhere near her, let alone anywhere near her arsehole! It's not right, it's just NOT RIGHT!"

I can't even make myself text the bloody words!

Terry *knows* he can't actually speak to Mercedes about this, he will just end up shouting the house down, so he eventually decides the less he says the better; he simply texts back: "Not the arse sweetheart", and checks three times that Mercedes is the only recipient – not a great idea to accidentally send that one to someone else.

***

Mercedes purses her lips to kiss her dad: this always makes him flinch a little.

"Full-lipper" treatment they had called it, just a very cheap lip-expanding treatment. It had been three months since Mercedes had spent £300 on having her face made to resemble a chimpanzee, both lips fat and protruding, the upper one jutting at a jaunty angle under her nose, but the lower one slightly lop-sided, less blown-up on the right than the left.

It was a treatment that the recipient was meant to have renewed every twelve months, so he guessed that meant it should start going down sometime, but clearly not yet.

Mercedes continually expressed satisfaction with the look, but she had started heavier use of lipstick since she had "plumped them up", straying slightly over the lip on the smaller right-hand side. All round, Terry thought it was a complete horror, but if it served to put a few blokes off, then it had its compensations.

He pecked her gently on the cheek, avoiding the slick of red lippy.

***

It had started on Facebook. Why they had thought it was a good idea to put that video up there in the first place was beyond Terry, and it had leaked out from one of Mercedes' "friends" onto YouTube, and now the video of his pole-dancing daughter had 21,326 hits.

He hit the "Play" button again on his iPad and there they were: Mercedes and her two equally chubby friends in their black bondage boots and huge tasselled bikinis, launching themselves onto the three poles lined up on the stage.

It all began quite well, in a comic-tragic sort of way: three tubby orange girls with too-tight bikinis cutting into their generous curves, one with a slightly lop-sided face, opening their performance by gyrating around the poles to Queen's "We are the Champions", remaining vertical, simply slithering, heavy footed, around the pole, almost in time to the music.

Then, the pole action started in earnest and quickly descended into flabby tragedy, ending in a close-up of Mercedes, upside down on the pole, now slippery with sweat and the baby oil they had applied, slithering headfirst down the pole and into the ground with a screech of "Fuckinell... Fuck!", as her cheek hits the ground hard, followed by the rest of her slamming onto the floor, rolling onto her back, moaning and clutching at the friction burn on the inside of her knee. The shaky video unkindly zooms in on her face, then on her left tit, which had escaped in the collision, and then back out before scanning up and down the fleshy pile.

Zooming back out to encompass all three of the girls (Terry only recognised one, the potty-mouthed Sharon), all in various stages of collapse, one still on her feet, but off the pole and squatting uncomfortably, and the third having met a similar, if less dramatic fate than Mercedes. All three gasping for breath, Mercedes shovelling her tit back in and clutching at her leg, the photographer clearly unable to hold the camera still while shaking with laughter.

It looked like the aftermath of a badly staged WWWF women's wrestling bout. The video ends to roars of approval from the audience, drowning out the pained expletives from the dancers.

***

"It had all gone so well in practice Dad. It was under the lights it all went wrong! It was so hot, and the poles were different, we just couldn't stay on. I knew we shouldn't have done the vodka shots first – and the baby oil. It was fucking Sharon..."

Bliss. It made him proud to be a father; or grandfather rather. Watching it produced a horrible sense of nausea and shame in the pit of his stomach.

What the FUCK do I say to Becca...twenty-one thousand, three hundred and twenty-six...fuck!

He was pretty sure she had not seen it, but it was only a matter of time before someone brought her the good news.

Terry pressed "Play" again – for the eighth time. It just got worse every time as he noticed extra reasons to feel sick with every re-run. You could see where the orange fake tan had run on her tit, and his eyes were magnetically drawn to her lop-sided lips in the final close-up; magic!

He was terrified about where this was all heading – *twenty* thousand fucking people and counting, watching his over-sexed daughter, tits all over the place, slithering around upside down and half naked. Terry had overheard Mercedes on her phone gushing animatedly about "modelling opportunities", "Instagram millionaires", and even "*The X Factor*". It turned out that Sharon had received a phone call from a guy saying he was a freelancer for *FHM* magazine and had arranged to meet up with them. Terry had intervened and bullied the mobile number from Sharon.

His mate Robbie T, who was a good bloke for a copper, had traced the number back to Clive Harrison who lived above the chippy, a far cry from an *FHM* freelancer! Everyone knew that Clive made cheap-shit hardcore porn movies in his grimy bedsit, but even that revelation had not completely stopped the girls' conversation about whether it might be worth "investigating" further!

Finally, it had been his description of little Chloe

watching a video of her mum on Clive's sofa that seemed to have killed the idea off…until the next one came along.

Twenty fucking thousand! About the same number you could fit in the O2 arena! Not sure which I hate more: the idea of the viewers laughing at her, or wanking over her!

Both thoughts were equally hideous, gut-wrenching images. He wasn't even sure whether you *could* wank over that. If it wasn't your own daughter you would just die laughing trying to watch it!

He knew this wasn't over though; normally he would receive at least half a dozen texts per day from Mercedes, usually a stream of inexplicably abbreviated trivia, the Klaxon making him jump every time. For two days now there had been radio silence, so he knew something was going on.

***

She was in his Amazon Prime account.

Fucking ridiculous; you could buy any shit from Amazon now, and because she was never at home when the post came, she had started having things delivered to *his* work address.

He knew it was bad news when he logged on to order printer ink – it came up with "Recommendations for You in Beauty and Home" and up popped a bunch of cheap and cheerful "Bondage Play Outfits and Sets". He knew it couldn't be Becca, firstly because it was cheap, and secondly because she wouldn't have it delivered to him! Two days later, Julie brought him a small, opened Amazon parcel, containing a set of twelve tacky little earrings with bits of coloured glass stuck to them.

Had to be Mercedes, but why would you need twelve?

Maybe she's planning to have her whole bloody eyebrow done to cultivate the Gypsy look!

Reading the back of the package, it became clear she wasn't having her eyebrows done at all and had opted to have her pussy turned into a diamond-encrusted sieve. From the looks Julie was giving him, she had read this too, and decided Terry planned to use them himself somewhere unspeakable!

What the fuck have I done to deserve this?

From then on, the Amazon account had gone completely out of control. Julie, who was not 100% unattractive herself, had appeared holding a package displaying a pair of pink fluffy handcuffs. With an awful smirk on her face, refusing to make eye contact, she deposited them wordlessly on his desk and sauntered out of his office.

That really is the last straw. What do I tell her: that this stuff is for my daughter? For Becca? There's nothing you can say that doesn't just make it fucking worse!

He had explained gently to Mercedes: "If you have to buy fucking sex toys online, I would rather you paid for them yourself and NOT have them delivered to my FUCKING work!"

Now though, he was glad she did. Although she had changed the delivery address, she was still using his account. The delivery confirmation of weight-lifting chalk – *Please God for the back of her knees* – alerted him first, but the giveaway was the three sets of nipple tassels and THREE different sizes of Madonna tit-cones and matching gold lamé G-strings.

They were fucking at it again…

10

MILTON KEYNES.

I mean, Come On! Dogfighting in Milton Keynes, you have to be fucking joking!

Scotch was talking of it as a "dry run", as he put it.

A dry run with my fucking money; I'm the one with skin in the game here!

But what else was there to do? He was *all in* now, committed, he *had* to lay his hands on some money fast, and nothing else had turned up to ease the cash shortage! All the drama was doing his sex life an absolute treat, which seemed vaguely ridiculous, but now it had to be followed through; no return. It all felt a bit too "real".

The caravan was ready. It looked like shit of course, but it *was* ready.

Only Captain Morgan and Mojito would be fighting this time, but they would take all the dogs, to get them used to the caravan. Becca in the back of the Rangey, Scotch in the front seat beside Terry.

What on earth was he doing? Saturday morning! He should be getting ready to head down the Den with his mates and his dad.

He told them he had to go shopping with Becca. Fucking shopping – when had he ever been shopping? His dad had made a strangled noise on the phone.

Terry knew *exactly* what his dad was thinking: "*Missing a home game against QPR to go fucking shopping?! Fucking pansy! It had been a mistake for you to marry her, boy: half gypsy, half Essex, what did you expect?*"

He had even asked Becca once if there was any "Romany" in her family.

***

Terry takes the M25, all the way round, rather than attempting to go through London; up the M1 a few stops, and they would be there.

What AM I doing?

He had been to three dogfights as far as he could remember, it might have been two: with his dad, when he was twelve years old, and he wasn't even allowed to watch! Now he was off to lose half his twenty-grand stake, watching his dogs get eaten alive in Milton-Fucking-Keynes.

Becca just KEEPS talking: stuff about her mum, Mercedes, little Chloe, her friend Denise…all just waffle, but it just gently goes on…and on…not requiring answers, just the occasional sympathetic grunt. And Scotch! He was no better: shuffling around with his too-big headphones on, legs twitching, lips silently moving to the tinny cacophony escaping the edges of the ear-pads plugged into the Kindle-sized screen he used as a phone. Ridiculous!

Turning off the motorway, Terry navigates the thousand roundabouts surrounding Milton Keynes like a protective reef.

Bloody dogs must be puking back there by now.

Scotch had made sure they got a special "slow-release, high-protein, low-emission feed".

What the fuck was that anyway?

"Got tae be ready Tel; at the right time, got tae have them hungry."

They are out on the western fringes of Milton Keynes now, onto the aptly named *Gravely Industrial Estate*. Becca is quiet at last, and even Scotch has turned off his personal disco, but still has his headset on, eyes lively, gleaming. Terry just feels sick. The sat nav had given up a few turns ago, but they had written instructions picking up where his Texan-lady sat nav voice (another gift from his talented daughter) gave up.

The caravan pulls into a grim concrete parking lot beside a grimmer ramshackle, breeze-block warehouse, metal windows rusting, glass cracked or missing. Thirty or so other cars, several estates, the odd flash job, and a couple of older Range Rovers.

Becca and the dogs are left car-sitting as Terry and Scotch head into what has to be the entrance. A couple of "hard nuts" are standing either side of the doorway, keeping lookout and vetting the punters, black puffer-jackets pulled up against the cold drizzle of another day in paradise. Eyeballing Terry and Scotch, shaved heads, a tattoo of an ornate black star around the ear of one of them, hand-rolled cigarette balanced on ear-top.

"Nice tat, pal."

Scotch's words almost acting as a password, they are nodded through.

Inside is just fucking dire, a real derelict. They pick their way through a couple of white, peeling doorways and into a larger room where a fifteen-foot circle of hay-bales and tyres form the pit: a peeling, painted concrete floor. A pretty comprehensive selection of human detritus seems to have been washed up here: grubby anoraks and great-coats, bald heads, hats, thick-set, a threatening texture to it all. A scruffy mixture of dogs, held close on heavy leads, growling, snarling, some barking, chains being snapped to keep them quiet or close by their handlers, shouts and laughter, unpleasant laughter. Terry starts to relax, not so different to the Millwall terraces, The Den, when the away team fans almost always used to turn up ready for a kicking. Only here there was just more barking and probably less real danger. Unless you were a dog. There was nothing new in the world.

Scotch picks out the big Irishman, drawn by the description he had been given and the babble and waving of money around him.

"You Dermot?"

Red-faced, a shaggy mop of ginger, unkempt hair nods in Scotch's direction; digits like a bag of fat sausages poke through fingerless, black wool gloves; Barbour jacket unzipped over a thick, knotted jumper.

Dermot is the fixer. The man who holds the money, not to be messed with. Takes 10% of the stakes and arranges the "contests".

Terry stands by while Scotch barters the details. They shake hands not once, but three times as they reach some sort of agreement; he can't understand any of it. Scotch's

Glaswegian drawl is hard enough to follow at the best of times and now he seems to have doubled it up. As for the Paddy, fuck only knows what he was saying; how could they understand *each other* when he couldn't understand either of them? They just seemed to utter a series of grunts and animal noises. He stands, hands deep in coat pockets, shifting his weight from foot to foot until they shake again.

"Gie us the ten Tel."

The bundle of fifties comes out of Terry's inside coat pocket: a grand counted off for Dermot, handed back to his ratty little money-minder, and the rest pushed into one of several inside pockets sewn into the Irishman's coat. Terry sniffs.

Probably the last we will see of that then. What the fuck are we doing here?

The Klaxon goes off on Terry's phone: "Dive! Dive! Dive!" Both men stop and turn to look at him. He smiles sheepishly at them and grapples for his phone in his pocket to turn it off.

Back in the car, he has Scotch translate what he has agreed: five grand for each fight against the other owner's five. They wouldn't be betting with the bookies this time, only having the ten grand at stake. Scotch's definition of a "dry run"!

"First time up Tel, let's not push our luck! Captain first, then Mojito, the little fucker. We'll see if he likes dog as much as he likes ma balls Tel! Haaaa!"

It was good to see Scotch wasn't holding a grudge now his testicles had settled back to their normal size, and it had made a great story down The Badger's once he had been able to walk again.

"You had better stay here Becca," Terry says, back in the caravan. "It's really not nice in there, not nice at all. Maybe get the table ready in here for when we get out, and the sewing kit on standby."

"If you think I am being your 'little woman' Terry, you are very much mistaken. They are MY dogs as well as yours!"

Eventually Terry manages to persuade Becca that as she *is* the only woman amongst approximately sixty blokes, she might distract the dogs from their business; promising that next time, once they knew their way around better, she could come in with them.

"Your bit is vital Becca; if they get messed up, they are SO going to need their mum."

"I'M NOT THEIR FUCKING MOTHER TERRY. Christ's sake! You tough MEN had better get on with it then."

Terry checks his phone for Mercedes' text. She always knew the wrong time to send them.

Brill news we will be in Sun – THE SUN ! :-) :-) brill – tell mum n call me wen u can.

I want to die…just let me die…

***

Cuba Libre whines plaintively as Mojito and the Captain are led from their cages and down the caravan steps. Thick leather collars and leads, the noise from the other dogs setting their hairs bristling, they trot almost eagerly towards the entrance, stretching their legs from the journey. Scotch reaches into his pocket and pulls out a small plastic bag of feed pellets, giving each a couple of small handfuls, "Jist to settle 'em down Tel," and they walk into the arena to wait their turn in the ring.

The fights are sorted into rough weight groups rather than breeds: Mastiffs, Dobies and Alsatians in the heavy weights; and the various terriers and "little shits" in the light weights. The Holy Trinity are clearly in the "little shits" section, but because they were faster and nimbler, little shits fights often made the best sport. The handlers, with padded trousers and thick leather gloves, as well as two big-set rough-necks, stand ready to leap in and separate the dogs when one owner shouted the surrender. Scotch has his full body armour and a cricket box to avoid any repeat of his first meeting with Mojito.

The fights run in no particular order. Captain Morgan is on third against a similar stocky-looking Bull Terrier, and Mojito fifth against another Pittie that Terry had not seen yet.

The noise as they start fighting is awful: each dog held, hands under front legs, no collars, by its handler. Winding them up; "showing" them each other from behind lines drawn on the pit floor.

"Let go!" shouts the referee.

Then, releasing an awful, primal noise, dogs snarling as they fly at each other, men yelling, screaming, roaring.

Scotch stands close, leaning over the makeshift barriers, quietly watching. Terry can't watch. No wonder his dad hadn't let him actually see this as a kid. When he thought about it, the more he remembered sitting in the car most of the time with a bag of crisps and a can of coke, his dad giving him a "clip" when he ventured out towards the excitement. He certainly has no memory of this bloody mayhem.

Both dogs from the first fight appear bloodied and limping, but clearly in one piece, but in the second fight, the loser is carried out on a blood-soaked blanket, a makeshift stretcher.

What are they doing here? What have my poor dogs done to deserve this?

And then they are up: Captain Morgan – glossy, deep brown, the colour of his namesake – teeth bared, straining against Scotch holding him firmly. Hissing rather than growling, eyes fixed on his white, pink-eyed opponent, similarly straining to go, both being wound up:

"AT HIM! TAKE HIM!"

"Let go!" the ref shouts again.

Released, flying across the ten feet separating them. Jaws locking together, a frantic scrabbling of paws and nails at each other. So fast! And it is almost over. The Captain, jaws locked on his opponent's shoulder, swinging him round, just like Razza had described in Starbucks when the Captain had attacked the Collie, tendons tearing and the white terrier is struggling on his side on the ground, not even a lot of blood, but clearly disabled –

"TURN!" screams his owner and the boys rush in to part them.

***

"Fuck me Tel, that's the easiest five grand we are ever going to earn!"

Terry has watched this one, unable to shout his support for feeling sick, but as Captain Morgan struts on his lead back to the caravan, mouth wet with foam and blood, he feels a deep pride welling up inside.

"Well done boy…well done my son…the old Collie move, that's what we like to see…well done!"

Becca beams as she sees the Captain walking unhurt towards the car.

"Good boy! I'll take him now Tel, you go and look after Mojito."

She helps the Captain climb the caravan steps, ruffling his neck as he wriggles his pleasure at the attention from the mistress.

Mojito is an entirely different affair…all the same preliminaries, the crowd really getting tuned in and excited now, a Pit Bull facing him, similar build and size. His owner, a giant of a man, all steroids and testosterone, wearing jeans and string vest, impervious to the cold, winding him up. Very odd: the huge man, the little dog.

Mojito is growling – a low, guttural sound from deep inside, like a big, liquid outboard motor, eyes on the prize and…

"Let go!"

A ball of unstoppable, lightning fury. They lock jaws, ripping at each other, teeth clashing, stop…check… lock again, snarling against a backdrop of screaming men yelling their instructions – if "Kill the little fucker!" can be considered an instruction that is. Mojito's aggression and speed simply overwhelms his prey. He gets under his opponent and his jaws lock on the throat, teeth sink in, crushing, suffocating. The towel is thrown in and it takes three men to unlock Mojito's jaws, while the giant in the vest picks up his dog in his arms as it struggles to breathe. Mojito stands alone, panting, calm, in the middle of the ring as Scotch moves to put his lead back on.

And the Valkyrie descends…

All eyes are diverted by the sight of Becca, moving at speed, hurdling the pit wall in her long, white Jaeger coat, above-the-knee skirt, fishnets and pixie boots, and flinging her arms around Mojito.

"GOOD, GOOD BOY!"

She hugs the little dog close to her chest, reaches into her pocket and retrieves a handful of chocolate drops.

"Good boy Mojito, Good boy! Choccy drops for my lovely boy!"

The crowd falls silent. Becca's white coat is now smothered in blood and dribble as she picks Mojito up in her arms – black flowing hair, freshly painted make-up – and sweeps proudly out of the pit and towards the caravan.

"Fock me!"

Then silence.

It is the first thing Dermot has said that Terry has understood.

11

NINE GRAND! AND they hadn't needed to fight off anyone, or do a runner for fear of their lives.

Probably a few quid to have Becca's coat cleaned up, a pretty decent return. Maybe Scotch was right about the dogs. They had looked pretty impressive, terrifying even!

Terry thought the locals had been scared off by Becca's dramatic and frankly surreal appearance. All that "Goood boy!" and choccy-drop shit, you would have thought Mojito had retrieved a ball in the back garden rather than nearly ripping another dog's throat out and smothering the place in blood. She had carried Mojito out through a crowd that parted like fucking Moses and the Whatsit Sea.

Now they all sit in the Rangey on the way home, quite elated, Scotch giving repeated running commentaries on each fight, each time elaborating a little more. Becca has gotten over her "Narnia" moment, and is now worrying about the impression she had made, while Terry is just turning over in his mind what to do about their daughter's imminent arrival on the world stage, courtesy of the *Sun*...

They had cleaned both dogs up once they were all back in the caravan; each had a few scratches and punctures, but nothing serious.

Cuba Libre was pacing, feeling left out, sensing the adrenaline flowing through his companions. Mojito had become entirely besotted with Becca, pretty much ignoring both Terry and Scotch, but hanging on Becca's every word and movement. *Pushover*, thought Terry, but she had been pretty impressive in an entirely weird sort of way.

They had learned a lot in Milton Keynes, and not many people can say that. What Terry knew beyond doubt, was that *someone* was going to need to learn a little doggy first aid.

***

Tasmin sits on Terry's sofa, tears flowing, shoulders shaking uncontrollably as she spews out the awful truth. She has dressed specially for the occasion, in what seems to be an avant-garde Mother Theresa cape: flowing layers of thick black patchwork material and a large, floppy, moth-eaten black and white hat; her face red and puffy, her green eyeshadow streaking unhealthily down her cheeks.

Most of the cash was gone, and Tas had unknowingly bankrolled the purchase of a large house in Tunisia.

Karma had started sending small cash parcels back home to his mother some time ago, sneaking small amounts from the bottom of the huge pile of cash in a large cardboard box at the back of the airing cupboard. Tas had considered this to be the most sensible way to store, and keep safe, her inheritance.

Karma had managed to pick up enough English to buy a new mobile phone from his friend who ran a tacky phone stall in the Peckham Saturday street market, along with a Lebara SIM card, complete with cheap calls to North Africa.

Now it was as if he had never left home. He talked daily to his mother, his sister, both his brothers and various friends and uncles, and had become a frequent user of Her Majesty's Postal Service.

The flow of cash had gathered pace once a successful channel had been established. It took approximately two weeks for the cash-filled envelopes to arrive in Tunis, and, after the second one had gone missing completely, a more formal agreement had been reached with the local postmaster. He would open the envelopes, remove his 20% rather than stealing all of it, *then* pass the balance to Karma's mother. A further 20 % disappeared in the process of converting Karma's fifty-pound notes into Tunisian dinar. He had been sending fairly decent sums of money to all the members of his immediate family for months.

Around £250,000 had left England in this manner and a large house had been acquired in a suburb of Tunis, in which Karma's mother, brothers and sisters, plus their spouses and children now lived, under the impression that Karma was now a successful sales executive for a mobile phone company, and doing well enough to send a small fortune back to his grateful family.

"He cried Terry, he cried! He knows he should have told me, but when he realised there was no more, and that he had hurt me Tel, he cried. Then we both cried and held each other. He is so worried that his family won't be able to pay the bills to run the house, and there isn't nearly enough left to pay what you said we owe the taxman. I'm so worried Terry."

Terry just sits and listens. Nothing surprises him except the element of responsibility his sister seems to feel for Karma's family over-extending themselves financially. She genuinely seems more worried that she hasn't had sex for two days – a fact he had not particularly wanted to be made aware of. He doesn't even feel the need to actually kill Karma, maybe hurt him quite a lot, but not actually kill him.

"So…he managed to send envelopes full of cash, sometimes EVERY day for over six months without you noticing Tas – every day?"

Tasmin just sits, head hanging low, looking at her brother through her tears.

"I know I've been stupid, but I love Karma, and the sex is SO good. He relaxes me, makes me feel calm and safe, and now I might lose him. And you hate me now! And the taxman wants to send us all to prison!"

She starts crying afresh.

Terry attempts to comfort her while she sobs, his arms clumsily around her shoulders as she sits in the chair. Hard to work out where the torrents of black, scabby material stop and where his sister starts.

"Nobody hates you Sis, and no one is going to prison. You were a bit silly with Karma, but it will all sort itself out in the end."

Where the fuck does she find clothes like this anyway? Does she make them? Perhaps they just fell on her from somewhere?

"Why, Terry? Why didn't I know, why didn't I feel it? From the Other Side; someone must have known. My spirit guide must have known, and I didn't feel it, I didn't get messages…nothing!"

Tasmin's despair deepens and her wailing intensifies as her brother attempts to reassure her through the shroud of dyed dog blankets she has hand-stitched into her own stinky canine-cape.

"My animal spirit guide is the Dog Terry! He showed himself to me in the shamanic lodge in Margate! I never SAW the Dog, but I BECAME the Dog. They said I was throwing myself around and howling. And that was it. The Dog has been by my side ever since. But where is he NOW? Where is the Dog now, when I need to know the way?"

"Not totally sure Sis."

Terry is desperate to get her off his sofa and out of his house with her dog-shroud thing before it starts moulting.

There has to be shit on it – only shit smells like that. It's not HER that smells, unless her "spirit guide" is actually dog shit… maybe that was it…they misheard…dog shit for a guide. It would explain a lot.

Terry's attention is briefly diverted as Scooter bumps into the wall again. His arse-wiping journeys are pretty much all he ever does now, his rear legs jutting forwards, not even touching the ground as he drags his little arsehole across the carpet. Terry sighs deeply as he notices Scooter is actually leaving a visible trail these days; he would not let anyone touch him, hissing and spitting demonically even when Becca came too close. He would have to go. Maybe his sister would take him in and get Karma to heal his horrible cat soul, and even his horrible cat arse. That was if anyone could even get near enough to the fucking thing to pick him up and stick him in a bag.

"They have nothing Tel. NOTHING! How can I be angry with him? He did it for love, love of his mother, and his need to heal his family."

Terry decides that pointing out that Karma's family ALL had their own mobile phones, and were living in a house paid for by money stolen from his – *NO* – *THEIR* mother, would not be productive; in fact, possibly the opposite. He was worried that any more tears wetting that awful piece of woven dog shit she was wearing might cause it to dissolve and flow into his shag pile, making Scooter's minimalistic poo trail seem quite benign.

Time for you to go… Terry helps his sister up from the sofa, but she just keeps whirling around in her fucking dog disguise, repeating parts of her story over and over, before finally saying, "I must let him have me Terry!"

Oh, holy mother of God!

"If I let him TAKE me it will prove I forgive him."

She rises up, spreads her arms under the cape.

"He must take me…TAKE ME like the DOG Terry!"

I HAVE to get her out of the fucking door.

He has been nodding enthusiastically to his sister's analysis on how to resolve a difficult emotional and financial situation.

She can let Karma fuck her in the ear as far as I'm concerned, as long as she goes away!

With promises to call round and to bring Scooter to see Karma for a bit of "hands on" healing, and even more importantly, to tell Tas what she should do when the tax letter eventually arrives, the door shuts.

Terry sits down, avoiding the sofa, in the living room. And he can feel an unseen weight settling around his shoulders, pressing on him, making him feel small. He draws in a deep breath.

A strangled hissing noise breaks through his thoughts as Scooter, clawing at the carpet, drags himself round again for the return leg of his journey.

12

THE GIRLS AREN'T talking.

It seems possible they will never talk again.

Becca had sat in absolute silence as she watched the video on Terry's iPad. He knew he would have to show her once Mercedes had decided to "go national" and talk to the *Sun*. Only her eyes gave any emotion away as they narrowed and hardened. He sat on the sofa opposite, waiting for the two-minute clip to finish. As the sound stops, Becca's jaw tightens, fighting for composure.

In an entirely false voice, full of forced normality:

"How many people have seen this?"

Terry explains the little he understands about how the video had arrived on YouTube – the "views" were up to 28,000 now.

"So, 28,000 complete strangers, including most of our friends too by now, have watched my daughter, *our* daughter, doing this. In fact, ANYONE on the whole planet could watch it…and you have known for how long Terry?"

It is a genuine venom whirlwind, made worse by the calm and cold way it is delivered.

Terry immediately feels a horrible sensation as his left testicle retreats back up into its cavity. This was becoming a regular and total unwelcome addition to his life; he instinctively moves his hand just below his belt where he could just sense it nestling. It never actually hurt, but just felt very weird.

It's like it knows when I have nowhere to bloody hide; so a bollock goes and hides for me.

It had started to happen during sex recently, and while he didn't *have* to stop, it was just such a bizarre feeling that he had withdrawn under the pretext of shifting positions, while gently trying to massage it back down into place with an inaudible "plop".

He knew he should see a doctor about it, but Google had explained that this was not actually terribly abnormal, and the idea of explaining his little problem to the young and rather attractive Dr Shah at their surgery hadn't become a priority for him yet.

Trying hard to ignore the shifting bollock, he gives Becca his usual feeble explanation for why there is yet another critical piece of information he feels should be kept from his wife, while 28,000 other people are aware of it, and waits for the shit-storm to blow over and around him, hoping it will soon settle on the real perpetrator of the crime.

Fucking hell Mercedes! It's going to be years, a lifetime, before I get laid again. It's just NOT fucking fair!

Terry attempts to explain that there "didn't seem to be a sensible time to bring it up", without the startlingly obvious caveat that he hadn't want to convey information that he knew would be the start of an extended period of complete sexual abstinence that he would rather avoid.

And then she is gone; car keys in hand, without a word, no handbag, no phone, just a verbal nail-bomb on its way to an unseen target.

An hour later, Terry hears the Range Rover brakes being heavily applied as Becca pulls up at the kerb outside. He reaches for the TV remote. He wouldn't want Becca to see he had been cruising the adult channels again, particularly at a time when he was meant to be providing a sympathetic, caring shoulder to cry on.

He never understood why anyone used the TV for porn these days, there was so much more decent stuff on the internet. But he didn't want a re-run of when Becca had googled "Leicester hotels" and after typing the first two letters had been presented with a drop-down list of fourteen searches Terry had conducted starting with the word "Lesbian". After a few seconds where his brain went into wordless shock as he scoured for a half-credible explanation, his face turned a deep shade of crimson. Becca had just laughed and whispered "Naughty boy" in that husky tone he couldn't resist, and given him a look that said he might not need to be searching anywhere other than right in front of him for a dose of naughtiness.

Nevertheless, it just felt wrong to be "found out", so he had abandoned the shared desktop PC in favour of TV or iPad in his periodic cruising for porn.

Slamming the door, face reddened, eyes puffy, Becca comes across the living room to where Terry is standing, puts her arms round him and squeezes very tight, her body resonating with bottled emotions. He squeezes her back, burying his head in her hair.

"I can't believe what I said to her, my *own* daughter. It just *all* came out: Little bitch! Ungrateful, stupid little bitch! I said the most terrible things…and she just doesn't care. Doesn't care about us, about *her* own daughter or anyone – she ONLY cares about herself. How did she get like that? HOW? What did I do?"

Becca is now calm enough to be sitting at the kitchen table, sipping the tea Terry has thoughtfully prepared. He doesn't know the answers, but at least it sounds as though he might be closer to grappling with Becca again than he had at first thought.

"Did she mention the *Sun* Becca?"

Becca's eyes narrow as she looks over the rim of her teacup at Terry; it is minus twenty-five in Siberia.

***

The upstairs function room at The Badger's was set up for the show. All very professional: lighting, a proper block stage, and three poles robustly secured from floor to ceiling. Tonto had been watching "Pole Dancing Disasters" on YouTube so was well aware of the damage an unsecured pole could do.

Terry had complained bitterly; it was his boozer too. "Who keeps you in fucking business, Tonto? The regular punters – that's who! So why wasn't one of your best regulars, ME, the first to know when the girls approached you to rent the room and sell the tickets?"

"'Cos you'd have tried to stop it Tel, s'ovious, and there's decent money in it mate. Sorry."

"Sorry?! You're not fucking sorry Tonto – you're just fucking me up the arse like everyone else!"

Fifteen quid each – and Terry reckoned half the tickets had been sold to his mates just so they could see his daughter make another tit-smacking, tragic display of herself at his expense! Her two co-performers didn't seem to have parents, or at least not ones who gave a toss.

Trying to talk to Mercedes about it was hopeless. She seemed to think she was going to be "discovered" by Simon-fucking-Cowell or something, and when she was with the other two she was much worse: their collective, foul-mouthed derision when they were confronted as a team was just shocking. Mercedes stood by just sneering at him as Sharon Potty-Mouth told him he had just better "Pay his cash to stare at the gash", with the rest of them. It didn't seem to occur to her that one of the "gashes" on display was his own daughter's; and that made a bloody difference!

Fuck it!

Becca had insisted he had to go and watch.

"I'm just not prepared to see something else on TV without being prepared. It will be fucking terrible Terry – but at least I'll know what's coming…"

***

The room is packed.

Best part of sixty people sitting on the rows of cheap plastic chairs, and another twenty standing around the edges. A dozen of the girls' friends are in the front row making more noise than the rest of the room put together, all with their phones in hand, texting and selfie-ing frantically as they shriek at each other.

Terry stands in the furthest corner of the room, as far away from the stage as he can without actually leaving the room.

There's no fucking hope!

Everyone apart from the front row has a pint glass in hand, average age of about forty-five – a decent number of them are clutching those electric smoking things.

Can't believe a proper pub allows half the punters to sit there looking like Gandalf puffing on their fucking coloured wands.

Tonto had something to answer for.

The girl's Essex-wannabe friends in the front row are split by an unsavoury-looking thirty-something grease ball from the *Sun*: long, greying hair swept back, a smoker's complexion and ratty teeth, his smartphone in hand and camera slung on a wide strap over the shoulder of his black leather bomber.

Terry had asked to see his *Sun* ID; but it turned out they hadn't even sent one of their own reporters. This lad just had a cheap bit of card with "Freelance" emblazoned all over it in gold letters. He wasn't sure whether to laugh or cry. At least the *Sun* didn't really give a shit, or they would have sent a proper journo, but a tiny part of him felt his daughter deserved better – *insanity*!

The girls in the front row are putting on the usual "screeching hooker show" for the *Sun* celebrity; the room is now full and the lights dimming.

Scanning the room, it looks to Terry that pretty much anyone he has ever known socially has turned up to "support" him.

Every time you think it can't get worse…even Scotch is there and that dirty bastard, Clive.

A hand touches him on the shoulder. He turns to see the smiling face of his sister.

NOOOOOO, noooooo !!

"Tas…it's you…"

Tasmin reaches up and does her usual miss-by-a-mile air-kissing thing somewhere near both his cheeks. Terry can barely breathe. Tas is wearing clothes that you could almost describe as normal, the first time he has seen her *not* looking like a fucking banshee since her wedding.

"What are you doing here?"

"Just supporting the family. Mercedes sent me a WhatsApp – told me about the show! I thought Karma needed an evening out, so here we are. See you later."

Tasmin moves off to take her place beside Karma. Terry had not spotted him in the crowd. It was clear from his sister's light-hearted greeting that she has no idea what the "show" is likely to entail. He feels a testicle on the move again.

I wonder what being dead is like? I must have done something pretty fucking terrible in a previous life to deserve this…

The speaker behind him bursts into deafening, pulsating life and the girls skip in from behind the stage, wearing golden G-strings and nipple tassels. To be fair, the nipple tassels are more substantial than the G-strings. The trio have clearly spent half their time down the fake-tan shop: a lurid orange, radioactive glow, smothered in body glitter.

They all have matching hairdos – black, piled high and pinned into buns – pretty clever given that Sharon was usually sporting a short mousey-coloured fringe. Apart from their waistlines, there is nothing on display that hasn't been substantially tampered with or painted an unnatural colour.

Terry has always been a closet Bon Jovi fan, not something you would admit down The Badger's, and as the heavy bass of 'Livin' on a Prayer' cuts in behind him, he feels a wave of panic as the girls prance heavy-footed across the stage.

They have invested, with the help of either Tonto or the *Sun*, in some decent professional poles with spinning external sleeves, along with strong base and ceiling fixings. Becca had caught Terry watching "X-Rated Pole-Dance Out-Takes" on YouTube, apparently to prepare himself for the worst, but the flush on his face and the speed with which he had attempted to close it down, had warranted a "For God's sake TERRY!" as she turned her back and stalked out of the room.

Terry feels his heart sink further as the lights dim, the manic strobes start up and the three girls launch themselves towards their poles, twirling around them in slow motion, large, dimpled bottoms hiding any sign of the G-strings.

Who WOULD wear a fucking G-string with an arse like that – WHY would you?

All three of them are now clutching the poles halfway up, heads hung back, tongues protruding – barely missing each other as their circling continues.

They're bending over now and slapping their own bottoms hard– a move clearly picked up from cheap porn movies. Pretty much every one of the dirty old bastards who had turned up to watch are on their feet, shouting their encouragement.

"Get yer tits out!"

"I'll slap that for ya!"

The *Sun* geezer is on his feet too, snapping away.

It's all out of fucking control; what am I going to tell Becca?

"FUCKING SIT DOWN, YOU TART!" an unseen member of the audience commands the *Sun* man blocking the view.

"WE'VE FUCKING PAID FOR THIS – NOT TO WATCH YOU AND YER FUCKING CAMERA!" The journo crouches a little, acknowledging his error.

The final chorus of 'Livin' on a Prayer', the mighty Bon Jovi almost drowned out by the raucous crowd. The seconds pass, then a couple of minutes, and thankfully, still little genuine pole action, or at least nothing that would result in the horrors he expected to be reporting back.

The music fades to be replaced by Terry's favourite anthem of all time – Joan Jett's foot-thumping 'I Love Rock and Roll'.

Why would she do this to him? It just wasn't fair – this was HIS, Tel's, music, and now he could never fucking listen to it again!

Slowly the girls, soundlessly mouthing the words, attempt some mild off-the-ground pole mounting. The crowd, who had been slightly restless for a while, have now fully embraced Joan Jett – everyone in the room bellowing raucously about dimes and juke boxes, half of them singing it, arms aloft, to each other. It is Saturday night at The Badger's after all…

The arse-smacking had almost taken over from the pole-action for a while, but now the girls start to tackle a more gymnastic set of moves: up the poles, if mainly vertical, slowly spinning earthwards, tongues still lolling, lips pouting, wordlessly miming along to the song, eyes glued on the camera lens. All three launch themselves upside down onto their poles, both hands clinging on, one leg wrapped around the pole above them, spinning, the other stilettoed leg almost at ninety degrees. Breasts now gravity-challenged, flapping under their chins; the crowd roar their approval as the G-strings struggle to perform even the flimsiest of disguises.

Terry feels sick: staring at his daughter's naked arse is one thing, but being confronted by her ripe genitals only split by a small piece of orange string in front of a pack of baying drunks *and* his sister, is quite another.

Got to get out. It's just too much…beyond awful, way beyond awful.

He starts to lurch towards the exit as Potty Mouth's leg loses its grip on the pole and both her feet fly out at right-angles as she hangs on, and slash across the exposed underside of Mercedes' left tit. Both girls plummet to the floor with a horrible impact, heads and shoulders striking first, hips and legs slamming into the stage. Mercedes is screaming, clutching her breast, blood seeping between her fingers, soaking her stomach, from the deep gash from Sharon's flying stiletto.

Joan Jett's bellowed "Dance with me" finale is projected into a horrified silence from the crowd, split by the moans from the stage as the strobe continues to flicker.

Terry races forward, barging through the watchers to find the *Sun* man standing crouched and snapping furiously with his camera zoomed in on his daughter. The crimson cloud descends and Terry slams into him, hurling him to the ground, and as the journalist gets to his knees, Terry swings a great barn-yard punch, catching him with his full weight between ear and jaw. *Sun* man collapses, poleaxed.

Turning now, he crawls up onto the stage on his knees. Sharon is laying on her side, clutching her shoulder, groaning. The third dancer, whose name he has never known, kneels beside a sobbing, gasping Mercedes, who is gripping her breast with both hands to stem the flow of blood between her fingers.

"Get an ambulance! GET A FUCKING AMBULANCE!"

13

THE AMBULANCE HAD taken forty minutes to get there, and then they had had to share it with that scumbag reporter and Tasmin.

Terry was worried about *Sun* man. He had been unconscious for fifteen minutes and hadn't really looked "with it" in the ambulance. He didn't seem to be aware who had put him there, and Terry was hopeful that he hadn't actually seen him before he had switched the little bastard's lights off. It had been a peach of a blow.

Might even teach him a lesson or two about respect, values, and all that good stuff they preach at the Sun.

Tasmin had insisted on coming in the ambulance with them, and had held Mercedes' hand all the way to the hospital, spraying her unique brand of half-baked spiritual mumbo-jumbo incessantly for the thirty minutes of beeping and yelling at the South London traffic, as they made their tortuous way to Lewisham Hospital.

In the ambulance, Mercedes was clearly in shock,

and was quietening down now they had filled her full of painkillers. Terry managed to stop Tasmin rubbing what looked like a mummified rabbit leg she had produced from her gigantic handbag into the wound; even the paramedic had been taken by surprise, telling the soppy cow to "Keep that fucking thing away from everyone," despite her protestations about its healing powers.

The hospital staff had parked them in a corner of a crowded waiting room, until Terry mentioned he was worried she had split the implant he had helped Mercedes choose for her seventeenth birthday.

It was ridiculous really, they were scary-big *before* the implants.

They had whisked her off pretty fast after he mentioned that. An hour later they wheeled her out and onto the ward to recover.

Sharon's heel had moved, but not split, the implant, so it had just been a simple matter of eighteen stitches to hold his daughter's breast on. At least the wound had cut along the implant scar, which for some unfathomable reason seemed to feel comforting. Her breast looked like one huge bruise, and they hadn't even thought to clean up the landslide of make-up, tears, false lashes and lipstick that had turned her face into a badly drawn cartoon. Terry stares hard at the ceiling, biting his lip.

"It will be all right, love."

***

Becca holds his hand tight, fighting back her own tears.

Even Tas is quiet, standing beside him, after she has

finally been convinced that none of the curious contents of her handbag will be either useful or welcome.

"I will help heal her Terry, I will. I know I can help; you'll see."

"I know you will Sis, but not with anything too dirty. Just hold her hand and keep talking to her. That will do it."

They are keeping Mercedes in overnight for observation, she had hit her head hard on the stage too. She seems pretty much out of it, so they had better push off and relieve Becca's mother from Chloe-sitting duty. Tas decides to stay to help "heal" the patient. Becca takes Terry's arm as they head out towards the car. They almost make it to the door before they hear the unmistakeable voice of Plod.

"Mr Granger, Mr Terence Granger, would you mind if we asked you a few questions please sir?"

***

"Don't touch me!"

"I'm just strapping you in Grandmo."

"You are NOT strapping me in, you are touching my breasts. DIRTY MAN! And DON'T call me 'Grandmo' – I am NOT your grandmother, heaven help her…"

Over an hour! Over a fucking hour talking to the Police. They didn't believe a word he said anyway. Then again, it wasn't very believable. Why *would* they believe he had just "knocked into" *Sun* man trying to get to his daughter, when his jaw was clearly broken? A few of the boys down The Badger's had seemed to think that being pissed off with someone actually made it legal to nearly kill them, so had told Plod exactly that, with a degree of pride. And now

111

Terry is expecting them to believe he just "bumped into him".

Pretty clear this one isn't going to go away.

And now here I am, with Becca's semi-continent bag of bitterness she calls a mother, accusing me of groping her seventy-eight-year-old tits. It just gets better and fucking better!

He had felt a warm dampness as he had helped Edith up into the Range Rover. He wanted to put a bin bag on the seat, but knew there was no chance he could get away with it.

"Sorry Edith, just trying to get you strapped in. We don't want you going through the windscreen now do we? I didn't mean to call you 'Grandmo', I am sorry, it's just because that's what Mercedes calls you. I am sorry…really."

She got a taxi over here. Why wouldn't she let me get her a fucking taxi back instead of putting me through this shit?

"Just STOP touching my breasts! You can touch my daughter's breasts if you like, though God knows why she would allow it, BUT NOT MINE! We are not ALL animals Terry!"

It is going to be a long journey back to West Norwood. Terry decides it is best to put his foot down; at least if the vicious old bint has to concentrate on the road she will have less time to moan at him. He would be lucky if he got her home without being accused of every sexual deviation known to man.

"I need the toilet."

Nooooo, surely not… They have only been in the car five minutes.

"Can't you hang on Edith? We are nearly there."

"We are not 'nearly there' Terry, and NO I can't hang on! I need a toilet."

He pulls the car up on a double yellow in Dulwich High Street by one of those round metallic auto-loos. They go through the "Don't touch me" ritual a couple of times as Terry helps Edith down from the Range Rover.

50p, the ever-increasing price of a piss, in the slot, and the door slides open and Edith actually backs in, alert to the possibility of her idiot daughter's fat, sweating, peasant-of-a-husband attempting to get in there with her; just the sort of thing he would try.

The door slides shut behind her and Terry gets back up into the car and waits. His head feels just *too* full. He doesn't have time for this. He really doesn't. He needs to be back with Becca, and he's *got* to talk to Tonto and find out who said what to the cops.

Time passes.

"Are you all right Edith?" Terry shouts through the door. He can hear knocking and muffled noise, but no response.

"ARE YOU ALL RIGHT?!"

"Can't get out. Can't GET OUT!"

"OK, Edith, calm down, we'll get you out. Can you see the red and green buttons?"

"Can't get out!"

"Edith, there is a GREEN button by the door, you just have to press it."

"Let me OUT! TERRY!"

"The GREEN button Edith, press the GREEN button and the door will open!"

The woman was just born stupid.

"I AM pressing the button. LET ME OUT TERRY!"

"Calm down Grandmo. Just slowly press—"

"I AM NOT YOUR BLOODY GRANDMOTHER, you horrible man – JUST LET ME OUT!"

"EDITH, just stop it. Stop it…and look around you at the buttons. Press the green one firmly and slowly."

"YOU'VE LOCKED ME IN HERE ON PURPOSE – LET! ME! OUT!"

There is quite a crowd gathering around Terry's toilet now, offering several less-than-helpful pieces of advice:

"Bloke stuck in there for three hours last week. I told 'em they shudda shut it; council fella said it was kettled."

Terry looks down and notices his friend with all the info is standing on a large, sodden piece of cardboard covered in Sellotape. The words "Out Of Order" are just discernible, despite it clearly having been trampled over for some time.

"I'M going to pull the black cord."

"Just press the GREEN button Edith."

There is a loud click and a scream from inside as the self-cleaning programme starts with Edith inside.

"That's what 'appened to the bloke last week too. Iss fukin' broken it is. I told em! In the end we had to put anuvver 50p in."

The sound of water spraying inside the loo can now be heard just above the screams of his mother-in-law, and an unseen hand tightens inside Terry's chest, his breathing laboured; his bollock retreats again, faster than usual, and horribly uncomfortable.

"Has anyone got 50p?"

The dozen or so people who have gathered for their free entertainment almost all look away as a unit. This is clearly just an act to extort 50p coins from them.

"She's gonna fukin' drown in there mate if yur not

careful. Fukin' tragic. What a way to go...I said, WHAT a way to go!"

"DOES ANYONE HAVE A 50p COIN? I WILL GIVE YOU A POUND FOR IT!"

The crowd *all* know this *is* a con now – some bloke, sounding desperate, buying 50p coins for a quid, must think they were born yesterday. Dodgy bastard.

The screaming inside continues as he finally manages to persuade the old boy who has been standing on the remnants of the "Out of Order" sign to change a pound coin for 50p, two 20p pieces and some coppers; all carefully counted out before the pound coin is taken with one hand and the change, including the 50p coin, is tipped into Terry's outstretched hand.

The spraying sound has stopped now. The screams have turned into deep, chesty sobs as the drying cycle starts in the toilet. Terry pushes his 50p coin into the slot, presses the now-lit green button and the door slides gently open, releasing a blast of warm, disinfected air and an old lady standing, drenched, naked apart from her white pants and thick black tights, both around her knees.

For the love of God! WHY has she taken her kit off?

A collective sharp intake of breath runs through the onlookers: this has been well worth 50p, whoever this bloke is.

"I think you had better get her a coat, dear."

Helpful, very fucking helpful.

***

"After everything that has happened today Terry, I fail to see how you can still think this is even slightly funny.

You made her get back into soaking-wet clothes and just left her in the house alone, drenched, and freezing cold. MY mother, an old woman! I know you don't like her Terry, and I know she doesn't like you, but even so…you just left and drove home? Just unbelievable! Only you Terry, only you!"

He shifts awkwardly on the kitchen stool, unconsciously massaging his abdomen, still trying to persuade the rogue bollock back into place. He still couldn't understand why she took half her clothes off in there, and *when* had she done it? After the wash cycle went off? Or before? How did she get it all off when it was wet? Why would anyone want to do that?

Cos she's fucking mad Tel. That's why.

"She wouldn't let me anywhere near her Becca, she thinks I did it on purpose! Made me stand at the garden gate while she let herself in, then shouts 'fucking rapist' at me! She would still be in the bog without me! She's ruined the car; it stinks of disinfectant and it's soaking wet! I don't have to put up with that Becca – a 'fucking rapist', I ask you! And why, fucking WHY, did she take her clothes off Becca?!"

They are interrupted by a pained, high-pitched howling emanating from the direction of the living room.

"God, are they still bloody here Becca, Tas and Karma? And what the fuck are they doing?"

He opens the living-room door as the extraordinary screeching intensifies.

Karma is sitting on the sofa with one hand, holding Scooter aloft by the skin on the back of his neck; the other hand clearly has an index finger inserted into Scooter's scraggy little rectum as Scooter's four legs scrabble wildly in the air trying to escape. Karma's head is tilted backwards and his eyelids are flickering, eyes rolling back, and then in a sudden movement he pulls his finger out of Scooter's arse as Scooter jerks even more wildly in abject panic.

Gently Karma lowers the cat to the ground, letting him go. Scooter bolts behind the sofa mewling loudly.

"Hush Terry," whispers Tasmin. "It's happening…*the healing*…it's happening…"

"HE'S FINGER-FUCKED THE CAT'S ARSE! TASMIN… I can't… I can't … DON'T PUT YOUR FUCKING HAND ON THE SOFA KARMA! DON'T! AGGHHH!"

"Terry, love, you don't see it do you? He has the gift. The cat will be healed…"

Scooter appears timidly from behind the sofa. The in-growing whisker that he has been desperately attempting to dislodge from his arse for months has gone. Cat bliss. No more wiping his bum across the carpet – and, for the first time, Terry sees Scooter walk normally, if slightly gingerly, across the floor…and nuzzle against Karma's leg.

Terry simply stands – he can see Karma gently wiping a dark finger on the arm of the sofa, with his sister gazing entranced at him. The ridiculous fucking cat rubbing himself on the bare patch of leg below Karma's shabby cut-offs. His brother-in-law beams at him, gleaming white teeth and a wide soppy grin spread all over his face.

From behind, he hears Becca's voice:

"Why don't you come and wash those hands, Karma love?"

His sister, open-mouthed, and clearly aroused, eyes fixed on Karma as he gets to his feet, says,

"Then, we MUST be going Terry. Things to do, you know?"

She winks lasciviously at him.

It is all quite beyond imagining. Terry's brain starts to shut down, numb. He just stands and feels himself breathing.

"DIVE! DIVE! DIVE!" breaks his trance. He reaches for the phone and reads:

Sorry I fukt up – tku for helping me – Rly hurt but B OK – Luv U dad xxxxx M

Another text bleeps. Terry absently flicks it into view. From Scotch.

Round 2 sorted – Hackney – decent cash – next Saturday. Fucking brilliant shot on the Sun Scumbag – what a tosser!

Terry sighs. It has been an interesting day, but not one he is keen to repeat any time soon.

14

BECCA IS BECOMING increasingly concerned about her role as chief "dog repairer". It was proving very difficult to find any relevant courses online, so she has sent Terry out on reconnaissance missions, first to the local pet shop, to peer along the bookshelves. Plenty of information on keeping your rabbit healthy, avoiding accidents with guinea pigs and the like, but when it came to dogs, it was all centred around training, healthy coats, healthy minds, and the most "clinical" it got was dealing with worms, a variety of "poo-related" issues, and clipping their toenails!

"Can I assist in any way? We have books covering pretty much everything."

Terry smiles at the lanky man before him, mid-fifties, checked shorts and very white trainers.

"I was looking for a book on sort of 'doggy first aid', but not really sure you have anything here. You know…for if they have an accident, or get in a fight or something."

"Really you should just take them to the vet for anything serious, but we have books covering the most common issues: fleas, ear problems, worms and tummy trouble…" He can see that Terry is not taken with this list of medical problems. "Helping with breathing difficulties is probably the closest thing to actual first aid, what breed is your dog?"

Breathing difficulties sounded more like it to Terry, but he quite quickly realised that his host wasn't talking "crushed windpipes", and the suggested "dab of antiseptic cream" for small wounds would not be entirely effective with large lumps of face hanging off. Similarly the ear issues did not seem to include what to do when one actually went missing.

Terry excuses himself as gently as he can.

Next is a trip to the local vet, at the tail-end of the high street, and its sterile, tatty white waiting room. A handful of concerned-looking owners waiting with their loved ones in small cages or boxes. A small girl sits with her mother, clearly distressed about her hamster, who appears to be lying stone dead on the floor of a small, clear plastic carry-box.

Terry's plan was to wander in unobtrusively and see if there were any useful pamphlets to be found on the shelves, but he finds himself standing encircled by seated patients and owners – the immediate centre of attention as the only pet-less person there, as if he had walked unexpectedly onto a small stage.

"Can I help you?"

Terry feels himself redden a little. The receptionist is blonde, a delicious lilt to her accent, perfectly made up, blood-coloured lipstick, plain black-framed glasses that heighten the "intelligent sexy" look she has cultivated, her gaze locked on his.

Unprepared for questions, or an audience, his imagination flies into overdrive – she is almost certainly Ukrainian, with a PhD in Sex Therapy, escaping Putin's mobsters. His eyes tear themselves away and dart around the room as his throat constricts, the only pamphlets anywhere on show are advertising insurance for veterinary bills.

"I was just looking for information on…sort of, wounds… how to treat wounds on a dog, my dog. Or injuries…"

God Terry, how stupid does that sound! Fuck's sake, calm down!

"If they are bad wounds you really should bring it in as soon as possible, we have a walk-in surgery for emergencies. Is it outside in the car, do you need help bringing it in?" The receptionist's gaze is directly on his eyes, unwavering, lips pursed slightly over perfect white tombstone teeth.

"Yes…errr, who?"

"Your dog."

"Ahhh, no. I understand what you mean! No, my dog isn't outside, and he's not actually injured. Not yet."

"Are you expecting him to *get* injured?"

"No…not really, no…it's just in case, you know, better safe than sorry."

"Can I actually do anything for you?"

"No, not really, I'll be off then, thank you though."

Her gaze breaks from his, shifts into the room, dropping him wordlessly into the trash. "Poppy the hamster and her owner please!"

How mortifying. Terry turns, moving towards the door, bumping into the little girl clutching Poppy in her plastic tomb. Poppy doesn't move at all; Terry thinks she is stuck to the bottom of the box.

***

Sitting in the reference section of the library, the only building anyone ever remembers in Peckham, a brilliant piece of modern architecture, Terry is poring over veterinary surgery books, finally finding *something* that at least shows a few pictures of wounds being sutured. Terry is not a member of the library, nor is he a fan of its funky modern interior design. It feels like he has been abducted by aliens and is sitting in their spaceship waiting to be experimented on.

Unable to take any books out, Terry defaults to taking photocopies of a few pages. He is not at all sure Becca will be impressed with the fruits of his morning labours.

"Why have you brought photocopies of things we can see better online? They aren't even dogs Terry – it's a picture of human open-heart surgery for God's sake, how does that help me learn to help a wounded dog?"

***

Becca signed herself up for a three-week first aid evening course, having been unable to find anything at all specific for mending and stitching up broken dogs; a week later, this wasn't going well.

"I need to do stitching Terry, pretty much everything else is useless. I am *not* going to be treating them for a stroke, or putting slings on them, *or* bloody resuscitating them – I am going to be *stitching* them up and treating wounds."

The next evening Terry gets home from work to find Becca sitting at the kitchen table, rubber gloves on her hands, stitching up lumps of meat with black surgical thread and long curling suture needles. The table is simply carnage, a leg of lamb, a whole chicken and a pig's trotter with several long rows of stitches down each piece of carcass where she has made long, deep slices, the table a slew of gooey blood and fat; Frankenstein's barbecue.

"I wasn't really sure what sort of skin dogs have Terry. They are muscly and thin-skinned, I think, so I thought I would have a practice with different things."

Becca has a tight, serious look as she pulls the needle through the flabby chicken breast skin, concentrating, not looking up, wincing. The spectre of having to do this on a live animal, a friend even, sits over them both.

***

Razza is taking them out in pairs now, wearing her leather wrist supports, the dogs wearing matching soft muzzles, wrapping the leads around her hands to make sure there is no repeat of the Collie incident; but when they were together no other dogs ever came within thirty yards of them anyway. It has been five weeks since the Milton Keynes massacre, and the dogs are proving expensive to run. Between the "clever" dog food, the vitamin supplements and Razza's wages, it was costing about £400 per week to keep the show on the road.

Terry walked through the door of the lock-up to the sound of a deep, rumbling growl, and found what appeared to be Mojito being hung by Scotch, presumably in revenge for his near genital amputation during the great "Dog Snatch" as Becca liked to refer to it. He had rushed over to rescue Mojito, only to find that he was hanging there entirely of his own accord.

"Whaddaya thenk of it Tel? This is what they need. Ah just fucken' wince every time ah remember ma whole ball-sack and tackle was there – it's a fucken' miracle ahm alive, Tel."

This was one of the dogs' main exercises: a spring-pole, basically a large steel spring with a metal loop on the end, hanging from the centre of the lock-up's roof, with a six-inch rubber ring wrapped in heavy material suspended from it, dangling about five feet from the ground.

The dogs would take obedient turns waiting to jump, catch the ring in their mouths and hang there, violently shaking their heads from side to side, growling through locked teeth, their whole bodies swinging from the effect. After a minute or so they would take a breather, just hanging, catching their breath, before the shaking movement started again.

Fifteen minutes each, three times a day. While one was up there the other two would just sit or lie quietly, but never taking their eyes off the one "playing". At the end of their allotted time, Razza would have to catch and hold each dog, one hand on the collar, the other wrapped round below the belly, taking their weight and shouting "Release", which after a while, they each did.

Poodle never seemed to want to join in this fun, but also sat transfixed by the gyrating, hanging dogs. It was hard not to notice the rapid deterioration of Poodle's twitch; now heavily pronounced like a severe Parkinson's tremor. It had made him a bit snappy with anyone coming near, but Terry had discovered that a sharp rap on the nose with a rolled up newspaper seemed to stop the tremor *and* the snappy behaviour, and sort of "reboot" him.

The stool-density testing, and slightly bizarre semi-science applied to the training and grooming routine was keeping Scotch happy, grunting his approval as he squashed a small turd on a white saucer with the flat face of a knife. He had a habit of doing this without warning. Terry would be sitting reading the *Evening Standard* and suddenly the smell would hit him, right between the eyes, and there would be Scotch sitting beside him, carefully examining a turd.

"You could at least fucking warn me Scotch!"

But to the extent to which Scotch found *anything* funny, this was clearly his favourite.

There were three large containers of vitamin additives, each with its own measuring spoon and labels hand-written on the side. The dogs were allowed one meal containing what Terry recognised as "meat" each day, mixed with Scotch's patent vitamin additive formula, plus two much smaller meals of different dry pellet food, all from the CSJ warehouse.

Scotch would stand beside Razza as she prepared the feeds, occasionally snapping at her in Glaswegian if he felt a measurement was slightly off, or the mixing not thorough enough.

It's more like watching the bald bloke from Breaking Bad *brewing crystal meth than someone feeding a bunch of dogs.*

But he had to quietly admit they were looking in very good shape: glossy coats, healthy lips and bright pink tongues, and they seemed to bristle with energy – *not to mention nice firm shit* – the various nicks and punctures the dogs had picked up on their first run-out had largely healed up.

Terry had been having a recurrent dream that always

finished with him sitting in his favourite chair in front of the TV, with a nice Indian takeaway on his lap. He looks down and it is the saucer full of squashed shit on his tray, with a poppadum on the side and a small pool of chutney. He *knows* it is shit, but he can't stop putting his fork into it, shovel-style, and lifting to his lips…and that is when he wakes with a shudder of relief.

The last, and most carefully worked out part of the feeding regime, was the "Last-Minute-Crunchy", a handful of which Mojito and the Captain had been fed a few minutes before their Milton Keynes fight. "Pure doggy Viagra," Scotch had been calling it. Terry had protested that they hardly needed the dogs getting massive hard-ons in the middle of a fight. He knew from experience that could slow a bloke down a bit when he needed to be running around. Fortunately, Scotch had been using the "Viagra" term very loosely to mean "up for a scrap".

Scotch would sit at the table in the lock-up making about ten of these in each session, mixing up a dozen or so ingredients in a small bowl, shaping them carefully into pellets with his fingertips, suitably clad in disposable surgical gloves, and laying them out on a baking tray to dry under a netting cake-cover. Twenty-four hours later, nicely dried out, they would be transferred to a jar, in which approximately sixty little pellets now nestled.

Why can't he just give them chocolate like any normal person would – fucking mad.

Scotch was adamant that this gave them an edge.

"Just like the Olympic cyclin' team, just lots ae tiny improvements can make y' a world beater! THIS was my old Da's fineshin' touch."

Terry's lively sex life was about as good as it had been when he first married Becca. But while he got on well with Scotch, he *still* harboured nagging doubts about his intentions towards his missus. He was *sure* he had caught the occasional glance between them he didn't like the look of.

Scotch would also unashamedly ogle Becca's arse, particularly when she wore her Catwoman leggings around the lock-up; but then again, they always gave Terry a "lift", so he could scarcely be surprised could he?

She really DOES have a spectacular arse.

Nevertheless, he didn't much like it – he would just keep his eyes peeled.

15

TERRY'S HANDS SHAKE as he puts down the letter from HMRC. Not only did they use the words "Fraud" and "Fraudulent" several times, and a load of legal bollocks about reserving their rights to prosecute, but then they seem to think they are doing him a huge favour by agreeing to a twelve-month repayment schedule of just shy of two-hundred grand, to allow him time to sell the house – with the first £40k due next month!

That's alright then, fucking generous of them really...

***

Terry has never liked "Norf Lundun", and thought the area round Hackney was particularly horrid, sporting various new housing developments behind heavy automatic gates with "*24 Hour Porterage*" – or "*Armed Guards*" as any sane person would describe it. The whole area had these little pockets of estate-agent wet-dreams, but, as soon as you were out of the "compound", you were treated to a high street full of Mr Chicken, pound shops, barbers' that carved strange shapes into your hair, and those spooky-looking cafés with painted-out windows and middle-aged Greeks in coats sitting round bare tables.

The closest thing to a department store is a fucking Argos.

It was one of the few places that made him proud to be Peckham born and bred!

Mojito and Cuba Libra had been packed into the back of the Range Rover – they had all agreed that driving a derelict caravan full of dogs across London behind an almost-new Rangey would be an invite to get pulled over.

Becca sits in the back with a couple of blankets and her slightly macabre dog-repair kit. She is wearing a mid-length bright-red coat – the white Jaeger one had cost over £100 to clean, but they had agreed over a bottle of Grey Goose that the "Becca Finale" at their first venue was quite entertaining, *and* had the effect of silencing the crowd.

Scotch reasoned that *both* of these things were good omens. One to encourage plenty of financial interest in the event, and the other to smooth what could potentially be a fractious getaway. They had agreed that Becca would wait in the wings and swoop in to scoop up the presumably victorious Mojito. Terry had agreed a hand signal to keep her away from the action in case anything went horribly wrong.

The journey across London in semi-torrential rain is horrible – mainly because of the smell. Repeated waves of horribly meaty, paté-like odours swept around the car without warning. Scotch's diet for the boys produces almost silent, but stunningly intense farts, which in the well-ventilated lock-up were pretty bad, but in the confines of the car create a need for immediate escape.

"Sick...I'm going to be sick!"

Becca has her scarf clamped over her mouth the third time the gas cloud spreads around the car, but it's too late. The smell has invaded and is running its course. The only solution is to have all the windows half-open and the heating blasting out full power as the rain sweeps through the car.

Terry is soaked down the door-side of his body as the rain streaks in; Becca is sitting dead centre, trying to avoid the wet, breathing through her scarf. All attracting far too much attention sitting at traffic lights in the rain with windows open and hot, stinky air emanating from within.

Welcome to Hackney.

***

They pull into the industrial estate, sandwiched between Orient Way and Hackney Marshes, not the same derelicts as Milton Keynes, but working units deserted at the weekend – but not this weekend: it is heaving.

Queueing at the car park entrance behind two other cars while a weasely man under an umbrella inspected each in turn through the window, peering back through the car – *Hackney passport control* – before waving them through to find a parking spot.

"Scotch, there must be eighty cars in here! How do you keep THAT below the fucking police radar?"

"You don't Tel. The cozzers are here too. It's the only way to have a decent crowd. Only costs a couple of small backhanders and free admission for a few of their mates; we should probably cultivate a few of our own!"

"Free admission? What do you mean free admission, it's a fucking dogfight Scotch, not the school fête – no one gets charged admission?"

***

Terry stands in front of the plastic trestle table at the entrance and hands £50 to the polite-but-firm tank of a woman sitting in her blue quilted anorak; she tears off two yellow and one green raffle tickets, handing them to Terry.

"The green one's yours love. Don't lose them or you won't get back in – and *phones off*, please! Anyone using a phone will be in serious trouble with the management."

£20 admission each, AND £10 for owners, you had to be joking!

"This one is proper job Tel, nae like that amateur shit-show in Milton Keynes. Proper rules here, proper breeders, celebrities and all."

Terry says nothing; this is all quite bemusing. They have turned up to what seems to be a well-organised charity event, with seemingly normal people about to watch a bunch of dogs tear each other to pieces. The police are there on a free pass and now Scotch is wittering on about celebrities.

What's the fucking world coming to?

Bigger money this time. Twelve grand a fight. A 15% cut for the House.

The House is a dour, wiry man in his early forties, wearing a grey suit, with thinning grey hair, sitting in a small room with a large window overlooking the open floor. He counts out Terry's money carefully; two discreet "minders" sit on their chairs in the corner as House unlocks a safe on the wall, deposits the cash neatly into it and hands him two receipts with £12,000 written on each and the fight number in the corner.

A poster hangs on the wall with "Cajun Rules" in big bold lettering and a long list of dos and don'ts below it. None of this was what Terry had expected; all far more up-market.

With 15% of the prize money, the door takings and undoubtedly a tax on the bookies, it is a gold-plated money machine! There seem to be three different bookies in weathered trilby hats, moving among the crowd, shouting prices like they are down the race track.

The pit in the centre of the open-plan office space is made of the same metal railing panels used for crowd control at any normal event, sitting on a large, freshly rolled-out carpet. Two white "scratch lines" are painted on, behind which the dogs are held before launching at each other.

Chairs are piled neatly against one wall, as are similarly stacked tables; office furniture all tidied away.

The crowd standing around the pit are starting to warm up as the time for the first fight draws closer.

Terry scours faces…

Fucking celebrities my arse!

His eyes settle on a woman's face he was sure he had seen on one of Becca's soaps – *Emmerdale* maybe? Unlike the first fight, there's a decent handful of women in the crowd.

Just popped in on the way down the shops for a scratch card.

Scotch had explained to them that this was a specialist Pit Bull and Bull Terrier event, not the mixed bag of sizes, shapes and breeds they had experienced before. Terry notices a number of the stocky little dogs on thick leads. They all seem to be squatter, more barrel-chested and bow-legged than his trio. He is not sure that is a good thing.

"Our boys are nippier than this lot Tel. Six fights on the card – ours are three and five, so we've got at least half an hour, probably longer."

Terry heads back to the car while Scotch gets in the queue for refreshments.

Becca is standing beside the car under her umbrella; it has almost stopped raining now, giant puddles everywhere, but the sun is starting to put in an appearance, typical end-of-April weather.

"I had to get out Terry, the smell is just ridiculous. They can't be well, smelling like that, surely? They have *never* smelt like that before. I'm sure Scotch knows what he is doing, but that just can't be right!"

Terry opens the back "flap" window of the Rangey to let the air circulate a bit. They hear a muffled roar from the crowd as the first fight gets under way.

"There's carrot cake or flapjacks," says Scotch, arriving with the coffees.

Exactly what you need for a good dogfight…

***

Scotch and Terry stand on their side of the pit entrance. The last fight was a bit of a horror; the two dogs just locked jaws and shook each other for fifteen minutes, neither really making great headway except to gradually gnaw off half of each other's faces. The carpet, which started a mottled brown, now has a variety of darker patches.

Cuba has had his little handful of Scotch's "Doggy Viagra" and is drying out nicely after his compulsory weigh-in and bath. The latter had taken Terry by surprise: a soapy pool set up with an official "washer" that each owner supervised while his dog was washed and had his teeth and paws scrubbed. Scotch had explained the various unpleasant practices of poisoned fur, teeth and claws. Terry became very diligent in observing the cleansing of Cuba's opponent.

"If there's anything we don't like the look of Tel, you just say, and we get the ref involved. They can ban 'em for life if anyone gets caught cheating. There are very fucken' serious rules!"

To Terry this sounded like the Hades version of the Jockey Club, and, not for the first time, a wave of shame swept through him...

What the fuck am I doing exposing Becca, these poor dogs and ME to this awful low-life shit?

But he knew the answer to that one. It was the wave of panic he experienced every time he thought about the money he had to find.

That's why you're here Tel, so better man up, son...

Cuba is up now – Scotch behind him, lifting his front paws off the ground – behind the scratch line, a mirror image of his foe. The noise from the dogs, the baying of the crowd has a thrilling, appalling, intoxicating intensity – and the room erupts in a savage roar.

"Let GO!"

The dogs are released.

Terry watches, transfixed. It's just fucking horrible! Cuba doesn't have the technique and dexterity of the Captain, or the speed and aggression of Mojito; he is just very, very powerful. So they just do what Pit Bulls have been bred to do. They lock jaws together and just crunch and shake until one of them is exhausted and gives in.

It takes fifteen minutes. Terry has stopped looking after five, but eventually Cuba's opponent, strength fading, starts to release and turn away. The referee shouts the end of the fight and the winner's name. Scotch and the other owner run into the pit and separate the dogs. They are both in a state, faces, mouths and snouts gashed and punctured, lips torn. Sweat and saliva mixed with blood. Terry just stands and watches, numbed.

Thank God Becca's not here, waiting for her Mojito-entrance. It had better not be like the last one – she loves that bloody dog!

Terry leads Cuba Libre: the little dog is sweating and staggering, on his lead toward the Range Rover. Why was this so much worse than the first fights?

He realises it is because they are all well-matched, the same breeds, all doing what they have been bred to do with unpleasant efficiency. Cuba's face is a mess, and he was the winner! His wounds stark, deep and seeping against his ginger-brown fur.

Becca is visibly shocked as they help Cuba up into the back of the car. She has spread a clean blanket out, her surgical kit ready and some Dettol in a dish. It all seems hopelessly inadequate.

Cuba lies down, head on his paws in front of her, panting, tongue out, as she swabs down the wounds with disinfectant; he doesn't seem to feel anything. This is the first time Becca has had to operate on a live patient. She has three wound-closing devices: steri-strips, vet-bond wound adhesive and a suture needle and thread.

The steri-strips are ridiculous, they just won't stick to wet fur, and, after three attempts, leaving patient and nurse exasperated, she starts on the vet-bond, a sort of "wound superglue", which seems to work pretty well on the smaller punctures and gashes – squeezing drops of the viscous liquid from the applicator onto either side of the wound and then gently holding them together until they stick.

Terry can see she hates the stitching, makes her skin crawl, shoving the needles in, pulling them through. Live flesh, not like her practice runs on butcher's meat, not a little bit like that, although there was a pleasing neatness to how the thread pulled the sides of the wound together. Each needle puncture making Cuba jerk a little, but he stays still, compliant, exhausted.

Eventually, with superglue on the face-holes, steri-strips on the lips and four lots of actual stitches on a couple of bigger wounds on his neck and head, Becca is finished.

Then large smears of antiseptic cream on each wound and a big collar to stop him worrying and rubbing at any of them. Now the fur on his face is drying out, Cuba is starting to look more like a seriously knocked-about version of himself.

Becca peels off her surgical gloves, sits back on her heels and starts to cry.

16

MOJITO SHAKES HIMSELF, spraying the last drops of water from his fur. He has had a handful of Scotch's Viagra pellets about ten minutes ago. He is in the zone, ready to go…

***

In the pit now, Scotch holds Mojito up as the dogs are "shown" each other behind their scratch lines. The chesty, bow-legged Troll-Dog opposite is having anger-management issues and is making a *lot* of noise and a *lot* of saliva. His owner, a sharply dressed thirty-something with slicked back hair and Essex written all over him, making a very obvious play of looking cool and unbothered, sneering.

Must be a City boy, what a wanker! Would take half an hour just to read the fucking labels on him…

Mojito is not as excited.

Terry is at the side of the ring and can see the lack of

snarling ferocity from his dog, but he can still hear him: a deep, loud rumble, like the liquid growl of a *big* outboard engine, smooth and penetrating, and he sees the look on Mojito's face, jaws set half-open, hungry and fiercely intense. The crowd sense it, something intangible. But more importantly, the slavering Troll-Dog senses it.

The referee, a gaunt, unshaven man all dressed in brown, with thick leather trousers and pads strapped round his arms and legs, has his hand outstretched in front of him; he lifts his arm quickly: "LET GO!"

The dogs fly across the ten feet of space between them and something quite unusual happens: as the dogs' jaws hit, the Troll-Dog pulls his head to the side, not engaging. Mojito's jaws close round the side of his neck, behind the ear…

"TURN!" screams the referee, both arms outstretched to the sides. "TURN!"

Both handlers rush across the pit to disengage their dogs, dragging them back behind their own scratch line. Scotch has explained the rules to Terry: Troll Dog turned his head away, disengaged, the fight does not start again until the dog that turned away is prepared to fight again. That dog is released first from behind its scratch line and, if it does not attack, the fight is over, forfeited.

The crowd has gone very quiet; Troll's handler, yelling, tries to rile him up behind his scratch line, but he is having none of it, just looks down. He has been carefully inbred for one single purpose, and that is definitely *not* to be looking down when he is 'shown' another dog.

Mojito is emitting the same deep rumble as before, eyes still fixed, but not straining to be released.

"FORFEIT!" shouts the ref, and it is over.

Terry is smiling, relieved, his hand aloft, thumb up for Becca to see. She appears, the sexed-up Valkyrie in full flight, black hair, red coat flowing, pale make-up and red-painted lips, hurdling over the barrier into the pit.

Without a real fight it feels like the SAS bursting into a children's tea party.

Mojito clearly likes this bit, and leaps, slobbering, into Becca's outstretched arms like a playful puppy. She picks him up in her arms: "GOOD, GOOD BOY MOJITO! WHO'S A STRONG BOY THEN? MY LOVELY MOJITO…THAT'S WHO!" and stalks out of the pit holding him.

The crowd are starting to recover. This is not the usual spectacle. One of the dogs many of them came to see, and bet on, has been completely faced down, led away in disgrace. Fifty grand worth of stud value evaporated…and then the Wicked Witch of the West appears and carries off the new champ. It seems more like that camped-up play-wrestling shit they have on the TV than a proper dogfight.

Conversation starting again in the crowd, slowly at first:

"That's not what I paid to fucking see!"

"How weird was that!"

"Thought he was a cert."

"Jimmy's gonna be fucking pissed."

"Just fucked with his head – Spooky!"

Terry makes his way out past the entrance.

"Got your raffle ticket, love? You won't get back in."

***

Back at the car, Becca is sitting in the open boot of the

Range Rover with the tailgate down. The rain has stopped, Mojito has his head in her lap, docked tail wagging as Becca scratches the folds of skin on his head; the other hand on Cuba's head in front of his big white collar, gently kneading, talking to both dogs.

"Poor Cuba, we need to look after him, he has been a *very* brave boy. We will ask Uncle Terry to make everyone a nice dinner to help him feel better."

Uncle Terry. UNCLE fucking Terry making everyone a nice dinner. It's not right; I'm their fucking uncle now...where does she get stuff like that from?

Seeing he is not needed at the "doggy love-in", Terry heads back, pausing to have his green raffle ticket carefully inspected less than two minutes since he passed by, to see if Scotch needs a hand collecting from the bookies. He has no idea what bets Scotch managed to place, but he *does* know he had twenty grand to spend if the price was right. Scotch appears, stuffing a wad of cash into the inside pocket of his coat.

"We've had et off Tel, fucken' had...ET... OFF! Haha! Two ta fucken' ONE! Can you believe et! That fucken' wuuss of a dog had won THREE fights. They all thought he would piss it. FORTY fucken' grand Tel!"

They call in to collect the prize money, less the House cut from the office. Troll Dog's owner is there, in a scowling altercation with House:

"Just accept it, Jimmy. You supervised the wash and checks, there was no funny business, your dog just bottled it; doesn't matter why, he just bottled it."

House is sitting, business-like behind his desk. Jimmy is not looking so cool now, and even Terry knows that snakeskin cowboy boots are a bit of a throwback.

"That was all a bit strange, wassnit lads? All a bit strange."

Jimmy seems to be speaking almost entirely through his nose, irritating before he utters a sound. Terry decides that business-like and friendly is the best response, followed by a nippy escape.

"Yeah, would have been a decent fight, mate, yours just had an off day I reckon."

"And there was me thinking he was worth a few quid. Well…he's fucked it now…and fucked himself. Got no use for a dog that doesn't fucking fight."

They all watch House wordlessly counting out Terry's money. He passes it over.

"Thank you, fellas. See you again, always welcome. The girly made quite an entrance; you can bring *her* along whenever you like! Must be fucking hard work keeping *her* under control!"

He shakes hands, dry and firm, and they are gone.

***

"So what does that mean – 'no use for him'? What will happen to him Terry?"

Standing round the open rear of the Range Rover, Scotch explains that the "Pussy Dog" will most likely not survive the night in the hands of Jimmy, or in fact of any owner playing the game seriously. He is badly damaged goods now.

Becca is clearly upset. The idea of that whining little City boy actually killing his perfectly healthy dog just because it was scared of Mojito is outrageous.

"Terry, I *know* a dog can actually die in one of these

fights, but this would be murder...a cowardly murder, and we are NOT going to let that happen!"

The thought that he might even *try* to keep this painted gladiator "under control" leaves Terry smiling inside.

17

THE JOURNEY BACK was ghastly.

The new Pussy Dog had to go on the front seat in case Mojito and Cuba ripped him to shreds, they growled and glowered at him all the way back. The farting had also started up again in earnest almost as soon as they were under way.

Need to fumigate the whole fucking car!

He had already cleaned off another turd parked on the bonnet that morning.

Terry seemed to be getting the "turd present" about once a week now, and every time it wound him up a little more than the last, if that was possible, and now the *inside* of the car smelt like a diarrhoea factory!

That's what I should be doing really, just a steady day job in a diarrhoea factory; coming home at night to a sex kitten who was turned on by the smell so I wouldn't even have to shower...

Scotch had agreed to review the meal mixtures to see

if he could reduce the intensity, if not the regularity, of the flatulence problem.

While Becca had asserted that Pussy Dog had a name, she obviously didn't actually know what it was. She objected to the name "Pussy" on the basis that it was clearly a male dog, and secondly, not a cat. What Terry *did* know was that it was pig-ugly and very "disturbed".

Becca's suggestion of giving Pussy to Tasmin really didn't appeal to him very much either; he would need to think about this one carefully. Even Pussy Dog didn't deserve to be turned into some sort of festering rug, or have his pickled body parts used as "healing devices". Tas had never had a dog, and now she seemed to think she *was* some sort of dog, Terry was concerned that this might not be the best time to make a canine present that was clearly off its rocker.

Meantime he had made some decent money. The original £40,000, half for stake money, half for bets, had come from raiding every bit of savings they had – cashing in their Premium Bonds, selling an old annuity for only half its value, and even raiding Mercedes' and little Chloe's National Savings accounts.

Now, after expenses and Scotch's 20%, he was sitting on about another £50,000 and would need to decide what to do with it. It seemed a lot of cash just to rock up at the bank with and park in his current account. Come to think of it, he couldn't remember the last time he had actually been *inside* a bank, but you couldn't exactly stick forty grand of cash in an envelope and send it to the taxman, so it would have to find its way into the bank somehow.

Becca can do the banking; give her one of nicer jobs after the horrid task of having to glue up dogs' faces all morning.

***

The smell is still fucking awful, even with the windows open.

Terry drops Scotch off on the high street so he can pop into Tats R Us to see how the day job is coming on.

Next stop, to get Becca and Pussy Dog back to the house, he clearly couldn't stay with the others, and then on to the lock-up with Cuba and Mojito.

As they turn into Hampton Close, they can see the police car parked outside their house. They peer through the car window as they pull onto the drive – two young coppers, one with his feet up on the dashboard, both drinking out of Starbucks cups. They jump a little as the Rangey pulls past them and start to gather themselves.

"You take Pussy out and walk him round to the house Becca. I'll go and see what they want; better if they don't see the other two, especially with Cuba all stitched up."

"Hello, officers."

They seem relaxed enough. He recognises one from somewhere: cocky lad, and after the pleasantries he manages to repel their suggestion to come in to chat. Terry suspects they just fancy another cuppa and to leer at Becca for a bit.

Good news from the cops, wonders never cease!

They only came to let him know that *Sun* man wasn't going to press charges despite a number of witnesses enthusiastically describing Terry "knocking him into next week".

The one he recognises chips in that, "Mr Williams may have had a word" with the reporter to plead on Terry's behalf.

Who the fuck is Mr Williams?

Seeing Terry's puzzled expression, "Mr Williams…you know…Tonto."

145

Good old Tonto…never knew he had a proper name.

Terry mentally takes back several of the darker thoughts he had been having about the publican. He thanks the officers for their help, saying he will be more careful to watch where he is going next time he is charging around to help "damsels in distress", and they start to head back to their car. The cocky lad turns to him as they walk away:

"Next time you belt someone though, don't hit them *behind* the jaw. You were fucking lucky not to kill him."

He realises where he has seen Cocky Copper – in the audience watching the pole dance fiasco. Terry gives his best half-smile and a sheepish wave as they climb back into their BMW and drive away.

***

Pussy has settled down nicely on a blanket that Becca has folded up in the corner of the kitchen; he seems much less skittish now that he is away from Mojito. He jumps a little when Terry walks into the room, less comfortable with men – *poor little bastard* – but relaxes again when he hears Becca's voice.

"You OK with him Becca?"

"Don't worry about me, Lamb; and we're going to call him 'Piddle'. He was SO scared Tel, he keeps having little accidents, but I am sure it will stop once he is shown a bit of love in his new home. You're safe now, Piddle…"

Terry smiles gently, noticing a small yellow puddle on the floor near the rug; Piddle looks up at him uncertainly.

"That's lovely Becca. We can chat about Piddle's future later."

Pecking Becca on the lips, one hand gently cupping her bottom.

I now own a psychotic Pit Bull called Piddle, as a pet! Just smile and say "yes" Tel…

***

The smell was *so* bad that Terry had needed to keep the doors of the Range Rover open for a couple of minutes before he could get in to drive back to the lock-up with the dogs; they actually looked quite distressed themselves.

What does a dog look like when he is holding his breath?

It hadn't seemed this bad in the lock-up; though there was a fairly constant through-draught. Scotch had clearly started feeding them something pretty toxic recently.

***

"You need to come NOW Terry – you told me just to pay the money in. They say they are getting a money laundering man, and I am in a horrible little room with no windows, just waiting, and they won't let me go. I have NO IDEA what they are talking about! They keep asking me where the money came from. I KEEP saying what you told me to, but they just don't seem to believe me. Did you know this would happen?!"

Terry feels a familiar scrotal movement as Becca's words hang in the air. He just didn't need more trouble; a quiet patch to catch his breath was what he needed; but *nothing* seemed to be settling down.

★★★

"No Mr Granger, of course it's not *illegal* to deposit money, but we need to know where the money came from, what its source is, sir. It's the money-laundering regulations. We have to be very careful; we *all* have a duty to be on alert sir."

The lanky deputy manager, with a lively dose of acne, sits opposite them behind a bare table, in front of an ageing computer screen, peering at Terry's bank details.

Becca had told them Terry had won the money gambling, as she had been instructed, but that wasn't enough for them. They wanted to know where from, which betting shop. Becca had panicked and said it was from playing cards, so they sat her down and waited while she called her husband.

Terry explains that his wife had misunderstood; they were just putting back the money they had drawn out over the previous few weeks as they didn't need it anymore.

They could prove where it came from, cashing in various policies. He explaining the cheques that had been paid in from National Savings, Scottish Widows and Aviva had been drawn out in cash for stake money for gambling, that was where Becca had become confused…

The deputy manager, whose pristine business card described him also as "Assistant Deputy Money Laundering Officer" is clearly unhappy with these conflicting stories and the entirely dishonest-sounding couple in front of him, but he agrees to have Becca stay at the bank if Terry can go home to get the paperwork to prove where these deposits came from.

"But the statement actually shows an £8,000 cheque

paid in from National Savings, and the same day you can see me drawing out £8,000 in cash!"

"I'm afraid we still need to see documentary proof, sir, these terrorists have complex ways of hiding and laundering money, sir, and we *all* have to be vigilant."

"You didn't ask for bloody proof when I took the cash out!"

"No, sir, but you stated that the cash was for building works, according to the forms when you withdrew the funds, and now you are saying it was for gambling, which is clearly inconsistent."

Straight out of school and into the anti-terrorist squad – HSBC! It was called Midland Bank when I opened the account, not someone in Hong Kong. And now they think I'm a fucking terrorist!

Becca lays her hand over the back of his fist clenched on the table. She can see the vein standing out against the redness of his bald, perspiring head.

"I think you should just go and get the papers the man is asking for, I'll wait here. Go on Terry."

Terry stands up, puts his coat on and turns to throw a parting verbal grenade at the spotty little fucker.

"Don't say ANYTHING. Just go and get the papers, please. This nice man will make me a cup of tea while I wait."

She is right of course, but then she almost always is.

18

"AHM GONTA STOP the cheese Tel; ah thenk et's brillyent, but the smell is juss tae much."

"What cheese? Dogs don't eat fucking cheese Scotch! How long have you been feeding them cheese? What SORT of cheese?!"

"Ahv been mixing et wi' peanut butter; Gorgonzola and peanut butter. But ahm gonta stop. Ah don't think they are digestin' et properly, the stools are terrible too; not digestin' any of et. It's just forming a sort of coating on their shite Tel."

Terry sits down and turns the pages of the *Evening Standard*. They all thought Scotch knew what he was doing, but fucking Gorgonzola! Dogs eat meat and biscuits. No wonder they smelled so bad, poor little bastards.

What would make you think cheese and peanuts would do anything for a fighting dog anyway?

Scotch explains that he came across it in one of the

"dark" chat rooms he frequented, which claimed that this little mixture eased the digestion of some of the drier feed he was preparing. To Terry it just sounds like Scotch must have had a load of it left over in his fridge and was using it up, but frankly even that seems unlikely.

The fucking idiot is making some decent money out of all this. But it's not HIS money on the line; just a 20% cut for his "expertise"! He just stares at Becca's arse all the time…and now he's trying to gas us all!

He resolves to keep a closer eye on Scotch.

***

Terry stares at the brightly backlit screen in Dr Singh's office; it was handy having King's College, one of the best hospitals in the country, just down the road, but he wasn't looking forward to this particular conversation.

"So Mr Granger, we can clearly see the problem: see how the left one just floats around? Nowadays, the solution is pretty simple. Just a tiny stitch and you will be back playing squash the next day."

The picture on the screen is the size of his head. You could clearly see one floating free, a little higher than the other. Terry had never played squash in his life, and the idea of starting the day after someone had stitched his left bollock to the bottom of his ball-sack didn't sound entirely feasible.

He stares, mesmerised, at the cunningly magnified X-ray of his testicles.

"What we will actually do is just pop a stitch in the bottom of each testicle, loop it down and place the other end of the stitch through a layer of the skin at the bottom of your scrotal tissue to secure them in place. Although the right-hand one looks fine at the moment, we don't want you back in here two years later to do that one – and once *one* starts this little game, the other one often follows, so we usually do both at the same time. But it's only keyhole, you'll be in and out in no time."

The whole thing had been thoroughly humiliating so far. Wearing a too-small, well-worn all-in-one while positioning his balls on the cold ceramic plate in front of the young female X-ray operator was not ideal, and when she had politely asked him to "Lift the penis out of the way", which he couldn't easily see over his belly, it had made the moment complete.

***

Becca had phoned the health insurance firm, pretending to be his secretary and booked the appointment. His GP had given him the referral letter over a year ago. He had protested, claiming that it had been easing off over the last few months, "*settling down…*"

"Yes Pet, I am sure it has, except quite often, when we make love, you suddenly start squirming around looking desperate, and pretending you've lost something. It's not really a turn on, Lamb, so think of it as *you* doing something for me."

She was right of course, and he vividly recalled the last time they had made love; he had tried holding onto the offending ball with one hand by reaching round his back, his arm not quite long enough, so he had to lean back at an angle in order to hang on to it at moment of entry. But as soon as he had let go, the little fucker was on the move in the most uncomfortable way. He had yelped and tried to pretend he was over-excited, attempting to convey to Becca, simply by staring at her like a maniac, that this was all part of a complex new position he had devised.

And here they are in front of him, his very own giant cartoon bollocks, just waiting to be stitched up. One day he is sure he will laugh about this, but right now it is hard to feel even vaguely hopeful.

"We used to do these with just a 'local', but you chaps tend to jump about a bit too much once we get going, so now it's a full anaesthetic, but the op itself is only a few minutes. In and out of theatre in half an hour!"

Dr Singh's bonhomie is starting to wear on him; he just wants to get out of there and lick his wounds, figuratively speaking.

"We can fit you in next week; no time like the present, eh? Book the date in with my receptionist and we will clear the payment with your insurers. See you soon then Garry".

"It's Terry actually…"

"Ahh yes…see you soon then TERRY – we will have you back on the squash court in no time!"

***

On the way home Terry drops in to see how Mercedes is doing and arrives to pass Darren, her slime-ball of a boyfriend coming out of the front door: he looks unwashed as usual, jeans worn around his fucking ankles, orange Polo boxers sticking a good six inches above the waistband. Already on his mobile, "giving it large" in the over-loud voice that swaggering "yoof" seems to adopt when broadcasting their presence to the world, a lit cigarette in the other hand.

He just fixes Terry with his fuck-you stare as he swaggers past him, not pausing for breath in the "street monologue" he is pouring down the phone. Terry has needed the shaven-headed, arrogant little tosser to "get his" for a long time now, pretty sure he is responsible for the shit on the car. Why does Mercedes keep letting him back after everything he has put her through? The father of his granddaughter, who never contributes a penny and spends half his life "inside" for things Mercedes swears he didn't do.

Try to say something nice to her Tel; don't let him wind you up mate…

"Hello, sweetheart."

He catches the door before it swings shut, calls round it into the hall, waiting for Mercedes to acknowledge him before just entering.

"Hi Dad, just a mo…"

He lurks at the door for several seconds and then enters, down the shabby hall into the shabbier living room.

Curtains pulled half-shut, though it is the middle of the day, his daughter is dishevelled, carrying an armful of glasses, a full ashtray and an empty vodka bottle. They have obviously been having some sort of sex on the sofa. It is only five days since his daughter had eighteen stitches in her breast.

He asks how she is, and cuts her off with "Good, good!" before she can really tell him. She seems slightly drunk and uncomfortable, and maybe in a little pain from whatever exertions have occurred. The odour of booze, fags and sex hangs in the room.

Terry can't cope with staying more than a few minutes;

turns down a cup of tea, excuses himself saying he must get back to take Piddle over to his new home with Tasmin.

Neither mention Darren, and that hangs in the air, a tainted presence between them.

19

BACK HOME, BECCA is out at work. He has felt shaky since his visit to Mercedes'.

Can't even speak to my own daughter, for fuck's sake…

"Come on then Pussy Dog."

He can't bring himself to call even the sorry Pussy Dog by a name as awful as "Piddle".

The "call of the kitchen" is quite strong. Time to raid the fridge and put together one of his "signature" sandwiches that will almost certainly make everything alright. The diet is coming along well, as long as you don't count anything you eat when no one can see you.

Piddle is not in the kitchen, and the ritual of white sliced bread, lashings of Flora, a slab of strong cheddar, topped off with a thick layer of dark, rich marmalade *and* a good twist of black pepper starts to take the edge off his shakiness.

Fabulous…food of the gods!

The "King of Sandwiches" is cut roughly in half, and

as always the first couple of bites require the careful kiss-hoovering of the marmalade as it squeezes out of the edges. Half-eaten sandwich in hand, Terry starts to wander the house in search of Piddle. He told Becca to keep him locked in the kitchen, but you just couldn't get through to her sometimes!

Piddle is laying on the sofa, his head hanging over one low arm; he looks somehow different.

"Come on mate, off to terrorise lovely Tasmin – you're going to love it there. Can't promise I'll visit you that often though!"

Terry has picked up the dog lead from where it hung over the bannister, moves back into the living room, not really engaged, chatting to Piddle, and he notices *why* Piddle looks different, his face is darker, particularly his muzzle. Piddle peers up uncertainly. He focuses in on Piddle's face as he reaches to take his collar and fix his lead. Piddle's muzzle is dark…and sticky.

What the fuck has Becca been feeding you? She is SUCH a soft touch.

In fact Piddle is clearly stuffed full, hardly able to shuffle himself off the sofa. A wave of unease sweeps over Terry, skin creeping gently. He looks around the room, and for the first time notices the obvious behind the armchair…

What the fuck is that mess in the corner?

Terry leaves Piddle and investigates. An area of carpet, roughly a four-foot circle: horrible mess, like a cherry jam explosion, splashed onto the skirting board and a little up the wallpaper, red-purple, sticky.

What the fuck is Becca going to say when she sees this, the carpet's bloody ruined? But what the fuck is it?

How stupid of him!

It's Scooter.

***

Terry squats uncomfortably on the footstool in the corner of the room to have a quiet think, surveying the scene. In one corner, Piddle is panting, his stomach distended, contentedly on the sofa, an element of pride restored. In the other corner, the sticky leftovers of another ex-cat.

How had he actually managed to EAT the whole fucking thing?

Terry scours the rest of the house, just in case some part of Scooter has been deposited somewhere as a "present" – nothing.

You wouldn't have thought it was possible, but he had seen "When Big Cats Hunt", and watched how a hyena finishes off the leftovers of a lion kill, crunching up all but the biggest bones with incredibly powerful jaws. And these boys *do* have incredibly powerful jaws.

Terry gets up and inspects the gory puddle. There really is nothing left, just a few bits of fur and what was probably part of an ear, and plenty of sticky stuff.

He hadn't ever grown "fond" of Scooter after all the arse-wiping, but you wouldn't wish this on anyone, and for it to happen following on from his awful rectal invasion by Karma and subsequent rehabilitation, it felt like Scooter had been dealt a fairly rough hand in life.

What had Becca been thinking when she let Pussy Dog, which now seemed an entirely inappropriate name, out of the kitchen to feast himself on her substitute cat. And how the fuck – really, HOW THE FUCK – was he going to explain this one?

A large glob of marmalade drops onto Terry's palm. He looks down and realises he is still holding the sandwich. He doesn't feel so hungry now, but it seems to be the right thing to do to finish it off. Scooter wouldn't have wanted him to throw it away.

It was not so long ago that Terry had got himself in terrible trouble over Tiger's demise, and it had taken weeks for Becca to get over it. Explaining to her that it was *her* fault that the dog she had rescued from being put down had actually eaten every last piece of her new cat seemed just too cruel. It was only a few days since she had watched Karma with his finger up Scooter's arse. But lying about Tiger had resulted in an awful chain of deception and outright lies – and a period of complete sexual abstinence. So maybe it was time to tell the truth!

***

Starting with the bucket of hot water and Flash, sponging down the walls and skirting board. That all goes well enough; the mess comes off the silky surfaces pretty easily, in fact they now seem cleaner than usual. Stepping back to admire the first and entirely insignificant part of the job, he feels stronger to confront the somewhat more complex task of the carpet. It seems hard to believe there was this much wet stuff inside a small, skinny cat.

Terry sponges at the sticky mass of blood and gunge, just succeeding in spreading it further around and deeper into the carpet; he is making no impression on this at all!

Terry knows they have a carpet cleaner in the back of the kitchen cupboard, just not how it works, but eventually, with the upper reservoir full of hot water and 1001 carpet cleaner with "Power Stain Remover", he plugs it into the socket and presses the red "Wash" button and fairly successfully manages a practice run on an adjacent patch of carpet. Now, pressing the "Suck" button, the now dirty carpet water fills up the lower part of the reservoir.

Excellent – here we go – do your stuff baby.

Back onto the "Wash" setting, he starts to encroach on Scooter's remains with his new weapon of war. The noise from the washer indicates that this is a little tougher than the practice run, and the foaming dark pink mess starts to bubble up all around the washer's path, thickening up as he wheels it into ever deeper, slimy territory.

"1001 cleans a big, big carpet, in less than half an hour...or half a pound...or something..." Terry sings the words gently from the ancient advert.

After four minutes of this treatment, Terry steps back to assess progress. It is quite horrible. Scooter's juices are quite clearly more powerful than the carpet cleaner, which he suspects is not designed for this particular purpose, and are now more evenly spread out, and encased in a dark-pink foaming scum. Switching to "Suck" he attempts to hoover up the thick viscous foam. He is not singing now, and the mild feeling of hopefulness he felt at the start of the big clean-up has evaporated, unlike the "cat smoothie".

The reservoir that holds the dirty water is full of flecked pink blancmange and the brushes of the washer are stuck and encased in what looks like sausage skin. The carpet is barely touched.

For a moment Terry considers getting the hairdryer, and trying to just hoover it up once it dries out.

Don't be so stupid Terry. Why hadn't the fucking stupid dog eaten him in the kitchen, on the tiles? It would just wipe off! Fucking inconsiderate!

It is getting harder to convince himself that the story he had been working on for Becca about the mild discolouration of part of the carpet was going to be convincing.

***

"Let's just make this a trial, Tas. I'm sure we can find him a home if this doesn't work out."

Tas, "The Dog", grins manically at on over-stuffed Piddle, curled up on his blanket in the corner of her kitchen. Karma is sitting at the table peeling a saucepan full of something unrecognisable again. Piddle keeps shooting nervous glances in his direction, clean again, following a good wipe with a J-cloth by the kitchen sink.

"Is that his *proper* name Terry, or just…like a 'pet' name?"

"He *is* a pet, Tas, so I suppose Piddle *is* a pet name – but he hasn't been called it for long enough for it to have really stuck – so I guess you can call him whatever you like."

Terry is pretty sure she will spend half the night moaning, dressed up in that awful piece of shit she reserves for "mystical traumas", waiting to see if the "Other Side" will reveal a more appropriate name for Piddle. He was starting to feel uncomfortable again. She always did this to him, setting off his "flee impulse".

"We will care for the dog my brother."

Fuck me, he's learnt some English, lucky old Piddle.

"Thank you Karma, that's very kind of you. Hear that Piddle? You behave with my sister now or Mr Karma will interfere with your arse. OK?"

He is actually quite concerned about leaving Piddle with his scary but unsuspecting sister now his more aggressive eating habits have been revealed, but he has briefed her fairly well; she knows he is a rescued fighting dog and that she needs to keep him on the lead whenever they go out.

"He won't need feeding for a bit. Don't forget to take him out for a crap later, Tas, and don't be surprised if his tummy is a bit upset. Moving house shakes them up a bit you know."

And with that, he escapes. No one will ever need to know about what happened. All he needs to do is develop the storyline he has planned for Becca and he can get back to what he laughingly considers normal.

***

"What the fuck Terry? What the FUCK have you done to the carpet?"

Becca stands beside Terry, having arrived home about fifteen minutes before him, in the lounge, staring at the four-foot square that has been cut out of the corner of her living room carpet.

Terry breathes in, the unpleasant sensation in his testicles adding to his complete inability to lie in an even vaguely convincing way.

He had cut the square out with his Stanley knife, making sure every trace of blood was inside the removed piece, rolled it up very carefully, stained underlay and all, taped the gory carpet roll together with Sellotape, and taken it down to the same charity clothes bin that had previously been his nemesis, and carefully, spitefully, jammed it into the metal-mouthed bin.

Let them sell THAT to someone for 50p.

It had made him chuckle all the way home. It wasn't "revenge" exactly, but it did feel like a certain balance had been restored.

"I'm SO sorry Becca. Ridiculous of me; it was that bloody ammonia mixture that we use for cleaning the lock-up where they all crap. I accidentally bought it in from the car with the shopping, put it down there on the carpet to unpack the shopping and nearly fell over Piddle – you know how nervous he is – and trod on the bloody thing, split it, and it sprayed all over the carpet. It started melting it all, and God it stank – really toxic fumes Pet. I was worried about anyone breathing it in, so the only thing to do was cut it out."

And that is it: another big, entirely unbelievable lie, just sitting out there waiting to be found out. He has an image in his mind of an organ-grinder's monkey sitting in the middle of the bare square of floorboard – the monkey has Terry's face.

What is it they say? "The truth is another country".

20

BECCA WAS VERY touched.

Terry had spent hours getting the "Cat Missing – £200 Cash Reward" posters ready.

Unfortunately, the only picture of Scooter was in the background of another photo, before Karma had "cured" him, dragging his arse across the carpet. But Terry had cropped Becca and Mercedes sitting on the sofa *out* of the picture and blown Scooter up. It was pretty good really; you could make out the discomfort on his little face.

Becca was surprised how easily Terry had been persuaded to put up the money – he didn't even seem to mind how much they offered for Scooter's return – *and* he had put his own mobile number on the poster.

He had put up almost forty posters, all over Peckham. Becca was pretty sure Scooter would be home soon with that sort of coverage, but Terry's theory just *could* be right: that Scooter had been so "rejuvenated" by his miracle cure that he had just taken himself off for a few adventures. That almost made Becca feel that Scooter deserved his freedom to wander and chase mice, birds and the like. Just having fun on the road after years of horrid, itchy-bum discomfort.

***

Ridiculous really that he had thought because there was *no* cat, there would be no response. Two days of texts, prank calls, ransom demands and several calls offering to sell him pet insurance had not been foremost in his thinking when supplying his mobile number to half of Peckham. After day two they had died down to only a handful per day, several to just let him know they hadn't seen Scooter, but were thinking of him, and were sure he would turn up.

***

Only a couple of days and the stools had returned to normal.
Amazing what a bit of cheese can do to a dog.
Scotch had restarted his routine of sitting beside Terry with a dark spoonful to test and study the grain and contents of the poo with a magnifying glass previously used by Terry's father for his stamp collection. "Iss lovely Tel, feel tha', very smooth…"
The dogs were all back on the normal training regime, Razza making sure they never came too close to other dogs while they were being walked. All three of them seemed to be able to hang from the spring pole indefinitely, each one of them having to be physically detached at the end of their allotted time.

Cuba's wounds were doing nicely, the stitches removed, and a good blob of antiseptic cream going on twice a day; Becca had done a nice job, all things considered, very nice.

The only blot on the landscape was Poodle. His tremors and accompanying snappy behaviour had turned into something quite unpleasant. The tremors now involved an exaggerated involuntary nodding action followed by a rapid change into comically vicious behaviour, his lips peeled back and mad eyes fixing in mid-air at some invisible foe he kept biting at. The whack on the nose now had to be quite powerful to calm him down. It didn't feel like this one would end well, and even the other dogs were now avoiding him.

***

Everyone had the task of paying in small amounts of cash daily to different branches of HSBC, between £200 and £300 each time. "Cash from the market stall," if the bank asked.

Terry, Becca, Scotch and Razza all took part in the cash runs: he and Becca up in town where they worked, and the others in the local branches. So far no questions asked. The spotty little git at HSBC had finally let him pay in £35,000, which was all he could find sensible documentation for, and although the weekly expenses were pretty high and they would need stake money again for the next event, having that much cash lying around made him very nervous. He resolved to pay in another £15,000 in these small cash runs, which at the rate they were going would still take weeks.

The first cheque, forty grand, had gone off to Her Majesty.

Tas hadn't even had a letter from them yet, but Jonny had a date to appear in court charged with a couple of complex-sounding tax evasion charges; but not for a couple of months yet. No one had seen Jonny for a while, and although Terry had provided half of the ten grand posted as bail, he was not sure he cared that much – *fucking idiot*.

Scotch had been working on a big fight up north, but was keeping it all pretty close to his chest, being unusually paranoid about ensuring his great brick of a phone never left his pocket. "Ah'll tell ye when it's done Tel, nae before."

***

Tas, on the other hand, seemed determined to get everything *off* her chest, and had invited them all to a "Sweat Lodge Baptism" in her postage-stamp-sized back garden. God alone knows what that meant, but the invite had come through the door on a piece of card which seemed to have been written on with a stick dipped in blood, with a small piece of feather stuck to the top-right corner. Terry had picked it up very gingerly off the hall mat, holding it carefully between thumb and index finger.

It was for this Saturday, two days after Terry's bollock-sewing operation was scheduled. They were all invited: Terry, Becca and Mercedes, but thankfully not Chloe. Maybe they would ask Edith to look after her again now she had recovered enough to be sending abusive, badly spelled texts about him to Becca once more.

"I understand what a baptism is Lamb, but not the sweat thing; and *who* is being baptised? Tas isn't even vaguely religious in the normal sense, so it must be either Karma or

Piddle, but not even your sister is bonkers enough to baptise a dog!"

***

Lying on the operation table, with his loose white gown flapping around his tummy, Terry stares at the ceiling above him, concentrating on a tiny wisp of cobweb hanging from one of lights. The pre-med is making him slightly drowsy, gowned shapes, green and white, all around him, the anaesthetist above his head with a mask in her hand.

The mask descends towards his face...

"Now count backwards from ten please Mr Granger."

He starts, reaches ten and feels his body fold up and slide backwards off the table and down...and round...and down.

Terry dreams: a gentle, meandering dream, about a cartoon dog in an aeroplane made of cheese. The plane is chasing cats – loads of cats –Becca is in there somewhere too...

***

His eyes are stuck together, and his mouth has been sealed up. Terry manages to peel his tongue off the roof of his mouth and slowly wrestle his eyes open. He is sitting up in a bed, a couple of tubes in the back of his hand leading to a small wheeled machine with a bag of clear fluid suspended from a metal arm above the machine. There are several other beds in the room, all occupied.

Smells like a fucking hospital.

And of course it should.

Becca gets up from the chair beside the bed as she sees Terry coming round and waves dramatically at the nurse at the end of the ward. She eventually walks over, picks up the clipboard from the end of the bed and reads.

"Excellent Garry. You have done VERY well now, haven't you!"

She moves round to the side of the bed and gently removes the needle from the back of his hand with the two tubes, and places a small plaster over the tiny wound.

Terry attempts to correct her regarding his name, but nothing comes out, so he relaxes back. Consciousness returning, and with it, his memory.

Just a little op – keyhole stuff.

The nurse is talking now, something about painkillers, and Becca is nodding. Coming round more quickly now, he tries to sit up a little straighter, but finds he can't feel much below the waist. The bedcovers are raised over his hips and groin by a stand under the material.

"It was a little more intrusive than the doctor had intended, but the painkillers will sort you out until it settles down. Otherwise it was very successful. No more trouble Garry."

The nurse smiles broadly at them both.

"Give it an hour or so and we will have you up and on your way home."

Terry pulls the covers down to take a look. His nightgown is untied at the front. They have put a protective purple rubber cover over his groin; he moves to lift it and realises it has a small pink penis gently poking up from it. They are his balls, of course, just four times the size they are meant to be, and the wrong colour – and he can't feel them.

169

Becca looks down at his groin in horror: "Terry, oh Terry! That doesn't look very nice at all!"

The nurse returns when he starts shouting to see the doctor, and informs them that the doctor will not be up on the ward again until tomorrow. She reads the notes at the bottom of the bed.

"It just says, 'Keyhole not suitable – incision method used' and that it will all return to normal in about five days. In the meantime, lots of codeine and don't get them wet. You can go home as soon as the drowsiness wears off, they need the bed back as soon as you can manage."

Terry tries very hard not to swear.

Playing squash in no time … who's he fucking kidding?

***

"Twelve fucking stitches Becca! TWELVE! What did they do it with, a knife and fucking fork?"

As soon as he got home Terry had taken a good look at the tapestry with a hand mirror: his balls were a livid blue-black colour over an inverted "T" shaped dressing. Becca had peeled the dressing back for him to reveal the stitches, six up the middle and three either side of the base of his scrotum. Black stitches – *carnage.*

The codeine worked fine, he could hardly feel a thing down there – *and* it made him feel pretty smiley about the world – but as soon as it started to wear off, as it had while he was sleeping, it was bloody agony, like being slammed in the nuts with a machete, which in some ways was actually what had happened.

He was moving around, but with two walking sticks

out in front of him, wearing his baggiest gym shorts, pulled down "gangsta" style so he could waddle along with his legs wide apart.

I'm a complete fucking spectacle!

The last thing on earth he needed right now was to be going off to his sister's freak-show baptism, but Becca had strong-armed him into being up, dressed (sort of) and ready before she arrived back with Mercedes, who had only agreed to come if she could bring her potty-mouthed friend Sharon with her.

What he actually found hardest was sitting. He could do it cross-legged with his balls resting on the floor, but not in a chair with his legs together, there just wasn't room for them. He had been checking them every few hours for some sign of them getting smaller, but so far there was no sign of any change.

Is there a pulse in your nuts? I'm sure I can see them pulsating. I suppose if you can take your temperature up your arse, there's no reason why you can't take your pulse with a finger and thumb on your bollocks...

He pops two more codeine and hears the car pull up outside, pulls his T-shirt down over his belly, reaches for his walking sticks, and swings his balls towards the door.

***

Becca had obviously called ahead and warned his sister about his little problem because no one makes any particular comment as he gingerly manoeuvres himself down his sister's dim, narrow hallway. He tries hard to avoid the various unpleasant items hanging from walls, from tacky "dream-

171

catchers" to pieces of barely cured fur just pinned up, and a number of posters carelessly Blu-tacked in place.

Terry leans forward over his sticks as Tas attempts a bizarrely choreographed air kiss without making *any* physical contact.

"What IS that round your neck Sis?" Instantly wishing he hadn't asked.

"It was a gift from The Dog Terry. He 'passed it' for me; it's a sign Terry, an omen for the Sweat Lodge. It's all connected, you SEE don't you!"

Terry studies it briefly: it seems to be a piece of jawbone with a couple of small teeth attached. "When you say 'The Dog' Sis, do you mean Piddle, or your sort of dog-spirit-thing?"

"It WAS Piddle Terry, but he was inhabited by the spirit of The Dog."

"Ahh, yes, I see."

Looking harder at the gory necklace, he feels a tearing pain in his groin. His testicle tries to move as a sickening realisation sweeps over him, draining the blood from his face. His sister is wearing a piece of Scooter around her neck. Not just a "piece" of Scooter, but a piece of Scooter's face that has recently passed through his murderer's bowels.

I'm not going to heaven; definitely nowhere near heaven.

"It's amazing Terry, all we had been feeding him was tinned dog food and then this appeared. It gave him terrible trouble passing it Tel, and Karma dug it out and fashioned it into this amulet. It's the "BITE of the Dog" Terry, a REAL sign. It *passed though* him…and we are all just *passing through* on this first part of our journey. This is why I knew it was the right decision to be baptised with you all around me in the lodge Terry – to start my new life…"

"That's really amazing Sis, really lovely, but don't say much to Becca about it though. You know how squeamish she can be."

21

TAS HAS SHOVED a pile of tatty old spiritualist mags into a heap in the corner, but that is as far as her "tidy up" has gone. There are still quite horrible "throws" over the two chairs and sofa, and the dimly lit room has the feel of a blindfold investigation of a tramp's underpants; an unpleasant surprise always just a moment away.

There aren't many of them there: Tas and Karma, two of his sister's friends (both called Karen) that he has met once before, sitting side by side on the sofa; a sad, straggle-haired pair in tatty black layers of skirts, dirty lace and jumpers. They blend in well with Tas's sense of decor. Terry nods with a grim smile at them, mouthing a silent "Hello" across the room. They sit very close, almost identical, giving off a sad aura of twins still in shock at being separated.

The only stranger, clearly the guest of honour, is a small, neatly bearded man in his early forties: ironed blue jeans, a red-checked shirt and bare feet. He wears a small beaded headband, with a handful of short grey feathers standing up round the front of it.

"I want you to meet Judd, our shaman. He gives off an INCREDIBLE light Terry. Judd, this is Terry, my brother."

Judd shakes Terry's hand just a little too firmly, and for just a little too long, giving off his incredible light.

"It's wonderful that you are here, brother. I have unconditional love for your sister, and now for you all here today to accompany her in her re-birth, her oneness with the Earth Womb, her *emergence*…it is a wonderful honour!"

Terry introduces Becca, Mercedes and potty-mouth Sharon, who looks like she has come straight from a two-day gang bang. Judd holds each of the ladies' hands between his, one top, one bottom, and lingers too long with Becca for his liking, and *far* too long with Potty-Mouth. Judd tells each of them how wonderful it is that they are there, and how deeply moved he is.

Judd breaks away from his hand-caressing and turns to Tas: "I think the Sweat Lodge should be ready now Tasmin, shall we explain how we proceed to your wonderful tribe?"

Tasmin smiles ecstatically and nods.

Through the window he can see a ramshackle tent that completely fills his sister's tiny garden: ropes attached to fences, left and right. It seems to be covered in old hairy rugs and skins, with smoke drifting out of a hole held open by a few sticks poking through the top.

What the fuck is that? And how did it get there? It's going to catch fire and burn the place down…

"We will enter the Sweat Lodge as naked as we came into the world. It is the Earth Womb…"

Judd pauses and smiles to show his empathy with his audience.

"Ha ha! But don't worry, nobody has to get naked unless you wish to, underwear is fine. All that matters is that you are relaxed, comfortable and open to the Spirit. Now, is anyone menstruating? The Sweat may not be appropriate if you are menstruating."

Mercedes and Sharon are standing beside Becca, open mouthed. Sharon is first to gather herself.

"FUCKING PERV! We're not getting our kit off in front of you, fucking perv!"

Judd is taken aback, a look of sympathy and understanding spreads over his face.

"My sister, you do not have to do anything. You can wear whatever you find comfortable, but it is very warm…" He is giving his broadest, engaging smile of forgiveness.

"We are NOT getting our fucking kit off, are we Sades?!"

"We certainly fucking aren't Sha, and we aren't inappropriately *menstroooating* either, for your information!"

Judd has not dealt with many "sisters" like Sharon and Mercedes before, but he is sure that the Earth Womb will comfort and ease their tension.

Judd goes out to tend to the lodge. Tasmin quietly speaks to her chosen tribe, explaining to each person, from a piece of paper, where they fit on her relationship wheel – family, lovers, spiritual community, her tribe.

She is unsure which part of the wheel Sharon fits on to, as she has only met her once at the pole-dancing fiasco, so she carefully writes her name under "Spiritual Community" and at the top, in his own box, is Judd.

Tas is *so* sincere. Explaining about the heater, the seven

rocks inside the tent, the cleansing; the need to be one with Mother Earth. So moving is her faith and her reliance on each of them that slowly everyone comes round to the idea that they should at least go along with this for a bit, for her.

Mercedes and Sharon agree that they will wear underwear, but with towels around their waists.

"I'm not wearing knickers anyway, fucking lost them last night," Sharon shares helpfully.

They all take turns in Tas's bathroom to prepare.

Everyone agrees…no one is menstruating.

***

Terry is last to embark on the crawl through the igloo-like entrance to the Sweat Tent. Top off, small towel around his neck and his baggy Millwall shorts loosely in place.

A bigger problem however, is watching from behind, while each of the girls crawl through the entrance into the dark, with handtowels tied round their waists, leaving nothing at all to the imagination. The big, sexy nearly naked bottoms wiggling their way into the tent. He looks away for his daughter and sister, but Becca, and even the pallid, slender Karens cause his heart rate to kick up a notch.

Potty-Mouth, who he has to admit, has a brilliantly voluptuous figure, wiggling her way in last, looks back over her shoulder at him as she kneels down and quite deliberately allows the little white towel to ride up around her waist, and puts on a slow, private show for him.

Terry had taken a couple of extra codeine, and everything is ever so slightly hazy and the doctor had warned him to avoid any form of sexual arousal for a few days, but this is *far* too much to be contained even by a Codeine overdose. As Sharon crawls her way to the far side of the tent, he follows, with a painful erection and giant bruised balls, his legs wide apart as he tries to navigate the narrow entrance to join the tribe.

***

It's fucking boiling in here!

Terry shuffles himself into a cross-legged position and peers across the smoky gloom: he and Becca are either side of the entrance, the Karens are beside him to his left, then Karma, his daughter, Potty-Mouth, Judd – and finally his sister, next to Becca. Judd is wearing a pouch, and a belt with various feathery, dangly items jangling around his groin. Karma is in his off-white underpants. The bras on show are quite varied, from the plain look sported by the Karens and Tas, to the low-cut sexy lace of his own little coven.

Judd throws his head back and moans; then cuts it short and throws a handful of sage leaves onto the big stones that cover the flames of the boxed gas heater, quickly followed by a ladle of water onto the stones.

The tent immediately fills with a thick mixture of toxic, herby smoke and steam, everyone coughs and puts their towels to their faces as it slowly clears through the central vent…

I'm being burned to death in a fucking pizza-oven!

His erection has subsided for the moment.

Minutes pass: hot, sweaty, claustrophobic minutes…

Judd had instructed that they should say anything they want to share, but that silence was often best: "Feel the Earth. Feel the love. Feel the womb…"

The tent is silent except for a continuous hum emanating from an entranced Karma, head held still above his wet, gleaming torso; and the sound of breathing, occasional coughing. Everyone sweating, wet, dirty from crawling on the mud. It is ridiculously hot.

Terry's head is pounding, sweat running in rivers down his neck, his belly, dripping from the tip of his nose. The codeine just adding to the haziness. Through the coughing he hears his sister start to moan and sway from side to side.

"It's here...it's HERE! I see it: Aaaayaaweee! Aaaayaawee!"

Tas falls quiet and sits still, a peaceful smile visible across the gloomy fog of the tent. Judd reaches across and rests his hand on Tas's arm.

More minutes pass. Terry is struggling with the heat, the smell, stinging sweat in his eyes. He wipes them for the twentieth time with his little towel, and tries to look around in the gloom; flesh, legs, breasts, sweat, everywhere.

His whole groin is pulsating, he shuffles painfully and tries to cup his balls with one hand to relieve the pressure of them being squeezed by his shorts as he moves.

Opposite him, Sharon catches his eye. She looks downwards; Terry follows her gesture and sees she has lifted her towel up, sitting cross-legged, her gaze fixed on him.

He gasps a deep involuntary breath. He has been breathing as shallowly as possible, the smoke and steam burning his lungs; he coughs, but cannot tear his eyes away. A sting on his leg. Becca has reached across and slapped him sharply; she cannot see exactly what Terry is staring at, as the heater and rocks are directly between her and Sharon, but she can see the shocked, desolate look on her man's face. She stares – livid – across at Sharon, who keeps her eyes locked on Terry. Judd senses all is not well in the Earth Womb.

His trance broken, he feels himself flush as if Becca has burst in on an act of salacious horror and shame. He looks across to Sharon, whose eyes are shut now. Biting her lower lip, her hand moves, touching herself…

A light goes off in Terry's head and he roars, "SHE'S JERKING HERSELF OFF! STOP HER DOING THAT! FOR FUCK'S SAKE!"

The rebirth appears to be over.

22

"GET THAT FILTHY bitch out of here!"

The words that have ended many a party. Becca is incandescent. She knew it was stupid to let Mercedes bring that toilet-mouthed little bitch along.

"Will you stop shoving me!? I'm moving as fast as I can Becca, I can't feel fucking anything!"

Terry shuffles his numb backside out of the hole in the tent.

"Playing with herself…actually PLAYING with herself… staring at YOU Terry! If I hadn't seen it myself I wouldn't believe you for a second! She arrives here WITHOUT any fucking knickers TERRY, and starts pointing her over-used pussy AT YOU! For God's sake, in front of your daughter Terry!"

"Please don't shout at me Becca."

The Karens follow them, then Tas and the wonderful Judd, attempting to look as though this was all part of the plan. Mercedes and Sharon following, sweating and muddy.

"I am *soo* sorry Sharon…he is *soo* embarrassing…he just ALWAYS does stuff like this Sha, lettin' me down in front of everyone. But you were wanking yerself off a bit – but OBVIOUSLY not AT him."

"Don't worry Sades, it's just blokes, they're all like it. I was just drifting off. Really Sades, and I didn't even realise I was ACTUALLY wanking! It was probably just the heat and the overhang of all the coke I did last night, and anyway Sades, I don't fancy him even a little bit…UGH, just think about it! It's probably all the drugs he's takin' that made him so weird Sades."

Terry lies on his back on the small patch of mud between the tent and the back door, he has to flop onto one side first and then slowly slump over until spread-eagled.

It's over, it's fucking over. I can have a bath, a cool bath, my balls can just float around. Fuck keeping the stitches dry, and a lager, a huge fucking icy lager.

***

Everyone is tending to themselves, towelling down the sweat and grime, getting back into "normal" clothes; only Terry doesn't have much to change, just to struggle back into his Millwall shirt.

He is coming round properly now, and as usual when visiting Tas, his "flight instinct" is up and running, and after the wanking outburst in the tent, he has a desperate desire to be almost anywhere else.

Tas neatly closes off the escape route: "Food and refreshments are in the kitchen. Help yourselves and we can sit down and share our experience."

Mercedes and Sharon appear from the bathroom, dressed in the clothes they arrived in, and head for the hall and doorway.

"She was fucking possessed she was. She told me. We've called an Uber."

And they are gone, the door slamming. Potty-Mouth hasn't said a word.

Their departure lifts the mood. Even Becca is concluding that something pretty bloody weird happened in there, and at least the dirty cow has gone now, though it seemed OTT even for one of Mercedes' friends.

Only Terry knows that Sharon had "flashed" at him before she even got in the tent.

He manages to shuffle into Tas's tiny kitchen before the crowd, and helps himself to a paper plate. Everything has a folded cardboard label in front of it: "Bacon Crisps", "Worcestershire Sauce Crisps", "Barbecue Crisps".

We can tell they're crisps, Sis…

A small plate holds cocktail sticks with a cube of pineapple, a square of cheese and a mini sausage on each, appropriately labelled "Cheese, Pineapple and Sausage Sticks"– nine of these, one per person. There is a gigantic bowl of mini sausage rolls, also labelled in case anyone didn't know what they were. The centrepiece was a small bowl of pungent dark-yellow mess with the label "Carnation Chicken", and finally a plate full of cheese slices beside another plate piled with sliced bread: "Mild Cheese Sandwiches".

He surveys the feast with a feeling of gloom. His senses have been assaulted on every front in the last few hours, but Tas can be relied upon not to stimulate the taste buds, or have any sense of proportion. You could feed an army here as long as they only ate sausage rolls. Sensing a moment of peace, he decides to search the cupboards for a pot of marmalade to at least give a sandwich a bit of a lift.

Tas's kitchen cupboards are a reflection of the rest of her house, everything should have been thrown out years ago; and what *is* in there is either unidentifiable or just disturbing.

The first, unlabelled jar Terry picks up is a stewed version of the things Karma sits peeling half the time. Ancient mustard pots sit beside half-empty pickled onions, dark and opaque. He picks up a small, open bowl, full of polished white "pieces"; strange, but not entirely out of place. Terry holds one up under the light…

"He spent all day passing this stuff. He suffered for us. Karma spent ages cleaning it up – but you can just *feel* the power coming from it."

His sister has entered the room, and Terry quickly puts the piece of cat bone he is holding back in the bowl and wipes his fingers quickly down his shirt.

"Got any marmalade Sis?"

***

Sitting down on the sofa beside Becca, her plate has one cocktail stick and a few crisps. Terry's plate is slightly smaller than the vast sandwich he has constructed: cheese, crisps, mini sausage rolls sliced lengthways and placed neatly on top of the crisp layer, all bound together with a thick layer of very old marmalade. Balanced precariously on his leg, it's proving difficult to eat gracefully.

Judd is holding both of Tas's hands, while she talks about what she saw.

"The Beaver and The Dog are cousins Tasmin, the fact that you saw Beaver doesn't mean you aren't a Dog – oh no, not the slightest – they are often found together, entwined. There is no need to be confused."

Judd is in full flow now.

"Let's move round the circle everyone, what did you see? What did you experience? There is nothing to be afraid of when the Earth 'touches' us."

The Karens saw nothing unusual, saying quietly that they were only aware of each other, and the rainbow that was wrapped around them.

Judd is excited about this, "The Rainbow of Enlightenment seldom visits us in a Sweat. Did anyone else see The Rainbow?"

Silence.

"Terry, did you see anything you would like to share?"

I KNOW I should just keep quiet.

"My eyes just stung the whole time Judd. My balls felt like they were going to explode – you know about my balls – and then my daughter's friend started wanking off while staring at me, in front of my wife. When that WASN'T happening I think I saw sandwiches: rows and rows of sandwiches…but there was blood coming from the sandwiches…"

He feels Becca dig her nails into his leg.

"That's unusual Terry. Was there an animal of any sort there?"

"No, just the sandwiches; the sandwiches bleeding…"

They all look at each other. Nobody says anything, all wishing they had seen The Rainbow, but *thinking* about blood-soaked sandwiches. There is a silence. Terry hates a "silence".

"Where's Karma?"

It took forever for the ambulance to get there – *again* – and this time the two paramedics, a man and woman team, had no real idea what to do.

Judd and Tasmin had managed to pull Karma out of the tent by his arms. He had stopped sweating some time earlier, completely dehydrated, and very hot, still emitting the same eerie humming noise he had started when they all sat there together. It was hard to say whether he was actually unconscious or just off with the fairies…

Terry had finished his sandwich, a fair amount of it had found its way onto his T-shirt and shorts, the marmalade making it difficult to wipe away. He thought Karma looked slightly swollen and quite red, though he was naturally such a deep black it was hard to say; but Terry was sure it was a "sort of red" shining through – but the more obvious feature was the "totem pole" holding Karma's baggy shorts to attention.

What the fuck is it? Can't be natural – you could kill someone with that!

All the girls in the room had noticed Karma's not-so-little problem, Becca looks away quickly when Terry catches her eye; a normally built bloke just can't help admiring something quite so ridiculous in a wistful "Why didn't God do that for me?" sort of way.

Karma lay on the floor where they had dragged him – breathing – humming quite loudly now, in continuous six-second bursts with a breath between each. Terry had been timing this in case it was helpful later.

Tasmin was in floods of tears kneeling by his side,

waiting for the ambulance. "How could I have forgotten him, my lovely Karma, stallion of my heart?"

Aware of how Karma has caught everyone's attention, she attempts to carefully press the totem pole down a little, only for it to spring stubbornly back into place, causing gasps and giggles rather than reducing attention to the problem.

Becca grins at Terry, leans over to him and whispers in his ear, "Don't worry, Pet, with his willy and your giant black balls, it would almost be worth having them stuffed and mounted on the wall."

"Maybe we should leave them to their grieving and get on home Becca?"

But it is pretty clear they are there for the duration. Tas's chest heaves and another bout of deep sobbing starts up.

The ambulance crew are wrapping Karma in a foil blanket, but the totem pole, apart from being undeniably noticeable, is clearly concerning them: "You had better take a proper look at it Bob."

The unlucky Bob rests his head on Karma's chest, looking south, and carefully lifts the waistband of his shorts for several seconds. "Nothing obviously wrong, apart from the size of it." He turns to the group. "How long do we think this gentleman has had his erection for? Does anyone know?"

Why is he fucking asking us?!

Tas is composing herself, Judd beside her.

"It could be a couple of hours now."

"And has he ejaculated in that time, miss?"

Oh God, it's getting worse.

"No officer, definitely not, we were all in the tent together and then he must have been in there unconscious for maybe another hour…" Judd helping now.

187

The two paramedics huddle for a few seconds.

"Let's get the foil round him, but be careful of the penis, and let's get him on oxygen and a saline drip. We need to get him rehydrated as fast as we can."

They put an oxygen mask over Karma's face; you can still hear the humming through the mask. The foil blanket is wrapped carefully round him to accommodate. The female para goes to look in the tent, and when she returns, leans towards her partner, dropping her voice:

"It actually looks like they might have tried to cook him." And in more of a whisper, "Just look at them: bloody nutcases. And a Millwall fan…"

Karma is finally driven off in the ambulance, still humming, with Tasmin and Judd.

Terry stands in the doorway resting on his two sticks.

"Don't blame yourself Sis!" he calls after them in his marmalade-encrusted football kit, waving them off.

23

"YOUR FACE TERRY – it was JUST a picture!"

"You couldn't take your eyes off it woman, never mind MY face!"

Becca is kneeling between Terry's naked legs, spread wide apart as he lays back on the bed, dabbing kitchen roll on his stitches to dry them after his soak in the bath.

"I'm not sure you should have stayed in there so long, Pet. It's all pretty gruesome down here: a bit 'grey' around the stitches. You just lay there for a bit and let it dry out; I think they *are* getting smaller though."

Becca is interrupted by an incoming text. He struggles to a more upright sitting position.

"Tas says they will have to operate on Karma's penis, or he may never have an erection again. She says it's called a slow priapism. How AWFUL Terry!"

"Maybe they could cut a bit off while they are there, it does seem a bit unreasonable Becca!"

"You *don't* mean that now. It really doesn't sound terribly nice. UGHHH! Tel, she says they are going to have to drain the blood out of it with a syringe, before it goes rotten."

"They'll need a bicycle pump, not a syringe!"

"That's enough Terry! The man is in a lot of trouble, and he *is* married to your sister. Spare a thought for her, and if it's any consolation, I think *you* have a lovely little penis!"

***

Evening back at the lock-up, he is starting to walk more comfortably. It's nice to be doing something half normal after the operation, the sweat thing, and all the rest of it.

"Lovely little penis; LOVELY little penis; lovely LITTLE penis…" sort of depends how you say it really. Maybe better than, "Big horrible penis; BIG horrible penis." "Look what I can do with my LOVELY little penis."

Terry tries humming a song to change the inner subject.

Razza is busy chatting to the lads while she feeds the dogs – true to his word, Scotch has been cultivating a few of the local coppers, and now half the police station seem to think they can just drop in any time they want to bunk off for a few minutes for some ready-made entertainment.

There are four regulars: the two who were waiting in the car outside when they came back from Milton Keynes, Terry's mate Robbie and his partner, Graham.

"I know it's handy not to worry about the Law Scotch, but this is all meant to be 'secret', not a fucking general invite for anyone with a bit of time on their hands! Robbie and Graham are OK, but the other two are lippy bastards."

The younger one, with the "work-out" body is clearly

more interested in Razza than anything else, which Terry found difficult to fathom given her butch looks and half a scrap-metal yard stuck through her face.

He has told them the house rules: Don't Touch the Dogs. Don't Touch the Staff. Don't Fucking Tell Anyone Else. He can't imagine them taking a blind bit of notice.

***

"Newcastle is on Tel. Et's a BIGGY. Unless your fucken' witch doctor says the tea leaves are blowin' the wrong way. Haaaaa!"

***

Fucking Karma. Witch doctor, my arse.

They had stuck a saline drip in one arm to rehydrate him, and had drained all the blood from his dick with just a local anaesthetic while he was still humming along. The doctor said they couldn't wait for him to wake up if they were going to save it.

The coppers had thought it was such a laugh to send the graduate trainee to interview the bloke with a giant hard-on; ask him how he knew the people in the tent with him, and if he thought they were trying to harm him.

The ambulance team had been sufficiently disturbed to call in a report, so despite no one down the station believing a word of it, they were obliged to follow up, even if it was just going through the motions.

Karma had come round after a couple of hours, but his English was so bad that he couldn't sensibly answer the questions of the young trainee policeman, and just kept nodding, gesticulating, and trying to show him his penis.

Despite Tas's repeated explanations, he had written up his report recommending that all those present should be treated as suspects and interviewed properly to try to find out the truth. Given that Tas was clearly a key "suspect" in the case, her explanations at this stage had to be ignored until verified.

"Sorry, Tel, mate, we have to take a statement. I really *am* sorry. *We* know you weren't trying to hurt the bloke, but now our boy has filed his report, we have to go through the motions."

Robbie had been the one with the idea of giving it to the trainee, for a laugh, and was beginning to regret it. He drank with Terry down The Badger's and knew he couldn't be involved in anything barbaric. It was clear he had trouble walking, let alone plotting to cook anyone.

***

Terry went down to the station and gave as slimmed-down a report of the Sweat Lodge party as he could.

"No, I didn't want Karma dead. No, I didn't see anyone 'handling' Karma inappropriately."

Terry had learned in his infrequent dealings with the police, that rising to any sort of bait was not smart, so he just smiled and stuck completely to the truth, without mentioning the wanking part, or his bollocks, or all the bits of cat in the cupboard.

None of the other witnesses suggested anything "criminal" had occurred, but they did, between them, paint a full and graphic picture of events.

While not the basis for any form of prosecution, it was a great story.

***

Interview over, he sits down to a cup of coffee. Robbie had said he needed a short "off-the-record" chat. Always worrying with a copper, no matter how well you knew them.

"Honestly Rob, you've never seen a dick like it mate," Terry said, breaking the ice.

"Bloody scary by the sound of it Tel! But that's not what I wanted to chat about." He drops to a whisper. "Bit sensitive really…"

They sit out in the waiting room on the cheap plastic chairs, no one else in earshot apart from the duty officer, bored behind the counter.

"It's these calls Tel. We've been getting them every other day for a couple of weeks now, she never leaves a name, but we know who it is."

Robbie pauses for effect.

"It's your lunatic mother-in-law! You've got to get her under control mate, really. She's wasting our time, and we can't get her off the fucking phone, and the stuff she comes out with. Really not nice. You don't want that stuff getting out Tel."

***

Terry, Becca and Scotch sit round the kitchen table, the takeaway curry tins in a line down the middle. He knows this is a poor idea, letting Scotch back in the house, but the lock-up no longer seems a place of privacy, for plotting plans and talking money. Nevertheless, watching Scotch squeezing ketchup in a careful lattice pattern over his chicken vindaloo seems a high price to pay for privacy.

The Newcastle plan is outlined. Mojito's fame has spread, and he has acquired an element of "notoriety".

Scotch is excited as he squeezes another dribble of ketchup onto his curry-laden piece of poppadum, and edges it into his gaping mouth.

"The secret is gettin' et inta yer mouth without touchen' yer leps."

Heaven help us!

***

The northern boys took their dogfighting, and breeding, very seriously.

"This lad's the Cappo, Tel – the Fucken' dog-breeding Cappo. *If* we win et Tel – WHEN we win et – Mojito will be worth a fucken' FORTUNE. The big boy will pay a shitload for him and his lettle doggy jiz, never mind the cash we'll take from the bookies!"

Terry has not really considered the "end game", he has just been desperately hoping to make enough money to pay off an instalment or two of the tax bill to avoid them selling the house – but clearly this would be a very happy ending if it came off. But he had watched Becca's face when Scotch was talking about selling Mojito.

"Maybe just renting him out as a 'sex machine' would work Becca – in fact, who *wouldn't* fancy that as a retirement option?"

For the first time in months Terry can see a glimmer of hope.

24

"**I THINK IT** was a bit early to try that Pet. We know it will be fine when it's better, and to be honest, it doesn't look very nice yet. Actually, to be truthful, it doesn't look *very* nice at the best of times, but right now, with all the bruising, it looks quite nasty. So I am not that upset; really not at all."

Terry lays naked on his back, Becca is on her side, one arm draped across his chest. His balls are throbbing to the point of gasping out loud.

WHY did I think it was a good idea to take that fucking Viagra, and before I had even taken the old chap for a "one-hand test drive"? It's only three sodding weeks since I had half a reel of cotton holding my balls together!

The Viagra seems to have applied its magic to his still slightly swollen testicles as well as its primary target. The more aroused he got, the more his balls hurt, and now he is laying there pulsating, and entirely unable to do anything about it.

"Terry, you have used that bloody stuff again, I can tell, and that's *after* you seeing what nearly happened to your brother-in-law. It's just dangerous, Pet, what were you thinking of?! You got yourself all wound up thinking about a bloke who nearly had to have his cock amputated, it's ridiculous! And *now* you are just going to lay there in pain until it wears off. Just *stay* there and I'll get a bag of frozen peas to wrap around it, that might calm it down a bit."

Terry lies there thinking. He could attempt to swerve this one; claim that his unnatural swelling was all just a product of Becca's allure and Mother Nature, but it was sort of stretching the imagination hot on the heels of the Karma fiasco. He gives in to the obvious truth.

"The peas would be lovely Becca. I've been pretty stupid. I'm really sorry."

She sits up on one elbow, lifting her head off his shoulder and looks down at the problem, bruised, stitched, and now quite angry; she gives it a playful flick of one finger, and as he gasps, she grins at him: "I'll get the peas, a cup of tea, and we'll turn on the TV and watch *Bake Off*, you know how *Bake Off* calms you down".

***

With Becca gone, Terry sits himself up a little. An evening of passion has turned into a complete embarrassment, a bag of peas around his bollocks and a painful night in with an episode or two of *Bake Off*. He preferred the "original" *Bake Off* team before they went off to some other channel for loads of money, and now one of the hosts of the show was this very strange man, a cross between a clown and a vampire, who seemed to know nothing at all about cakes. There was something incredibly restful about watching the hotchpotch of contestants stressing about whether a sponge had risen, or their jam was jammy enough.

As the closing titles scroll down the screen, Terry allows his thoughts to flood back, his anxieties only temporarily held at bay. His defences are down, and there is a trickle of condensation between his legs as the peas defrost.

Becca lies quietly beside him, listening as Terry unloads a stream of worry: about money, about the taxman, about his failed potency, his stitched-up bollocks, the dogs, the awful dogfighting world, the coppers, his beloved nightmare of a daughter and that fuckwit boyfriend she is still seeing, the shit that *still* keeps appearing on the car, his stupid fucking job, and his mother-in-law, and just EVERYTHING!

It just flows out of him in little soundbites, like compiling a list of all the things you *don't* want to deal with. He can't stop, it just floods out.

Becca knows he needs to let this all out, and he will feel better afterwards. She was worrying about most of it too, but she didn't realise his work was a problem; he always put on such a front, and she didn't understand why her mother was in there with all the rest.

Becca asks him about work.

"I haven't sold anything for weeks, Becca, nor has my whole bloody team. I know it's always slow in summer, but it just feels more serious than the usual slow-down. I'm sure it will be fine though."

What he doesn't say is:

"As well as selling sod-all for an age, our fucking PA has signed herself off with stress, and I'm just waiting for the letter

from her doctor saying it's because of all the "shock and offence" caused by opening MY DAUGHTER'S bloody Amazon packages delivered to me; she's always been a complete bitch, and now she's going out with a fucking lawyer. You can just see it coming!"

"So what's the problem with my mum? I know she can be a pain sometimes, but she really means well underneath it all, you know that Lamb?"

He takes a deep breath; he knows he can't avoid this one.

"You know how sometimes a couple have to discuss something really sensitive Becca? Like when I found your drawer full of naughty toys?"

It was years ago that he stumbled across her little hoard of "things a girl needs". There *were* quite a few of them: eleven in fact. Becca had explained that they were "like shoes: heels, flatties, sandals, boots, platforms…" she just ended up acquiring them over the years. Every time she went to a friend's Anne Summers party she "sort of *had* to buy something" – and that's what she bought, and she could never bring herself to throw any of them away. Like shoes, they still fit, and every one had a little memory associated with it, she clearly quite liked teasing him with it. Normally when Terry mentioned her "collection" it was an attempt to turn it into a spectator sport, which she never actually allowed.

"I'm not *at all* sure you should be thinking about that right now Lamb. You know what it does to you, and we've only just managed to calm it all down!"

"No Becca, I mean, like a 'proper' talk, like about your mum."

Terry recounts his conversation with Robbie down at

the police station almost word-for-word to an increasingly horrified Becca.

"So she tells them my name Becca, refuses to say who she is; but they all bloody know. That's probably the only reason they haven't pulled me in for questioning. That, and the fact that Robbie knows me. A 'pervert and a sodomite' Becca, and, 'grooming old-age pensioners'. And then she starts describing stuff straight out of *50 Shades*. Robbie reckons she is actually reading from a book down the phone line. I mean it's just horrible Becca. And they're bloody recording all the calls! I reckon they sit around with a beer and play them back for fun. We've got to stop her Becca."

"I should NEVER have bought her that bloody book Terry! I am *so* sorry! Bloody woman!"

"Robbie even played me the tape where she describes me kidnapping her, stripping her, and locking her in a public loo on the high street; *then*, while she is locked in, getting a crowd to gather round before setting off the washing function and then opening the door in front of everyone! The worst thing Becca, if I didn't know better, I would actually believe her!"

Becca is completely gripped in a tide of emotion and tears: first her daughter, selfish little bitch, and now her mother. Her stupid fucking mother!

"Don't cry Becca, it's not your fault she's just gone a bit loopy. All we have to do is work out how to get her to stop now Doll."

"What *am* I going to say to her Terry? She'll just deny it. We have to think about this for a while. I am *so* sorry."

The tears flow, and Terry knows he has caused them, but what could he do?

25

ALL SO FUCKING predictable.

Terry sits at Tulip's desk, waiting as she arranged various papers in front of her, peering at him over the top of her glasses.

Terry shifts around in his seat; it is still difficult to sit with his legs closed, and the narrow, high-sided chairs are impossible, so he sits, very unnaturally, on the edge of the seat so he can splay his legs, giving the impression that he is about to launch himself across the desk. He feels himself reddening slightly, throat tightening; tense, though Tulip hasn't actually said anything yet. Tulip is Ghanaian, *very* tall and *very* serious, the word "Amazon" always leaps into Terry's mind when thinking of Tulip.

"As head of Human Resources, I am sure you realise I have to take *any* complaints from staff members seriously – and *this* particular letter of complaint from Julie Addison is quite unusual, and quite serious. I hope you realise that Terry."

"Could I actually *see* the letter please Tulip?"

"No, I am afraid you cannot at this stage. If there is any need for a formal disciplinary hearing, you will of course be allowed to see any materials forming the basis of that hearing, but at this stage this is just an informal fact-finding meeting."

Methodically, Tulip reads out, point by point, the complaints that Julie had listed.

"I felt humiliated and embarrassed by being expected to deliver various sex aids and play items to Terry Granger in front of the other team members."

"I suffered from shock and anxiety when I had to deliver packets of 'Sexual Performance-Related Drugs'."

"The packages I was expected to deliver had clearly been opened, so that the contents were clearly visible before being given to me for delivery to Terry."

"My decision to visit the doctor arose after reading a truly horrible article in the local paper about Terry, which gave me nightmares and has made me nervous and stressed in Terry's presence."

"Terry looks at me in a strange way, which makes me nervous and stressed."

Along with the letter are two articles cut out of the local papers about the emergency services involvement in the rescue of Karma from what was described as a "Black Mass". A picture of Terry in his Millwall strip and his two walking sticks outside his sister's house while his brother-in-law was stretchered past had inexplicably found its way into the article accompanying the story. Terry is clearly laughing in the picture.

A doctor's letter accompanies the newspaper cuttings –

stating that Julie was suffering from stress induced by Terry's behaviour, and had been so adversely affected by the stories in the press to the point that she was scared to come into the office.

"Julie, or the lawyer that wrote the letter for her, is requesting a formal investigation into your behaviour, a formal apology from the firm and a written assurance that this unacceptable working environment will be dealt with. She also asked that to allow her to cope with her anxiety attacks she would be allowed to move to a three-day week.

So, Terry…Julie Addison has been asking to move to a three-day week for the last couple of years, a move which the firm has resisted. Now, however, we can hardly refuse *anything* Miss Addison might ask for, and *you* have put us in that position. What on earth were you doing having nipple tassels delivered to work anyway?"

Terry tries gamely to explain that it was his daughter sending the parcels, but that doesn't seem credible when seen alongside the packages of Viagra.

WHY had they bloody opened all these things down in the post-room anyway, nosey fuckers? It was THEM that should be in leg-irons, not me!

"You know there are company policies prohibiting personal shopping deliveries to work Terry."

Terry explained that the newspaper articles had completely misrepresented the accident to his brother-in-law, and that no charges had been brought against anyone.

"But you *can* see why an article suggesting you are involved, in some way, in attempt to 'cook' a man of colour, alongside another article about cannibalism in Papua New Guinea, *could* lead to Miss Addison, or in fact anyone who works with you, becoming upset – now you *can* see that can't you Terry?"

Fucking Streatham News. It was a ridiculous story, and *how* did they get that picture? It looked like it was taken on a mobile phone, and while Terry was not central to the picture, he was clearly visible, and his shorts and walking sticks immediately drew the eye to him – and he *was* laughing.

"I don't really know what to say Tulip, except that I am *so* sorry to have caused Julie distress, the post-room opening the parcels – and I *know* it looks terrible, but it *really* was my daughter…"

Terry tails off. It is all just so horribly incriminating and fucking embarrassing – this is worse than visiting his sister.

"You do not have to say any more Terry, but you just mustn't bring your personal life in to the workplace – *we* don't judge people, what you do in your own home is *your* business – and I *have* seen the YouTube video of your daughter, so I understand that some families are just *different.*"

She's seen the fucking video…that means they had ALL seen the fucking video…my life is just SO over…

Terry's mouth falls into a slack, open smile, no words. He wonders if he had a heart attack on the spot, or some sort of stroke, whether Tulip would give him mouth-to-mouth. He quite likes the idea of Tulip giving him mouth-to-mouth – being "lipped" to death…

"I will talk to Julie and see how far she intends to take the issue, but it is possible that we will have to conduct a more formal investigation depending how those discussions go. In the meantime you are to stop *any* deliveries of personal items to the office in line with company policy. Do you understand Terry?"

Tulip stands, moving towards the door, signalling the meeting is over. Terry passes her, towering above him, and she rests her hand firmly, comfortingly, on his shoulder, giving him an encouraging squeeze.

***

Something had to be done with Poodle.

He seemed to be becoming more psychotic with every passing day, spending more time in the midst of his personal fugue than out of it. Terry had considered giving Poodle to Edith, to replace her beloved spaniel, Bitsy. She had become even more of a titanic pain in the arse ever since her dog *and* her husband had died a couple of years ago. It might give her something else to think about apart from how best to piss off her favourite son-in-law, but given his success with animal husbandry lately he abandoned the idea before even attempting to sell it to Becca.

The three of them, he, Becca and Scotch, toyed with the idea of taking Poodle to the vet – but the two possible outcomes of either extended treatment for his psychiatric disorder, or simply putting him out of his misery, were both expensive. Truth be told they didn't want the mad little fucker back, and Terry's sentimental move to rescue him from the police pound was not looking so great now.

In the end they made a collective decision that Poodle should be taken somewhere and dropped off to fend for himself – but where?

The choice was simple; they either had to just let him

go somewhere to run free, or leave him tied up in a location from which he would have to be removed, effectively passing the problem to whoever was unlucky enough to get the job of dealing him.

***

Very early Sunday morning Terry drives Poodle across to Morden Underground station, the first stop on the Northern Line. He waits for the Edgware train, right out the other side of London, but more specifically, the branch of the line passing through Hampstead.

He likes the idea of Poodle heading, screaming mad, to Hampstead.

Boarding the empty train and attaching his lead to one of the handrails as the train approaches Tooting Broadway, Terry says goodbye as Poodle enters the "Alien versus Predator" phase of a particularly nasty fit. He hops off and crosses the platform to reverse his route as Poodle speeds north in the empty carriage, teeth bared, snarling and frothing.

He would make someone a lovely pet.

26

NOW TERRY KNEW. And he really wished he didn't.

Knowing fuck all, absolutely fuck all, was bliss!

Finally, he had discovered Scotch's secret recipe for his "Doggy Viagra" pills.

As they approached the Newcastle date, Scotch had begun feeding all three of them a carefully timed, carefully rationed pellet from his special supply. But he had been stressing about not having enough of them and Terry had walked in on him mixing up a batch, moaning quietly to himself in guttural Glaswegian.

"Not much in here eh Scotch. What is it mate?"

Terry had picked up a clear glass jam-jar with a smear of thick, opaque fluid in the bottom.

"WILL YOU FUCKEN' PUT THA' DOWN TEL!"

Taken aback, Terry quickly replaced the jar on the small table where Scotch was mashing up a small quantity of other "magic ingredients". He reached for the jar, muttering, carefully spooning in the mixture, and started blending it together.

"Come on Scotch, enough. Fucking enough. WHAT IS IT, you tetchy bastard?!"

Glaring at Terry, irritated, his "colour" up, Scotch says, "If you HAVE tae fucken' know Tel…it's JIZ! MA FUCKEN' JIZ!"

Terry sat down. He was pretty sure he understood what Scotch had said; a revulsive shudder runs through him as he thought about holding up the jar of what he has just been told is cold sperm.

He's been feeding his own sperm to the dogs – Nooooo, surely not! It's beyond fucking belief; first, fucking cheese, now cold gobs of spunk. How much of it, for how long? Is it even FRESH?! Fuck me!

Unusually, Terry was actually speechless.

"It was ma Da's secret Tel; he told me, sorta passed it down through the generations his secret recipe. Told ya, it's pure Doggy Viagra."

"Scotch, mate, that's just fucking horrible. It's not 'Doggy Viagra', you're just feeding your own jiz to the dogs Scotch; to the fucking DOGS Scotch!"

What should you say? How could you ever explain this to anyone?

"I'm not sure I want to know any more. What are you doing man? Sitting at home jizzing into a fucking jam-jar Scotch? And then what do you do? Walk along the road holding it in your hand, or what? Tell me you're fucking joking Scotch, please!"

"No Tel, no fucken' joke! It has to be pretty fresh. Ah usually do it here. Just quietly. It's nae always easy, but it has tae be done; they rely on me, the dogs. Becca niver told ya Tel? She's a good girl, can keep a secret."

He stopped for a second, letting the words sink in.

"Becca knows. How does Becca fucking know Scotch?"

Scotch was caught in the headlights: mouth moving for a moment or two, with no words.

"Caught me at it, she ded. Everyone had gone, ah was trying to wank off watching some shit on ma phone and suddenly she was fucken' there Tel! Ah could hae fucken' died a embarrassment.

When ah told her it was for the dogs Tel, she kinda understood. She laughed when ah told her the porn on ma phone would nae work properly. Ah would NIVER have touched her Tel, not after the tattoo and you kicking the shit outa me. NIVER touch her Tel!"

"I never said you would touch her Scotch. Why are you even saying that mate? What do you mean 'never touch her'?"

"I ONLY fucken' look Tel, just look. She's got the best arse Tel. You're a lucky, lucky man!"

***

"He just liked me walking up and down in front of him in my onesie, the black one, like a cat-suit, and heels, but he never touched me. I never *saw* his actual thing – he sat behind the desk just doing it into a jar. He said he couldn't do it on his own, so I just walked around, wiggling a bit; it's harmless…REALLY! I did it for the dogs, and it *does* help them, you can just see it! I think it might even be why the dogs love me Tel. It sort of 'transmits' itself to them; it *is* possible now, isn't it? And they have just gone and won *every* time Pet, haven't they? Blokes do it *all* the time anyway. YOU do it all the time!"

Terry sits at the kitchen table opposite Becca, feeling numb, the pasta-bake slowly congealing as he pushes it around the bowl with his fork. She seemed to think this was OK. He had to calm down, keep this under control.

HOW can she think this is OK? Keep calm Tel.

"YOU THINK IT'S FUCKING OK! MY WIFE THINKS IT'S OK TO PARADE AROUND WHILE A BLOKE WHO HAS ALREADY TATTOOED HER FANNY SITS AND WANKS OVER HER! IT'S NOT FUCKING OK…FUCK!…FUCK!"

Terry is on his feet, the chair pushed back, his fists bunched by his sides. He can barely speak; the red mist has descended.

"He doesn't wank OVER me. He wanks into a jar… TERRY!"

"OH! SORRY! I HAD MISUNDERSTOOD. HE'S ONLY WANKING INTO A JAR WHILE YOU TOUCH YOUR TOES IN FRONT OF HIM. THAT'S FUCKING FINE THEN! SO WHEN…WHEN WERE YOU GOING TO TELL ME? I SIT TALKING TO THAT FUCKER EVERY DAY, AND MY WIFE IS LETTING HIM WANK ALL OVER HER WHENEVER HE FEELS LIKE IT FOR FUCK'S SAKE – AND I, STUPID FUCKER THAT I AM, DON'T KNOW ANYTHING ABOUT IT!'

Still on his feet, he feels like his head is about to burst. He is spitting the words out in a foaming rage.

Becca, still sitting opposite, trembling. He looks like he could do anything.

"I don't touch my toes, and he DOES NOT wank OVER me! You need to calm down Terry, you are really scaring me. Sit down Terry. Sit down NOW!"

Terry stops, breathing in gulps, pulls the chair around and sits down.

"HE'S FUCKING DEAD. Fucking dead…" and he goes quiet; spent.

"I'm so, so sorry Tel. You know I would never do anything to hurt you. You get *so* angry. Nothing happened at all Pet. It was just silly Scotch with his silly magic potion. Nothing sexy. I wouldn't ever let him touch me, especially after you got so upset because of the tattooing. I am *so* sorry, it won't happen again Tel. I love you, you know."

Becca moves round the table, puts her arms around his head, sits on his lap and just holds him while he calms, starts to breathe more normally.

His arms reach around her waist, his head cushioned by her breasts through her cashmere jumper. She feels him stir against her thigh. He will be all right.

They sit like that for a while, Becca holding him, shifting slightly. Whispering into his ear: "I *know* men look at me Tel, you know they do too, and…I know what they are thinking of doing to me Tel…and what they want me to do to them…"

Becca went ahead and did it to him, carefully, and let him do it to her, less carefully. It was fucking outrageous, and Terry could see months of very naughty "game-playing" stretching ahead of him, and it just wasn't worth jeopardising that by putting Scotch's lights out just to make himself feel better.

"Ah noo ya think it's mad Tel, but it's handed down through generations, and ah just cannae, and I willnae stop now! It *works* Tel – it just fucken' works."

Terry has made his peace with Becca thanks to the outrageously naughty "making up"; but now he has to work out how to handle his thoughts about Scotch, and even how to feel about being licked by a dog full of Scotch's jiz.

"And ah swear, no more lookin' at yur missus Tel. Ahll just find another way. Ah can just shut ma eyes and think ae her instead."

"Fuck's sake Scotch. NO! Don't look at her! And don't fucking think about her, and especially not while you're playing with yourself. Think of someone else!"

"Ye don't realise Tel, what a fine and sexy woman you have there! There are a lot of men who look at her and fancy her pants off; it's not a fucken' crime! How would you like to be married to a woman that *no one* would want to letch over Tel? It *must* be why you fancied her yerself in the first place. You are just fucken' lucky! But ah swear, ah SWEAR, ah willnae think about her; look at her; or anything while ahm milkin' masell Tel; ah SWEAR!"

"Don't call it fucking 'milking' Scotch! It's horrible. You are wanking for God's sake! Just wanking! Milking sounds even worse!"

27

"**IT'S GOT TO** stop Mum. It's got to stop *now*."

"What's got to stop dear?"

Edith peers over her knitting glasses, the fat needles in a state of perpetual motion, glancing across to Terry every few seconds.

"The calls to the police Mum."

"I can't really hear you dear."

"Well why don't we try turning the television down a bit Mum," Becca says, raising her voice over the ambulance sirens on *Casualty*.

"I want to see what happens to the man who had the accident with the bus – he looks in a bad way, doesn't he, and his children are very upset. I think he will pull through, but you never know on *Casualty*."

"We came round to talk Mum, it's important, more important than a man in a hospital soap pretending to have been hit by a bus. Really Mum, so we need to turn it down a bit."

The football-sized ball of wool lies to the side of Edith's armchair, slowly turning as she draws more thread into the clacking needles. The remote control is on the wide arm of her chair, the thread running protectively over it as she knits. Her right arm moves just an inch closer to the controller, elbow extending protectively over it with each slight tug on the wool. Her gaze intently focused on the unfolding drama.

"Please Mum, it's important."

Terry sits at the corner of the triangle, his mother-in-law at the apex directly in front of the TV, he and Becca in small matching armchairs either side of the screen. He has no idea why he is here, Becca insisted that they would both go and "flush it all out" – an appropriate expression he felt. He intends to keep very quiet, and just be ready to pull Becca off the vicious old bint if it gets out of hand.

Becca is having to shout above the TV, while Edith's answers are delivered in a normal tone, so it is almost impossible to hear.

"I miss the company you know."

"I know you do Mum. We all miss Dad a lot, but let's just turn this down a bit so we can talk, eh?"

"Not your father dear! I don't miss him at all – it's Bitsy I miss, she was such a comfort to me, she got me out of the house for little walks. Your father just wanted sex all the time dear – sex, sex, sex – it was a blessing when it all stopped really."

Angry now, Becca is out of the chair and over to wrestle the TV controller away from her mother. A slightly slapstick faux fight over the six-inch piece of plastic ensues, with Becca stepping back victorious, theatrically pointing the controller at the screen and turning the volume down to a whisper. Edith's face is contorted, as if she is chewing a mouthful of nettles. She sits back, upright, jaw set in place, eyes still firmly locked on the screen.

"How *can* you talk about Dad that way, going on about sex! He was disabled for his last five years!"

Almost spitting the words, Edith says: "Just because he couldn't walk, dear, doesn't mean he didn't have constant, distasteful physical demands – non-stop, sex and more SEX. Just like HIM in the corner, just sitting there all smug, saying nothing. I'm an OLD WOMAN, I can't cope with constant fornication, not at my age. Bitsy didn't need sex, NO, she just needed dog biscuits and an occasional walk."

"We are going to stop talking about this NOW. You never took Bitsy for walks, you just let her into the garden to shit all over the place! WE know that! The gardener who came every fortnight – that WE paid for – used to spend half his time just scooping up poo everywhere. You NEVER took her out. Let's just stop this now Mother, there are things we have to talk about, not your flights of fantasy!"

"Sex and more sex – you'll never understand."

Terry is totally impressed that Becca is managing to keep this all together, but it doesn't feel like a good constructive discussion is anywhere close by. He has his serious, concerned-but-supportive face on.

"So, Mother, it has to stop. These calls to the police – they have to stop."

"What ARE you talking about, who is talking to the police? Has he been reported? Him over there, sitting all smug, trying to look serious, has HE been reported yet?"

"Mum, the police know it's you, they told us, and they

traced the number – it's your number, here at the house. So let's stop pretending."

Edith sets her jaw ever firmer, her gaze locked tightly on her ungrateful Judas of a daughter.

"It's my duty. If I don't do it, report him, then who will? YOU certainly won't because he has YOU under his control! He PRETENDS to help me up into the car, and before I know it he has half his arm inside me! PERVERT! If I don't say something, have him stopped, then nobody will, and he will be out there, out there with his horrid, HORRID appetites!"

"He's just helping you into the car Mum, he is *not* assaulting you. You have to stop it. Anyone who comes within fifty yards of you, you tell me is trying to have sex with you. They aren't Mum, they just aren't, they don't want to have sex with you. You are just upsetting everyone. So it stops – now – or I won't be coming to see you again until it does. And nor will your granddaughter. And nor will Chloe. You can ask social services to get your shopping. Do you understand?"

God she's beautiful.

Terry sits, awestruck. It was all just delivered with a quiet, steely calm. His woman. Vampire Slayer. Awesome.

Edith doesn't even begin to acquiesce, jaw still set, glowering at her daughter, but both know that the balance of power has shifted. The hotline to the police station will fall into disuse, and for now, Edith understands that no one – no one – wants to have sex with her.

28

TAS LOOKS LIKE shit.

She is sitting on one of her "animal sacrifice" sofas with her leg resting on a footstool. The footstool looks as if it could once have been alive, but the blood leaking onto it from some hastily arranged bandages is definitely hers. Karma sits opposite her, a look of concern and anxiety clear on his face.

Terry's mobile had gone off three times with his sister's name flashing up on it. It was Saturday afternoon. Becca had called him up to the bedroom and he had found her standing there in the middle of the room: in the cat-suit, heels, and nothing else, the zip undone as far as it could go. Down to her tattoo. It was years since he had even *thought* about performing *twice* in quick succession, but it did seem to be happening! And then the bloody phone kept going – and now here he was.

"It wasn't his fault Terry; he only attacks dogs, and he sensed, he knew, I AM a dog!"

Piddle is outside in the yard, no longer a danger to anyone now. Karma had skewered him with a garden fork when he realised that Piddle really wasn't going to let go of Tas's leg.

Terry looks out the French window at Piddle's lifeless form: he lies on his side, the fork still sticking out of his back.

It could have been worse, mate; he could have finger-fucked you up the arse first!

Poor Piddle. He had never liked him much at all, but like Scooter, you wouldn't really have wished this on him; but why the fuck had he attacked Tas anyway?

Maybe she is a fucking voodoo she-dog thing after all?

Terry reaches across, asks if he can take a look, and lifts the bandage carefully, stickily, off Tasmin's leg.

Oh God that's a mess. Fucking dog. Deserved all it got.

"We need to get that properly looked at, Sis. Can you make it to the car if we help you?"

It was my idea to bring that demented fucking thing, a trained fighting dog – no idea what had been done to it in its past life – round here AFTER it had killed and EATEN my own cat. And now I should be surprised it's attacked someone? Fuck!

***

"It was after the Inland Revenue people came round that he got all agitated Tel. They're nasty little people. They never actually *call* you a liar, but you know that's what they mean."

The three of them sitting in casualty in Dulwich Community Hospital, a sea of groaning and damaged people of every shape, size, age and race.

This is the problem with community hospitals, people from the bloody community are in here.

They have been there for an hour now after the tired-looking receptionist had given them a number, 107, to wait for; they had started with 89 showing on the screen, but are now up to 104.

"I can't believe we just sit here for hours while you fucking bleed to death Sis. You're gonna need a tetanus jab or something for those bites. So how long have you known the tax filth were going to be coming to call?"

Karma sits to Tas's left, his hands in his lap, just rocking back and forth. The skewering incident has upset him; he seemed to be fond of animals, so killing a big-ish one with a garden fork doesn't sit easily with him.

"Couple of weeks ago. I didn't want to bother you about it. I know how much you have been dealing with Tel. I got the same letter as you, telling me to pay all that money. All that money I haven't got. So I rang them and just explained what had happened to it.

They obviously didn't believe me, so said they would send someone round to interview me and I *had* to pay them the money. I wouldn't even believe it either I suppose, it's a ridiculous thing to have done, to not notice that much cash had actually *gone*. But I've never *had* any money before! They were just horrible on the phone Tel."

"So you told them Karma had just given all the money away; what did they say Sis?"

"There were three of them. They already knew that I work in the housing department, *and* what I earn. Bloody cheek! So I showed them my bank accounts online, with about £400 in them, and all my payslips. They searched the house – bastards! Then, when they didn't find anything, they started asking Karma about it – really threatening and everything. We had to lock Piddle outside because he was starting to growl at them. Karma just told them I am 'very kind'. He saved my life you know Terry! 'Very kind' and 'much money', he just kept saying it, over and over. They made him write down where he sent the money, and they made him give them his mobile phone number. You don't suppose they will go over there and make them sell the house Terry, do you? That would be SO awful!"

"I really don't think they'll go over to Tunisia, Sis. I'm not sure there's much they can do; you haven't really got anything they can take away Tas. Your house is council property, nothing in the bank, you haven't even got a car to flog, and what do you earn now down at the housing?"

"About £12,000 for my three days a week; I just don't think I could manage to work more! Oh Terry, you don't think I could go to prison!?"

Terry slips his arm around his sister's shoulder; he can see she is about to start crying again.

"No, don't be daft Sis. The worse they could do is try to make you pay a bit back every week; we didn't *know* the tax hadn't been paid, and they can't prove we did, that was all down to Jonny, fucking idiot. Just keep telling them the truth. It's so bizarre that they might just give up on you!"

"They kept asking me if I had seen Jonny. It's just so stressful. I just try hard to think, 'What would Judd say?' He wouldn't be scared. I hate them, I really do! When they left, we let Piddle out and he seemed really disturbed, jumpy, like he was looking for something, and then he just went for me Terry. He just went mad! Karma couldn't get him off; and then…"

Her voice tails off and tears entirely overtake Terry's sister.

That must have been pretty fucking awful seeing Karma driving the fork into the dog while it was still attached to her leg, poor kid.

107 flicks up onto the screen and they help Tas over to the waiting nurse. Karma goes with her while Terry goes back and sits, staring into space, in the middle of the rows of plastic chairs, surrounded by South London's groaning casualties.

***

Disposing of animal remains is becoming a regular pastime.

He had headed off while Tas was being stitched up, to tidy up the carnage back at the house.

Terry stands in Tas's garden, pondering over how to deal with the latest little problem, with a fork sticking out of its back, right in the middle of the tiny lawn.

You don't see many of these around. Maybe you could sell them down the fair-ground next to the toffee apples "Dog on a Stick! Who fancies a Dog on a Stick" – it probably won't catch on…

He looks back and up at the windows of the neighbouring terraces. Both sides would have had a grandstand view of the battleground, and while everyone talks about South Londoners being a friendly bunch, getting any help from them was another thing! It was pretty certain the neighbours would have seen what was going on, or at least heard it – must have been a fucking terrible row. To the left, the bottom windows were actually covered up with black plastic bin liners, taped up from inside, the top windows with thick tatty curtains pulled tightly shut even in broad daylight. Tas had said they didn't see much of the gaunt, pallid, middle-aged couple who lived there.

Most likely vampires. Can't get away from them these days.

The other side was far more typical, pairs of cheap net curtains, partly opened at the bottom where Doris, the old girl who lived there, liked to stand and watch anything that was going on. This was better entertainment than the TV. Doris had appeared for a chat several times while the Sweat Lodge was being prepared, and had opened up the nets properly and pulled up the armchair at her bedroom window for a front-row seat of the proceedings – hours of fun!

Surveying the body, Terry sees the four smaller holes lower down Piddle's back, where Karma must have had a practice run before deciding that the "full monty" was the only answer. Nice.

He had better just get on with it. Picking up a spade from the grubby collection of tools propped up in the corner, he selects a nice corner spot and starts digging, only to find that the grass is sitting on a thin layer of topsoil and a huge amount of muddy rubble, broken bricks, bits of concrete. He soldiers on for a while, but is barely six inches down after thirty minutes, and the rubble just keeps going as he levers out each obstacle. His shoulder isn't particularly enjoying this either.

"He can't go *there* Terry."

Tas appears at the kitchen door, her leg heavily bandaged.

"It's the aura – an evil aura, a terrible omen. It would be like knowing Satan was buried in your back-garden Terry

– how would you like that? Knowing Satan's remains were only a few feet from you while you were having dinner?"

It isn't a question that Terry has a ready answer for, but the digging is fucking impossible, so he is easily persuaded that there might be better ways of disposing of the body. The idea of a bonfire doesn't go down well with Tas, and there isn't really enough burnable stuff, unless you included the entire contents of his sister's house, which Terry feels would have been a blessing for everyone.

With Karma's help, Piddle's remains are lifted up and lowered into a black bin bag. Once properly obscured, Terry puts his foot on the bag, yanks out the fork and returns it, bloodied, to the pile of tools. Tying the bag neatly, it feels as if the body had vanished, to be replaced by something far less gory, just a shiny black bag, neat and tidy. He then puts the bag into *another* black bag to avoid the problem of leaks from the now-unplugged wounds, and ties that one up neatly too.

***

It had all been a bit too "deja-vu", driving the car with a bin bag containing a four-legged, deceased furry friend. Tas had been insistent that Piddle was not just put in the waste, even though Terry had been very clear that it would be "general waste" rather than recycling, she had developed a very strong feeling that Piddle's remains housed some form of evil spirit, and that having Satan, or any of his closer friends in the bin just outside the front door for the remaining five days before the refuse collection was simply not acceptable.

They had considered a number of ideas: burying it in the

local woods or the local park would be slow, hard work, and likely to attract attention; dropping it in the river, with a few stones for ballast felt faster, but not a particularly hygienic option. In the end, the simple task of taking Piddle down to the Southwark refuse centre and slinging him in a bin seemed the quickest and least sinister alternative.

***

Quite why the local dump, as Terry prefers to think about it, is so fucking popular on a Saturday afternoon, he just doesn't know, but he has queued for three or four minutes just to get in there. Everyone seems to know what they are doing – purposefully heaving their loads in the direction of specially signed bins for each particular waste category.

"What's in the bag mate?"

None of the giant metal containers have a sign for "Waste Animals". Several have metal steps alongside, so that the items can be dropped in, others are open at one end, so heavy loads can be humped and dragged in.

There are several refuse and recycling attendants herding and directing people, and it is one of these that call out to Terry as he mounts the steps beside the "Household Waste – Non-Recyclable" bin.

"Nothing much, me-old-shagger, just a dead dog or two."

"Ha! You might joke mate, but you wouldn't fuckin' believe what some people bring in here – nice one tho!"

Piddle disappears over the edge of the bin.

Even Satan wouldn't be terribly chuffed to wake up in there.

***

Jonny hadn't been answering his phone or texts for over a week.

Standing in the half-lit hallway on the eighth floor of Jonny's block of flats, Terry takes deep breaths of almost-fresh air. The lift has hosted a urinating contest over the weekend, and the smell mixes nicely with the disinfectant used to swill it every Friday by the cleaners.

Aimsbury House had been part of the great "social housing" jamboree of the early 60s that now brought so much joy to its residents while they prayed for the demolition order to be served on it.

Eventually, he knocks on the doors of almost every flat on the floor. Most of them don't open, even though he can hear movement inside.

"It's Terry…Jonny's brother – from 806."

If I lived in this fucking place I wouldn't answer the door to anyone either. Don't suppose any of them even knew his name.

Eventually, the old boy next door opens the door a couple of inches, two security chains firmly in place.

"'Asn't been 'ere for fucking days, mate. Plays that fucking awful music all fucking hours, bin a fucking relief. Hope 'ees not fucking coming back!" The door shuts.

He hadn't even known Jonny liked music, let alone playing it "all hours". The possibility that JonJon had done a runner now seems more like a certainty, *and* with five grand of *his* money, half of Jonny's bail, after the filth had frozen Jonny's bank accounts, the little tosser.

As Terry turns to go, another door opens along the corridor, just a few inches, and a pale, pudgy face peers out at him.

"Jonny's brother, are you?"

Terry can barely make out the words through the noise of the TV.

*****

After a brief shouted conversation through the gap in the door to establish his identity, mostly consisting of Terry shouting, "Yes, I'm Terry! Yes!", the man asks: "You want to get into his flat then?"

Terry nods over the racket. The chains are rattled aside and he stands back as a short, rounded figure dressed in a heavily stained, powder-blue *Star Trek* outfit, bundles out of the door with a TV controller in his hand. "Hang on" he says, as he reverses back in and waves the controller in the direction of the TV. The noise slowly subsides and then falls silent.

"Just putting it on pause. It's my favourite, 'The Search for Spock'. Bloody brilliant."

Extending his hand, the man says, "Elmo."

"Sorry?" Terry carefully shakes the limp, wet fingers, caked in the orange coating of some disintegrating snack.

"Jonny always calls me Elmo, like everyone else, it's my red hair. You know, Elmo the Muppet, the red-haired one."

Terry nods, a thin smile. "Ahh, of course, Elmo the Muppet – the red one."

Elmo sweeps his hand through thinning ginger swept-over hair, leaving small flakes of the pungent snack he had been eating clinging to the greasy strands. Terry tries to stay as far away from him as seems reasonable, the dark armpit stains and the residues of an all-day beer and crisp festival smeared down the front of his outfit. He does recognise the smell of Quavers – prawn cocktail Quavers if Terry is correct – combining nicely with powerfully seasoned armpit odours, but after nearly suffocating with no escape in the lift, at least he can move away from this latest nasal assault.

"I go through phases. Switch between *Star Trek* and *Star Wars*. The fans don't usually mix though, one thing or another. It's like being Jewish one day and Catholic the next, but I don't care. They don't have nicknames you know."

"Sorry. Nicknames?"

"*Star Wars* fans, no nicknames. Not like 'Trekkers' or 'Trekkies', you can't really be a 'Warsie' – takes me a while to switch between them, have to get your head in the right place, you know."

"Yes, it must be difficult."

The inside of Jonny's flat is quite a surprise; while the rest of Aimsbury House is disintegrating, his brother's flat is crisp and cleanly decorated, high tech even, with two enormous Kef tower speakers either side of a very slick turntable dominating the room. Enough wattage to blow the roof off the Albert Hall in his brother's living room.

Shelving along one full side of the room holds perfectly ordered and labelled old vinyl LPs and singles. On the other side, there is smaller glass shelving, with row upon row of perfectly organised painted figures and models – fighting figures in space suits, armoured fantasy beasts, orcs, troops and soldiers of every sci-fi magazine imaginable. Hundreds of them – possibly thousands.

Terry is silent, just taking in the extraordinary collection, unable to associate any of it with JonJon. *None of us really knew him at all.*

"What…what this fuck is all this?!"

"Pretty impressive isn't it? I guess you've never been up here before. We've got everything. Every Warhammer set, all the *Lord of the Rings* and *every* Codex ever published – the Codexes are like the bible, with a new testament for every set of figures and every battleground. Jonny leaves me the keys so I can come and set up the games."

Elmo gestures at the wall opposite the speakers as he scratches hard at the right side of his groin, dark Quaver stains suggesting a well-attended itch. What seems to be a fold-down bed is clamped against the wall. He presses the huge board in towards the wall, and it gently clicks, releases, lowers smoothly down, the legs dropping into place. The most detailed model "battlescape": craters, hills, rivers, bridges, wrecked buildings and mechanical detritus – all sitting waiting to be populated by the tiny figures.

"We usually have between four and six of us playing. Most weekends. Jonny would get up and really smash out the sounds on the deck while we play, and smoke some. We haven't seen him for ages. Do you think he's on holiday?"

Elmo wipes the back of a damp hand across his mouth, chasing the Quaver crumbs away. He looks forlorn, a piece of his life in jeopardy.

"I'm not sure we are going to see much more of Jonny for a bit Elmo – but I'm sure he will be happy if you guys just keep on playing."

Terry moves towards the bedroom, sticks his head through the door – the wardrobe doors ajar, a chest of drawers looks ransacked, signs of packing in a hurry.

It is starting to feel a bit lonely.

***

"Terry! Have you used this? For Christ's sake Terry!"

The couple of weeks running up to the Newcastle trip have passed quickly, and Peckham is gripped in an unusual heatwave, Summer actually arriving when it was meant to for a change. The lock-up is like an oven though, even with the all the doors open, breezeless and smelly, although the cheese-generated flatulence was just an ancient memory. The dog training regime had slackened off a little just because they got overheated so fast.

Terry's balls are back to their more normal size, though he finds it hard to feel grateful. Big balls and a relatively small willy seemed one of God's poorer jokes.

"Oh shit, sorry Pet, I had meant to clean it up. Won't take a sec."

"That's not the bloody point Terry, did you ASK if you could use it? Did you? This is horrible Terry. This is mine. My PERSONAL property, and you just use it, don't bloody ask, and leave it in a disgusting state! It's just NOT ON Terry!"

God's teeth! Why didn't I clean the thing up before sneaking it back into its little pouch? What were you thinking Terry? So busy admiring the handiwork you forgot to clean up the tools! Shit.

Holding it up, Becca's face contorts: "What on earth have you done with it Terry?"

While his lips move gently, soundlessly, in Becca's direction, his brain quickly processes any even vaguely credible response other than the truth, and gives up. Terry has noticed the trend on the various bits of porn he managed

228

to watch, that not only are the girls almost exclusively hairless these days, but also most of the blokes are at least a "short back and sides" if not similarly bald and smooth.

"It was after the stitches were out Becca, I just realised what a tangle everything was down there. You usually don't really see much of it, as a bloke, with the old tummy and all that, but I've had to have a proper look with the op and everything, so I thought it would be nice for you if I tidied up a bit down there."

Becca looks at him with mounting disgust etched over her face. She marches into the bathroom, returning with one of the nappy-disposal bags kept in reserve for Chloe, makes a display of opening it up, and gingerly lowers her best Braun Lady-Shave, holding the base carefully between thumb and index finger, into the bag, quietly tying the top securely.

"Terry. Take this, and throw it away somewhere; NOT IN THE HOUSE! Then, go to Boots and buy a new one, please. Do it now. And if I EVER find you using ANY of my things again, I will kill you; slowly and painfully!"

Becca passes the pink parcel to Terry and informs him that she is going to go and clean her teeth because she feels sick.

"I really am sorry Becca. I tried using my beard trimmer, but it kept nicking me without the cover on. I ended up with blood all over the place."

"I know there was blood Terry, because quite a lot of it is on my Lady-Shave, as well as the rest of the jungle you were trying to remove. It *is* a nice thought. Please don't go overboard with it though, it won't look very pretty at all. If you *really* want to do something to make yourself look nicer down there, maybe a couple of inches *off* the tummy that hangs over it would be a better idea. Now, off you go."

It's the TEACHER voice. I hate the fucking teacher voice, like telling a ten-year-old to wash his hands after visiting the toilet!

***

There is an air of anticipation and excitement about the lock-up as the final preparations are made for the trip: Razza is giving motivational pep-talks to each of the dogs, even Scotch is referring to Mojito as "my beauty", which was about as friendly as you could get to an animal that, on first meeting, had attempted to bite your tackle off.

The dogs themselves look good, sleek and sharp, glossy coats and a spring in their solid steps.

This will be the first time all three of them will be fighting at one event, so the medical supplies have been topped up and the van has been cleaned out and spruced up; even the chemical toilet has been emptied and the chemicals replaced. Everything is in its place, functional on the inside, shit on the outside.

"Proper money Tel, seven and a half each for Cuba and Captain, and a magnificent twenty fucken' grand for Mojito! If…NO…WHEN he wins, ah reckon we are looking et eighty, maybe even a hundred grand for him tae live a life of 'forni-fucken-cation' Tel, maybe even more. This'll be like winnin' the Grand National!"

It had seemed daft having to take out so much of the cash that had so painstakingly been drip-fed into the account.

"Thirty-five grand is a lot of fucking stake money 'at

risk' Scotch. We are 'all-in' mate, between the prize money AND twenty grand of betting money."

"Ahm in for ten of ma own, pretty much all ah have from ma 20 percents so far. Gets the old 'drenalin going doesnae? Don't worry Tel, we are sittin on a GEM!"

"You know we are all done after this one Scotch. *If* we pull it off, I can pay down most of the tax filth, and we all just go back to quiet little lives. All this lock-up business goes, sell the van, dogs retire, no more fucking ripping and tearing. They can lick their wounds and become nice family pets, and they bloody deserve it!"

"One step at a time Tel, let's line the duckies up, step at a time."

"Tomorrow afternoon, meet you here about four."

Sounds like 'game on'. Off to the other end of the country with a van-load of dogs, the Snow Queen, a mad scotsman and a handful of spunk tablets – the Invincibles!

29

BYKER, NEWCASTLE, A super little area as long as you had extremely low expectations. An industrial estate is an industrial estate; just here there seemed to be more razor-wire than usual.

It had been just like going off to the seaside with your mum and dad. The dogs neatly shut away in their cages aboard the "Wankavan", and the whole of the UK enjoying an unseasonal heatwave for the end of June.

They hadn't got to the cheap-shit hotel until nearly midnight, and then had to pay an extra £30 to park the caravan there overnight. It had taken Terry ten minutes to understand what the "equal opportunities" night security guard was trying to say. It ended with him writing down "£30" and a lot of pointing, which was presumably what "Thutty gid fu garaven" had meant.

Geordies, you had to love them, but no idea what fucking language they're speaking.

They hadn't slept much. He insisted Scotch had a separate room, but the walls were paper thin, and stoked-up pissheads seemed to be arriving all night, loudly shouting their way down the single corridor and slamming doors.

No air-con, so the window had to stay wide open as he and Becca lay there sweating, until a fitful sleep eventually claimed them.

World War Three started outside as the hen party disgorged from their minicab, it was 5am, and the sun was already streaming through the flimsy curtains. Terry was jerked awake by a huge thump on their window and the most extraordinary yelling directly into their room.

Lurching half-asleep to the window in "battle-mode", he found two paralytic girls fighting, half-naked, smothered in some sort of body paint, up against their open window, screaming at each other.

Becca had run into the bathroom, convinced they were about to be murdered in their beds, when Terry ripped back the curtains, naked, his belly and untidily shaven groin level with both girls' snarling faces.

It's so hard to know where to stop with a Lady-Shave once you get going.

They had immediately quietened down, calling, "Wankaaaa!" at him as they backed off, staggering on their four-inch heels, into the car park; the aural barrage restarting in earnest as the girls located their rooms by shouting at each door in turn until they reached one that didn't shout back.

By eight thirty he gave up attempting to sleep: the heat, bright sunlight, and now the road noise harrying him from his bed into the shower – long dark hairs in the shower tray left as a memento by the previous occupant and a shower head that sprayed in every direction except where it was needed. It was time to get going.

The caravan was in need of cleaning out after three hot, stinky dogs had spent the night in it, but a short walk calms and cools them down. The tiny cavalry on the dawn of battle.

***

Dog owners are being guided by a couple of heavies at the front of *H. Evans Storage Warehouse* towards the small car park. Spectators and others are told to scatter their cars around the largely deserted sprawl of ageing workshops, warehouses and storage units along the estate.

None of the bullshit commercialisation of the Milton Keynes fight, just an aura of hard men doing something professionally.

"I just get SO nervous Tel!"

They sit in the Range Rover, all the windows down, in the car park.

"Over soon Becca; one way or another."

"All right boys?" says a familiar voice as the two coppers, Graham and "Work-Out" – *Fuck knows what his real name is* – walk nonchalantly past their car.

Terry hadn't been expecting any "home supporters" this far away, and it seems best not to acknowledge them publicly. "Lads." He nods through the open window as they move by, towards the entrance, hands tucked deep into pockets.

Terry steps out of the Range Rover and opens the windows on the caravan to get a bit of air circulating. It's hot in the van and the dogs are panting.

"Better get you boys out of there before you all melt!"

Four cars down in the parking bays is a gigantic, metallic gold stretch Hummer, nearly as long as the Range Rover *and* the caravan together. A huge, heavily tattooed and tanned bodyguard is standing guard at the rear.

"Will ya fucken' look at THA Tel! WAY too far up his own arse!"

The bodyguard slowly and deliberately turns to curl a lip in a mild sneer at the flash Range Rover pulling the near-derelict caravan, and adjusts his sunglasses on his nose. It is already hot, and the sweat is running from his shaven head onto the collar of the crisp white shirt worn under his leather waistcoat. He curls the thick chain around a right hand leading down to the biggest Bull Mastiff Terry has ever seen, sitting on the ground beside him – its head comes up to the bottom of his ribcage.

"Ahm sure I recognise him from the wrestling Tel. Ah think he used to be 'the Tank' or something. Definitely him: it's the Tank, ah know it is. What's he doing here Tel? Ah hope he doesn't think Mojito is fighting *that* bloody thing!"

One of the far-side doors of the glittering Hummer swings open and a well-built man in his late fifties gets out, straightens the sleeves on his tan suit, and, in a slow ritual, puts on his dark glasses in the bright sunlight. the Tank is swiftly by his side as the three of them walk towards the entrance, not glancing in Terry's direction.

"Will you look at that syrup Becca? Looks like Donald-fucking-Trump! Why would you wear a wig that makes you look like you've put a fucking ice cream cone on your head? And it IS the Tank; used to get the crowd chanting 'Pump it up for the Tank'. What the fuck!"

"He had to retire, I remember. It was in *Hello*: he married that funny-looking ginger girl from that Rap band 'Tiny Tinny' or something. He had a problem with a vasectomy. You could tell the baby wasn't his Tel – it actually looked a bit Chinese. And then he just disappeared off the TV. And here he is, a glorified bouncer or something."

Surreal conversation over, Terry and Scotch take a look around the warehouse arena, getting past the two muscle-bound tattoo adverts on the door. "Owners," Terry explained. The bemused looks and barred way prompting him to repeat, "Owners, dog Owners," but that still doesn't seem to register until one of the heavies turns to the other with a thick Eastern European accent, sounded Polish, and translates his words into Geordie, and the two take half a step back to allow them to squeeze past.

***

The cosy atmosphere of a typical 80s-built warehouse, whitewashed breeze-block running up to a high flat roof; barren offices along the end, with all the activity centred on the middle one, which must be The House, bankrolling the event. Beside the offices, a couple of rigid paddling pools serve as the dog-baths. Thick plastic panels on stands, about three feet high form the pit in the middle of the room, orange and yellow, almost certainly nicked from a building site.

"It's getting pretty fucken' full already, will ya look at the ontoorage round the big mon! 'Sa fucken' circus Tel!"

"He's got to be the breeder-bloke you told us about Scotch, looks like he owns the place."

Scotch looks hard at the circus: must be right, but not

what he had been expecting from his research. He just knew the Cappo was monster rich – a hard bloke, and a total dog nut – but no one had mentioned the freak-show dressing-up and the support team!

There is a steady stream of people filling the place up now, no air-con and even the Geordie spivs in their sharp suits and ties are loosening their collars, sleeves rolled up.

The two coppers have faded into the crowd. Graham, the older of the two, being a Brummie, helped stop them stand out too badly.

"Tha's the stake money done for Captain and Mojito. They're nae sa sure Cuba's fight will turn up so ah've hung ontae tha. Ahm gonnta see what the inside track is with the bookies. Don't worry Tel, the dogs are dosed up on the old jizzy viagra. We cannae go wrong!"

Terry goes back to the car to see Becca and bring out Captain Morgan. She is sitting in the car, windows open.

"Don't worry Becca, they'll be alright, they're tough dogs; and now they're full of Scotch's jiz pills, even *I* don't really want to go near them!"

False bon-homie, you are fooling no one Tel!

"I just *hate* them getting hurt Terry, it feels wrong. It's OK while we are just training and feeding them, but then we get here, and it sort of sinks in; why we are here. These people are just horrible, all of them, I just hate them, those bloody coppers too."

"I know Becca, but this is the last one babe, really. I don't like this stuff either. After this one, we are out of all this, I promise. We'll be getting going in a few minutes and Captain is on second fight, so I'm going to get him ready to roll."

"OK Tel, I'll come out for Mojito's fight, I can't just sit here waiting, it's just too nerve-wracking!"

As he leads the Captain round for his bath, the first fight is starting: the noise, shouting, yelling, the dogs snarling, all blending into one huge, repellent crescendo. Terry winces; Captain Morgan bristles, an urgency to his step now.

The bathing area is just out of direct earshot of the fight under way, as Terry washes and scrubs the battle-scarred terrier, long white snout and pinky eyes, under the watchful eye of his opponent's owner, a scrawny street-fighting Pikey if there ever was one. He says nothing, he just nods.

The Pikey rolls his sleeves up and goes through the ritual of washing Captain Morgan, who stands disdainful as the scruffy stranger scrubs him. One of The House "helpers" stands watching, cigarette hanging from his lips, disinterested.

The Pikey looks over to Terry. "Propa radgie, like, I'm ganna set-a-had to tha fuckin' dog."

He hears the noises, but they just don't mean anything. "Sorry mate, say that again."

"Fuckin radgie! I'm ganna set-a-had to tha dog, ya fucker."

It's just a string of unrelated noises, the expression on the Pikey's face suggests it's probably not a compliment, but fuck only knows what he's saying.

"OK mate, sounds good, see you out there, eh!"

"He says, you're a chav and he's gonna set fire to your dog," the smoking helper translates for Terry.

"Ahhh, I see! Good. Could you tell him to go fuck himself *and* his mangey little fuck of a dog, please? I don't think he speaks any English."

Bath-time was never like this when I was a kid.

Captain Morgan shakes the last few drops of disinfected water from his fur and leads Terry away.

30

YOU CAN SMELL the blood.

Sweat, cigarette smoke and definitely blood.

The first fight was a long, sweaty, gory mess. Both dogs barely making it out in one piece, the loser carried out in a filthy, bloodied blanket; the "winner" led out limping with bits of his face hanging off.

"Fucken' 'orrible Tel, ah hate et when they just hang on tae each other like tha. We don't need tha."

The pit is being swept with a soft broom to clear away any slippery patches. Terry and "Morgan's" names are called.

Can't tell them it's fucking "Captain" Morgan, they'll all just take the piss.

He feels shaky after seeing the last few minutes' carnage of the first fight.

You can't go all soft over these bloody dogs. There's every chance one of them doesn't make it. Fucking SHAPE up Terry.

Scotch is holding the Captain's front legs up, behind the

scratch line, "showing" him to the beady white bull terrier being held and shown the same way by his ratty owner. The warehouse is pretty packed now, all hard men, no women here. Donald Trump, the Tank and his entourage take up a good quarter of the ring, interested in this one as the precursor to Mojito taking on their champ.

"Fucken' AT IM! TEAR 'IM UP boy!"

The noise level reaches a baying crescendo as the ref nods to the holders:

"LET GO!"

They fly at each other, jaws scrabbling ferociously, neither getting any sort of grip. Everything happens at high speed: heads, muzzles, cracking together with sickening noise, bone against bone; teeth scratching, gouging, saliva and blood spraying as they clash jaws repeatedly. A space opens between them for a fleeting instant and the Captain slams his head into his opponent's chest, driving him onto his side, and as he flips himself back upright, the Captain's jaws lock around his front upper leg.

And hangs on.

He is too close in for the white dog to get his jaws around anything except some flesh around his back and shoulders, but nothing to lock onto.

The Captain shakes his head, four feet planted firmly on the floor, tipping the terrier off balance, hopping around on three paws.

The Captain keeps shaking, the crowd are roaring, and the terrier is starting to panic, to free himself rather than bite now, and the Captain shakes some more, jaws pounding pressure, eyes wild. And the terrier just stops, turning his head away in pain.

"TURN!"

The ref screams and the handlers leap into the pit with their gauntlets to part the dogs.

Captain Morgan is brimming with adrenaline, slobbering, eyes wide, growling furiously as Scotch pulls him away, a rubber bar inserted to lever his jaws open.

The terrier's front leg is completely mashed, useless, he stands pathetic on three legs, and collapses painfully forward. His ratty owner ignoring the yelp of pain as he roughly picks him up, shouting incomprehensible obscenities over his shoulder as he manhandles his mangled dog out of the pit.

"Niva sin anythin' fuckin' layk et!"

"Propa knacked it!"

"Howay man!"

A general air of respect for a "killer move" they hadn't witnessed before spreads around the arena; even Donald is looking animated beneath the sunglasses, Stetson and fake tan.

Scotch is jumping with excitement: "Dya see that focker?! Dya see hem?! Foooooken' brelleant!"

Captain Morgan has calmed now, quietly panting as Terry holds his lead, proud winner for his master.

He did it again. If that's what he did to that poor collie a couple of months ago, we are lucky he didn't rip it right off and bring it home with him! Someone must've actually taught him to do that...

"Fefteen fucken' grand Tel! Even-money with the bookies, that's another fefteen grand on top of the seven prize money! And it only took five minutes Tel, and NOT a REAL fucken' mark on hem! I LOVE thess fucken' dog!"

"Calm down Scotch, we're being watched by the

'mutants'; let's just play nice and cool, maybe a bit surprised; you don't want to spoil the betting odds for Mojito."

Donald's 'camp' had steadily been growing, most of them looked like they had stepped out of the Newcastle version of WWWF. All flashily dressed, pumped up muscles, tattooed, dodgy haircuts.

You can almost see the fucking steroids leaking out of 'em; all sweating their nuts off in this heat, soppy bastards!

A muffled shot from outside breaks the atmosphere, all noise stops for a few seconds, and then slowly restarts.

Captain Morgan's opponent is not in any pain now. Terry just looks at Scotch, pale-faced, as the excitement of the win drains, to be replaced by an awful dose of reality.

"Teach him a fucking lesson."

He and Scotch both clearly hear the words from across the pit, and Donald waves one of his mutant heavies in the direction of the gunshot.

"I've told the cunt before, use the vet, it's what he's fucking there for – NO SHOOTERS – I've told him. Teach him a lesson."

The Tank passes the chain of the giant Mastiff and slips away. Donald has softened his accent, almost a cross between Home Counties and Newcastle, but with none of the softness of the Geordie lilt, a blade-edge control to it.

The pit is being tidied up for the next fight, with Mojito to follow, the last of the Pit Bulls. The fights scheduled in order, another four fights to come after him, as the size of dog breed increases.

***

"That caravan is a fucking heat trap Becca. Let's have Mojito out to let him breathe a bit before his fight; then I'll take him over to the washing pool. Scotch is just walking the Captain for a bit, let him cool down; he was fucking brilliant."

"I thought I heard a gunshot Terry! I didn't see anything and then that Tank bodyguard dragged a scruffy little man across the car park by his hair! I just have a bad feeling about all this. I really don't like it here. You be careful. I want to get away from here as soon as Mojito wins. *If* he wins."

"He'll win Becca, and we're out of here the second he does, just as soon as we collect. We are way ahead on the Captain. He was a star – all over in a trice, with hardly any nasty stuff."

Except that he nearly ripped the thing's leg off and then its owner fucking shot it…pretty civilised really.

"I'll give you the signal Becca, to come in and get the champ; it always shuts the crowd up!"

***

Scotch stands holding Mojito from behind, hands under his front legs, behind the line, showing him his opponent; he can feel the dog's deep rumbling growl building against his palms. The entire Donald entourage are pressed close round the opposing side of the pit, a buzz of anticipation around the room, shouts blasting out from the bloodthirsty crowd.

Donald's champion dog is a real rough-house, going crazy in his handler's hands. Snarling, barking, slobbering. Mad Max has won seven fights, making him a grand champion on the professional circuit. He looks "Mad Max"

– tufts of shaggy black hair around his neck, low and stocky, scars around his face and a vicious insanity in his eyes.

Never been scared of a dog before. It just oozes fucking madness!

"Max – Mad – MAX!" chant the entourage, just adding to the barely contained fury of their favourite. "MAX – MAD – MAX!"

Mojito, if anything, is even quieter than normal, taut, tense, focused.

***

"LET GO!" bellows the referee.

The dogs fly across the ten feet divide. Fangs rip at each other's snouts, jaws and teeth crashing together, audible above the crowd's roars and their own snarling; jaws not locking together, Mojito is briefly knocked over onto his side, but springs back to all fours as the mad dog scrambles to pounce upon him. They return to the awful open-jawed slashing and biting at each other's faces, Mojito clearly the faster dog, but Mad the stronger.

All Terry can say is a half-whispered, "Go on son…go on." He has barely remembered to breathe, adrenaline and fear filling him in equal measure.

Mojito is wrestled over onto his back again, this time with the mad dog astride him biting at his face. He manages to rip himself out from under the squatter dog. Fists hammer around the top of the pit barrier, visceral roars from the transfixed crowd. Blood. More blood!

"MAX – MAD – MAX!"

No…oh no, fuck's sake, NO!

For the first time he realises, truly realises: his dog could not just lose, but die in there, the mad thing a yard stronger than any Pit Bull he has seen before.

The dogs return to their face-to-face ripping, slashing, both muzzles and snouts gashed and bleeding.

"UNFANG!" cries Mad Max's handler.

The ref holds his hand aloft and Scotch moves to unravel Mojito from the brawl, while Mad's handler does the same. Mad Max's fangs are stuck through his own lips on one side. The only time a fight is ever held up without a dog conceding or turning away.

Mad's lips are carefully lifted off his teeth, still wild and shaking with fury and adrenaline.

Terry gasps. He feels lightheaded through lack of oxygen, breathing to the rhythm of the fight; sweat pouring off his head, not just through the stifling heat of the arena.

The dogs are back behind their scratch line and released again, Mojito setting off the slower. Mad sensing his opponent slowing, smashes low beneath him, tipping Mojito onto his back, bearing down over him, jaws wide; this will be over soon – and it is.

Mad utters a screech as Mojito arches up from the floor still on his back, his jaws clamped from underneath, round his opponent's throat; locked, crushing.

Mojito is still on his back as Mad desperately tries to shake him off, dragging him across the pit floor, clawing with his paws. But Mojito's grip is unbreakable now, flipping himself onto his feet, still locked on; shaking powerfully, as they were all bred to do. Mad's adrenaline keeps him going, shaking and dragging them both around the pit, but with every movement Mojito's fangs dig deeper, jaws vice-like.

Mad Max is on his back now, no longer fighting, just pawing frantically.

The referee yells for the end of the fight. The crowd quieten, stunned. Scotch steps over to unlock Mojito from his victim, flinching as he remembers the bloodied jaws locked around his groin, months ago now.

Mad Max just lays, convulsing, unable to breathe; airways crushed. His handler drags him from the pit, on his back, by his front legs, looking over at Donald and his muscle-bound cronies: "Done for, boss."

Donald flashes eyes at him.

"I can SEE he's fucking 'done for' son, I'm not fucking stupid! Someone get the vet. The little fucker doesn't deserve to suffer."

All eyes are on Mad Max as he is dragged, dying noisily, from the pit.

In shock, Terry feels Becca take his hand, pressing the Captain's lead into it; then, she vaults – the Valkyrie – over the pit wall in her low-cut lurex cat-suit, shiny leather high-heeled boots and a white faux-fur coat flailing behind her, all eyelashes and rouge. She sweeps the bloodied, victorious Mojito, as he whimpers with delight, up in her arms and turns, dramatically, coat flaring behind her and stalks across the pit in the direction of the exit.

The crowd are gobsmacked, largely standing open-mouthed. Their odds-on winner has been massacred, and now the Wicked Witch of Anne Summers has swept in like a fucking Panto character!

***

The Tank is *not* open-mouthed. He has made his way round to Terry's side of the pit, and as Becca swings one leather-clad leg over the pit edge, he smashes Terry aside with a blow from one giant forearm and grabs Becca's shoulder and neck with one hand, the other tearing Mojito from her arms by the loose skin on the back of his neck, holding him aloft, helpless. Becca screams out in pain as his hand digs into the nerves round her neck. He leans down and growls an obscenity into her ear. He turns to stare at Terry lying on the floor as he forces Becca to her knees.

Terry on the ground starts to pick himself up, stunned, as Captain Morgan, released by Terry as he falls, flies forward and locks his teeth round the Tank's ankle and hangs on.

"FUCKER! YOU FUCKER!" spits the Tank as he tries to viciously shake off the Captain, whose teeth have now found bone, from his leg. "FUCKER!!"

The Tank first drops Mojito, who immediately launches himself at his other leg, biting through the thin suit material. The Tank *may* be full of steroids and testosterone, but he *can* feel pain. He shoves Becca away, onto the ground and starts to beat at the dogs savaging him, getting nowhere.

Screaming, pulling himself upright, Tank reaches round to the belt beneath the back of his suit. A gun is in his hand, pointed at Mojito's neck.

The room explodes.

31

THE TANK LAYS on his back, writhing; his hands pressed against the spreading red stain just above his belt, wheezing, a Pit Bull attached to each shin and a bullet lodged in the general area of his appendix.

The Mastiff hellhound launches itself past the Tank and the little Pit Bulls at the greasy Scot in the coat, holding a smoking pistol.

Another explosion and the Mastiff hits the ground, stone dead.

"Fuck…FUCK! Fucking hell Scotch! Becca. BECCA!!"

Terry and Becca stagger, stumble and sprint out of the warehouse, Mojito and Captain Morgan trailing behind them. Scotch is half running backwards, waving his gun around: "GET DOWN! ALL OF YOU! FUCKEN' GET DOWN!"

He shoots into the air.

They stampede across the thirty yards between warehouse

and the car, the dogs following, Mojito first, then Captain Morgan, trailing his lead along the ground.

Pandemonium in the warehouse: orders being yelled, and the heavies burst out of the doorway, running, Donald with the Tank's gun in his hand.

Scotch shoots into the air again and they pause momentarily.

Becca has the car keys. As she stabs at the unlock button, the car lights flash and it unlocks. Terry hurls himself into the passenger seat as Becca starts the car, gunning the engine, Scotch and the dogs scrambling through the caravan door.

Blind panic. Becca jams the car into reverse, the caravan behind them, reversing hard straight into the oncoming crowd, who scatter. Oblivious to the angle the caravan swings as she turns the front of the Range Rover towards the exit, she slams into "Drive" and jams her foot to the ground, heading for the road, almost jack-knifing the caravan on its tow-bar.

There is a bump as the caravan wheels hit something, and they are through the exit. Sharp right onto the road, caravan wheels skidding, only one on the ground, and away, with the caravan swinging from side to side, righting itself. Two shots above the sound of the engine, "plunking" noises from the caravan as the bullets penetrate tin.

"Oh God, oh God, oh God TERRY! Fuck! Fucking hell Terry!"

"Calm down Becca, calm down…well done girl… steady down a little, we're going to make it."

Becca is starting to hyperventilate, gasping, squeaking her words out.

"Breathe, just breathe, slowly… it's OK, just drive. I'll

tell you when to turn. Just breathe. Well done, well done, we're away; just breathe slowly."

Terry had seen Donald and the heavies running towards their cars. Donald had jumped into the driving seat of the glittering gold stretch Hummer, his cronies attempting to get in the side doors as he screeched into reverse. The others piled into a huge, glossy, blacked-out 4X4.

"Next left, Becca" Terry hunched down to see what was happening behind them in his wing mirror: the gold brothel is about four-hundred yards behind them, closely followed by its sleek, black back-up.

"Straight over the roundabout…next left…left at the roundabout…next right."

Terry is on autopilot. The Range Rover's power is tossing the caravan from side to side, its door still flapping open, pulling away a little from the Hummer, which is even clumsier round the bends and turns than the caravan.

"WHERE ARE WE GOING?!" Panic in Becca's voice. She can see glimpses of the chasing cars in the mirrors as well as he can.

"Don't worry, I know where we are, just follow what I tell you."

They are both sweating heavily, the car like an oven before they even got in. No time for seat-belts, windows or air-con, Becca in her heavy white coat, driving the automatic in stiletto boots, make-up spread all over her face from tears and sweat, wiping her eyes with the back of her hand.

He has no idea at all where they are or where they are going, the seat-belt alarm is now at maximum volume.

They are out of the industrial estate now, onto grimy

backstreets, heading north, Terry thinks, the roads narrow, winding.

"They are still there Terry. Still FUCKING there! They're going to kill us, and all because of that Scotch idiot with the gun. WHY DID HE HAVE A FUCKING GUN TERRY?!"

"Calm Becca, calm. We can sort that out later, you just concentrate on driving…left here Becca."

Finally, they are out of the suburbs, onto a narrower country lane, the gold Hummer closing as the Range Rover/caravan combo twists and turns, Becca's adrenaline subsiding, tears starting as she drives.

"Don't cry Becca, NO TIME TO FUCKING CRY. Just drive, it will be OK." Terry shouting over the blaring seat-belt alarm is adding to the sense of utter panic.

The roads narrow, but they're still just about two-way, and Becca drives, a woman possessed, accelerating and braking like a seventeen-year-old boy-racer behind the wheel of his first car.

Must be like a fucking food mixer back there in the caravan. They'll live…if we get away.

The stretch Hummer is struggling around tight bends at speed. Donald has never driven it before, and its sixteen-feet length doesn't handle like his 911; at least the caravan is on a hinge.

One fast bend too many, and the Hummer rear wheels catch in the verge on a tight left-hand bend; the back skids out to the right-hand verge and slams to a stop across the road.

"IT'S STOPPED TERRY! IT'S STOPPED!"

Only able to see with glimpses in the extended wing mirrors on the straights, the caravan blocking sight on the bends, Terry strains down to see out of his passenger side mirror. No sign of the golden trucker.

"GOOD GIRL Becca; good girl! Just drive, go girl, GO! We're gonna make it Becca, you beauty!"

Elated, Becca kicks the Range Rover on, three more bends…four…onto a straighter patch, she sneaks a peak in the wing mirror: NOTHING. Fucking brilliant!

***

As Becca peers into the wing mirror, the sharp left hander comes up *just* a bit too fast at sixty miles per hour; in a panic Becca jerks the wheel hard through the ninety-degree angle of the bend.

"BECCA!!"

There is a sharp snap, the Range Rover jerks and leaps forward. Looking across Becca, Terry watches the caravan arc through the air, upside down, almost clearing the five-feet hedgerow completely, as if it were in slow motion.

"JUST DRIVE BECCA. DON'T WORRY. DON'T TRY TO LOOK!"

Becca has no idea what has happened until she realises she can see out of the rear-view mirror.

"TERRY!!"

"It's alright, don't scream, just drive Doll."

"WHERE'S THE CARAVAN!? TERRY!!"

***

Terry pulls the Range Rover onto the forecourt in front of the Clam Bay Guest House, a couple of roads back from the sea-front in Whitley Bay, parking between a campervan and the building, tucking the car well forward. Becca has been repairing herself as much as possible in the mirror. Terry unclips the remnants of the caravan cable and slings it in the back of the car, the ball of the tow-bar completely sheared off.

They are a twenty-minute drive from where the caravan disappeared. There has been no further sign of the golden Hummer.

"I'll see if they have a room Becca. We can just lie low for a bit, find out what's happened and then make a plan."

She hasn't spoken at all since we swapped seats, need to get a stiff drink inside her.

It's still sweltering, but as it isn't school holidays for a couple of weeks, Clam Bay has several rooms free. Terry takes the deluxe en-suite double at £60 for the night. The whole place smells of stale cigarettes and cheap room freshener. Badly in need of redecorating, or even rebuilding, it's the last place he would ever want to stay, but exactly what they need to just hide away, get their heads together, and decide what to do.

***

"They'll have killed them all, if they weren't dead already. I killed them Terry."

"Noo, of course you haven't killed them. REALLY! We don't even know if you could see the caravan from the road, it almost cleared the bloody hedge Becca. Who *knows* what's happened? It might have just rolled to a stop in the field, we just don't know."

He doesn't mention that the caravan was upside down as it cleared the hedge.

"I don't know Terry, I can't see how anything would survive that, and those horrible people have guns! They would have killed us – they WILL kill us! Scotch SHOT one of them!"

He holds Becca close as they lay on top of the almost-clean bedspread and she sobs, chest heaving.

"It's alright Becca, don't cry. You did SO well. You saved our lives, you were brilliant. If the caravan hadn't gone they would probably have been able to follow us forever; you were SO brave."

"I hate it up here Terry. It's like we're in a foreign country. I don't understand what anyone is saying. Those people were just SO horrible, all of them; and the AWFUL strutting little man with that ridiculous car. And WHAT was Scotch doing with a gun? Did you know he had a gun?"

"I couldn't believe it either Becca. I didn't even know he owned a gun, let alone brought it up here."

He is half-watching the TV. BBC News North East is playing quietly on the cheap little screen sitting on the white melamine corner unit. No "Breaking News", but then again, it had only been a couple of hours ago.

"I smell Terry. I smell of sweat. I have no clothes, only that fucking stupid fur coat, and it must be nearly thirty degrees! AND this room smells nearly as bad as I do. AND it's probably hotter in here than outside! You need to find out what happened to the caravan, and what happened to Scotch and the dogs Terry."

32

"**HAVE YOU GONE** completely fucking insane Terry? Two black lace thongs and a silver G-string!"

"You asked me to buy you underwear Doll!"

"I didn't even ask you to buy a bra at all, so a *quarter* cup bra is *not* what I expected you to come back with. It's not a bra, it's a bloody display shelf, and it's going in the bin where it belongs."

"I did get everything else though Becca, I just got a bit carried away."

"I asked you to buy me a couple of pairs of knickers; not dress me up for a fucking sex party Terry! For God's sake! We are hiding from men who want to kill us; in a boiling hot dump of a hotel; at the seaside in the arse end of nowhere. Our friend is probably dead in a mangled caravan, along with our dogs and you go shopping and come back with this lot! You make me SO angry sometimes!"

Park View Shopping Centre, a sweltering twenty-minute walk from the guest house, had yielded a Sainsbury's, for a few basic supplies, and Peacock's clothes shop. Armed with Becca's sizes, Terry had bought underwear and polo shirts for himself and jeans and T-shirts for Becca; enough for a couple of days. He had also noticed the Foxy Roxy shop window as he was walking through the shopping centre and had been unable to resist.

"I'll just have to stay in these knickers and wash yesterday's out in the sink. In this weather they should dry in about ten minutes. And Terry, just to be clear, we will *not* be having any sort of sex in this hotel; and the way you are going, possibly never again Lamb."

***

It HAD seemed like such a good idea at the time.

They'll trace us back to London for certain; find out where we live, probably using the emails from Scotch to the organisers, or his number plate. They had plenty of time to get that off the caravan while they chased him. People like Donald always had a pet copper or two to help them trace a car or a phone number.

What to do? What to do?

Got to find out what happened to the fucking caravan; to Scotch. If he's OK he might even be able to negotiate a way out of this. IF he's OK, and IF they haven't already found him and shot him.

Looking at the map together on Becca's iPad, they attempt to work out roughly where the caravan went off the road to within about a half-mile stretch. Terry has rung Scotch's mobile a dozen times. Nothing. Now it seemed to be dead, probably the battery; but at least no one else had answered it.

***

No fucking idea what he is saying. How many times do you have to say you don't understand before they slow down a bit?

Eventually Terry communicates where he wants to go to the Indian-Geordie cab driver by tapping on the iPad, but when he tries to change the scale by moving his fingers around on the screen it turns into a satellite picture of somewhere. He sits in the front seat of the battered Nissan, eventually giving up with the iPad and tracing the area on a dog-eared A to Z.

"Here Andab, *here* is where we need to go. You drive *here* and we look…OK? And then we drive back…OK?"

"Wey aye man, nee way a problem."

"Do you understand? We need to go *here*, look – *here*."

Terry stabs at the map with his finger.

"Ah said wey aye, nee problem, we go heya."

What's he fucking saying? I THINK it's yes; why can't he just say "Yes" instead of the sing-song Geordie-Punjabi?

Slowly, Andab and Terry learn each other's language and the old diesel chugs its way towards the general area that Terry is "fairly" sure they were speeding through earlier.

The roads are very quiet: it is 8pm, but warm, the sun still fairly high. They drive around for forty minutes, up and down, almost back to the area of the industrial estate. Terry's new friend is quite jolly as the meter ticks round, driving slowly up and down the country lane, chattering amiably, if completely unintelligibly. Terry is peering high, trying to see through or over the hedges lining the sides of the road, hoping to see a broken area where the caravan crashed through.

Nothing.

Retracing their route again, with a different strategy: eyes low on the mud verges to see where a car might have caught the verge at speed, and finally they come to a bend with a great lump chewed out of it: the Hummer, Terry is sure.

"Along here, Andab mate, just a bit further, this is it." A tight left-hand bend about a quarter of a mile further on. "Stop here please, put your 'hazards' on."

***

The caravan lies: smashed, on its side, door side up in the overgrown field.

As Terry approaches, a dog barks urgently.

"Heeelp, heeelp…"

Weak, but obviously Scotch.

His heart skips a beat.

"Hold on guys, just hold on, help on the way."

Mojito's barking becomes frantic as he recognises Terry's voice. He clambers up the underside of the caravan, the only part of it that hasn't burst apart. The door is missing, just a hole, and he peers down into the carnage.

***

"I'm going to have to call an ambulance Scotch, I can't get you out of here."

Scotch swigs greedily at the bottle of water Andab has retrieved from the car.

"They're both fucken' broken Tel, ahm sure! Fook nose where Cuba is, think he was thrown clear and just pissed off. Mojito stayed with me, mebbe 'cos he cannae get out, haaa."

Scotch coughs painfully. He is a complete mess. The state of the field and the distance the caravan is from the road suggests it must have somersaulted two or three times. He is covered in blood and livid bruises, a deep gash in his head, dark congealed blood matting his hair. His legs in front of him, but at slightly strange angles. The entire contents of the caravan are smashed all around him, the cages ripped from their fixings; a bombsite.

"The Captain, Tel, he's gone."

"I know Scotch, and Cuba, no fucking sign."

"No. The Captain's gone. She ran over him; poor little bastard."

Scotch describes the panic of trying to get himself and the dogs into the caravan, Captain Morgan slipping out of the open door as Becca jerked into reverse, and then the awful bump as the wheels of the caravan ran him over as she accelerated forward again.

They are quiet for several seconds: Terry is speechless, sitting amongst the debris, a tear visible in Scotch's eye, pain making way for emotion.

"He was a fucken' good dog Tel. A good dog."

"We ran him over Scotch, are you *sure*?"

"Ah heard et, and ah felt et."

"You know, I think I remember a bump. Fuck Scotch. Fuck!"

They are quiet again, just looking at each other, unspoken grief.

***

Andab's face peers down from the open door: "Haddaway… shite!"

"Who the fook is tha? What's he sayen?"

Terry tentatively searches around the caravan, glass and breakages everywhere, and finally locates Scotch's phone. He drops it into Scotch's shirt pocket, touches him briefly on the shoulder and clambers out of the caravan.

"What were you doing with a fucking gun Scotch? A fucking GUN! We could have all been killed, you mad bastard."

"Nasty fucken' pieces a work Tel. Just insurance. Didnae expect to be usen et."

Scotch groans as the pain from his legs intensifies.

So he had a gun; and he shot a WWWF wrestler – and his dog – who was guarding a thoroughly spiteful, rich gangster, who is now chasing THEM with a gun of his own. All going nicely according to plan…

***

"You go back to where the caravan is, and you call an ambulance. OK? You WAIT for the ambulance and show them where to go. You DON'T mention ME; OR the dog. OK?"

"Wey aye man, nee problem."

"Good man Andab. Remember: NO me; and NO dog. You were coming back from a drop off and just noticed something in the field – stick to the story and we'll all be fine."

"Wey aye."

Fucking "wey aye", where did plain old "OK" or "got it" go?

Terry pushes his door open, back at the taxi rank. He and Mojito, a solid little ball of muscle, who, miraculously, is knocked about but basically unhurt, apart from a few gouges and gashes from the fight, climb out of the ancient minicab, the caravan number plate folded in half under Terry's arm. He peels off £100 and gives it to a beaming Andab, the meter switched off ages ago. He hasn't had so much fun for years. Stories to tell his pals, his kids.

"Purely belta man!"

33

"**HE SAVED ME** from that steroid-bound piece of shit Terry. We *are not* going to leave him rotting in a bloody car park. How do we even know he's dead?"

Tears of anguish and anger streak Becca's face. Terry had explained how Scotch saw the Captain run over by the wheels of the Hummer during the great escape. The lie so close to the truth it made *him* cry telling it.

"Scotch was sure he must be dead Becca. There's nothing anyone could do."

Mojito is laying on the bed, his head resting on a towel in Becca's lap as she cleans up and patches his war-wounds. His ears pricked up, alert. He doesn't like it when she is distressed, and she is distressed now.

"He's family Terry, he took on that great lump, ten times his size when he saw him hurt me. He's just roadkill to them, but *not* to us; he's a hero and he *will* get a decent burial."

There are times when she is just a force of fucking nature! A decent burial…why didn't I just say he had run off like Cuba? But she is right. Oh bollocks!

***

"Here Andab, here on the fucking map, mate. We go HERE!"

At least she hadn't made him actually go last night. Trying to find the place in the bloody dark. Sunday today, everywhere pretty quiet. Maybe he will have gone, they might have gotten rid of him.

The industrial estate wasn't hard to find now that Becca had given him lessons with the iPad map. Andab had stayed with the ambulance for a while. They just took his name and phone number and said they would be in touch. Now, in the bright morning sunlight, the day heading for another scorcher, Andab drives Terry via the caravan crash-site. There was a lot of yellow plastic tape across the hole they had cut in the hedge. The caravan looked empty.

Andab warbled along in his quirky lilting voice. Terry still had no real idea what he was saying, and couldn't quite decide if the accent was funny or irritating, but it was certainly fast!

They pulled into the parking area of the warehouse: empty, not a soul in sight. An involuntary shudder ran through him as the memory of panic and flight rushed back.

No sign of a body. There was a dark patch that could have been blood. But no body.

About to leave, Terry glances up at the pair of green plastic waste bins at one end of the car park. One lid slightly raised, overflowing, and he realises it looks like a dog's leg keeping the lid from closing.

Captain Morgan is not looking his best. A day in the sun hasn't done anything for him either. The Captain is starting to smell.

Andab is putting up serious resistance to the idea of a dead dog being put in the boot of his minicab. Terry has some sympathy for this, the smell is not good at all, but he knows what has to be done. This dog is a hero, a battle-scarred hero. Who has been run over by a caravan, driven by Terry's wife.

"It reeeally smells, man!"

"We'll wrap him up well, it's only a short journey, Andab mate; your cab won't smell at all, I promise."

The promise of an extra £20 for boot-cleaning convinces Andab to allow Terry to gently lower the Captain's body, now encased in several Aldi plastic carrier bags retrieved from the bin, into the boot of his car.

Got to find something better to wrap him in, it's a fucking long journey back to London. He will be high as a kite in this heat. What are we going to do with him anyway? Take him home and bury him in the garden?

He gets Andab to stop for a few minutes at a local Spar, pops in and buys three economy rolls of cling film and a spray-can of air-freshener.

Seal him in, that's the way, and the spray just in case a bit of residue escapes.

"I'll walk from here mate."

Cautious to ensure no one knows where they are staying, Terry has Andab drop him a couple of roads down from Clam Bay, who makes a fuss about the smell in the car boot.

This hasn't been as exciting as the previous excursion, and Andab makes it pretty clear that if Terry needs a cab again, he should probably look elsewhere.

He waits until the minicab is out of sight before heading towards the guest house, awkwardly holding his Aldi-clad dead dog beneath its tummy, trying not to have direct contact with his macabre package.

***

Captain Morgan is leaking onto the bathroom floor.

After a couple of false starts trying to wrap him in the bath, Terry had given up. It was just too awkward to manoeuvre the cling-filmed roll in the confined space. The Captain lies on his side, quite squashed, as Terry tries to work out how best to wrap him up. His legs won't really fold in against his body, so he starts to wrap him in a "dog shape", cling-filming each of his legs first.

Becca can't stop the tears. Sitting on the bed, she turns the TV up to drown out the crackling noise of cling film unrolling and Terry's light panting and sighing from the bathroom.

Terry, in turn, is trying to keep quiet, balancing the Captain on the bathroom stool, his legs hanging down either side, he is not terribly straight after being run over. First mummifying his head and shoulders; and now his leaky backside. The smell is making him retch even with the window wedged wide open. Eventually, only his middle is unwrapped, and Terry stands him up on his stiff, cling-filmed legs, passing the roll under and over repeatedly.

It looks so fucking easy when they wrap up your suitcase in the airport!

Propped up against the bath, held rigid in his cling film tomb, Captain Morgan starts to resemble a strange dog-robot-mannequin as his rich brown fur colours disappear below layer after layer of film.

Can't afford the little chap to leak in the car.

A bit like hoovering in awkward corners – or using a Lady-Shave – it is hard to know when to stop. Round and round, up and down the legs, lengthways nose to tail. Eventually, he had used up all three rolls of cling film and the Captain is no longer leaking; the floor has been cleaned up with toilet paper, and he can be easily carried around.

"Oh my GOD, Terry, what is THAT?"

"He was just getting a bit too smelly. If we are going to get him back to London he needs to be well sealed."

Even Mojito is staring quizzically at the bulging cling-film package.

"It's just very weird Terry, like something off *Doctor Who*. I don't like it *at all*. Take him out to the car. You *will* unwrap him when we get home to bury him, won't you?"

Terry checks that the coast is clear, but Clam Bay Guest House has been largely free from staff since they arrived. The only exception being the bulky teenage girl behind the reception counter, never looking up from her mini iPad, wires hanging down from each ear under long, straggling hair shrouding her face.

The mummified Captain Morgan under his arm, Terry passes by with his package concealed from view by the counter, without attracting a glance.

***

"Don't look at the house love, just keep wheeling the push chair and talking to me. Look straight ahead *and* don't look at the car again until you are well past it."

"What the fuck Dad, who are they anyway? Where *are* you? Is Mum with you? Are you OK?"

"Just keep walking away from the car. We are fine, just having a couple of days away at the coast. How many of them do you think there are in the car? It might be something to do with the insurance claim for the carpet; you *know* what these people are like."

"You are fucking joking! I'm *not* stupid Dad. They are in a blacked-out 'bad-boy' Lexus, sitting across the road from your house, with the engine running, wearing sunglasses. That doesn't sound like insurance men worrying about five hundred quids-worth of carpet, DAD!"

Shit. Shit, fuck and bollocks. Shit!

***

"So, we just can't go just yet Becca. Not until we get this sorted out."

"We can't stay here, surely? How are we going to sort things out by sitting *here*? Are you sure it isn't just a mini-cab or something? We know she's a bit of a drama queen."

"It's definitely not a mini-cab. I'll talk to Robbie down at the nick, see if he can gently move them on or something, but he's not very good with his mobile. It might be a while, I've left him three messages *and* a text, but Becca, it's dangerous; we're safer here for a while. We could always see how that bra fits if we need something to do…"

"Don't try to be funny Terry, that's not even slightly fucking funny! It's in the bin, as you well know!"

***

A quiet Sunday night in the heat of Newcastle, taking Mojito for a walk: Becca in badly fitting jeans and T-shirt, hair tied back, no make-up. Unrecognisable from her performance the day before. Terry in badly fitting jeans and T-shirt, bald head, belly – exactly as he looked the day before.

Sweating in the balmy heat of the Newcastle seaside resort, unable to go home. No plan but to wait.

Nothing from Robbie, their only lifeline. Nothing from Scotch, despite repeated calls and texts, just voicemail.

The klaxon goes off on Terry's phone.

Robbie: *Stay put, got yr message – lads briefed me – they had to get out fast – know what went down – stay there until I call – R.*

Thank fuck!

34

"**JUST TELL TULIP** I've still got raging diarrhoea, I'll wrap up a sample of it and bring it in for everyone to have a look at! And tell her I'll get a bloody sick note from the doctor when I'm well enough to get TO the doctor!"

Terry hangs up and glares at his mobile.

"You'd think I was always off fucking sick Becca. Bloody woman. She's just constantly dropping me in it. Call her a fucking PA – personal assistant – how can you be a personal assistant working from home two days a week? Permanent arse-ache more like!"

"Just don't go there Terry. Three bloody days here… doing NOTHING! Sitting on a boiling, stony beach in deckchairs, afraid to take the dog out in daylight; waiting for your mate to let us know if we'll be fucking MURDERED when we go home! I've cancelled two days at work, Pilates, a hair appointment AND my weekly visit to mum, and YOU'RE surprised that your PA, the one that cited you for 'mental harassment' to HR, is not covering for you when you lie through your teeth about where you are. So now you are in trouble with everyone at work over it, you tell her you are going to bring a handful of your own diarrhoea in for her to have a look at for Christ's sake!"

***

All they have had for three days is the occasional text from Robbie telling them to "hold on", a number of texts from Mercedes confirming the continued presence of the blacked-out car, interspersed with details of the continued mayhem of her sex life.

The only bit of good news from Mercedes was that "Sha's getting married." Terry and Becca asked her to send their best wishes to her, and sympathy to the monosyllabic West Ham footballer, with too much cash, that she had managed to nab. Clearly the Sweat Lodge had been a cathartic experience for everyone.

They had kept up the insurance story, texting rather than talking to Mercedes; easier to keep up the lie on text.

Radio silence from Scotch.

Conversation is now completely strained after endlessly picking over what might or might not happen to them when they get home. Becca, unable to settle to anything more consuming than *Hello, OK, Cosmo, Elle* and endless magazines, has now started Christmas shopping on the iPad, but the intermittent Clam Bay Wi-Fi is not improving her mood. He had managed to persuade the hotel to let them borrow a DVD player for their room. Becca had made him sit through season three of *Sex and*

The City, a full *Bake-Off* competition and season one of *Downton Abbey*…again.

Purgatory.

***

Moved them on Tel – safe for now – but not sure for how long – Robbie

Thanks R. Can we come back then?

Yes – but wait till tonight – still very awkward sitch – careful up there tho Tel – they are still looking for u – stick to back roads for a bit – R

***

"Thank God Terry, this is driving me *mad*. Is it actually sorted out, or are we just going home to wait around to be murdered?"

"Yes, we'll probably be murdered pretty much as soon as we get home…I DON'T FUCKING KNOW BECCA! I am trying to work it out, but it's no bloody good just sitting here watching soaps on a twenty-year-old TV, and buying fucking Christmas decorations on Amazon; it's still only June Pet!

At least if we are home we can talk properly to Robbie; make plans; find out how Scotch is, all that good stuff. They've got our sodding money too – so we could do with sorting it out before the taxman sells the fucking house out from under us WHILE we are being murdered!"

FUCK – why did I say all that, she's going to cry for an hour now!

"It's OK Becca, I'm sorry. Just frustrated and a bit scared. I know you are too. Let's pack up and get ourselves ready to go."

***

Tel – it's Scotch – that nasty Donald fucker been to visit me – they know where you live – I reckon they are going to bloody kill me – nurse threw them out – they want to talk to you. Legs in plaster up to the hips – fucking hurts – call when I can – gotta keep mobile off in here – S

***

Terry opens the rear door of the Range Rover to put their bags in, it must be one hundred degrees in there, and a simply foul smell makes him reach almost instantly. Hand over his nose, he opens each door in turn and heads back inside to find the air freshener.

Back with the car, he throws the holdalls in the boot on top of the wellie bags, boxes of toys, and accumulated detritus. He gingerly moves round the side of the car and peers in.

Captain Morgan has grown. Substantially.

Inside the car, in the full sun for three days, Captain Morgan's gasses have gradually escaped and expanded. His plastic tomb is no longer dog-shaped: more like a giant dough balloon; more white now than silver – and at least 50% bigger, laying there on the beige leather back seat, the smell less pungent now. Terry empties half the pine bathroom spray around the inside of the car.

Not really a good development this. How are we going to drive home with the smell? And how the fuck am I going to get him out of that lot to bury him?!

***

Terry squints as he peers through the darkness of the windscreen at the teeming rain. The oppressive heat had to end some time, they could have just done *without* the torrential fucking rain tonight, but at least it should give them cover!

Only one headlight seems to be working, and all the windows open despite the rain; déjà vu! Heading south, but sticking to minor roads for an hour or so, they should have reached the motorway a while ago, he is sure; the sat nav helpfully shows their position as a cursor slowly moving across a field, no roads in sight.

Useless piece of shit, you would think we were on another fucking planet rather than sunny Newcastle.

Becca sits beside him, a scarf pressed over her mouth and nose, her shoulder wet from the incoming rain.

The smell keeps catching in his throat: a rich, gamey, rotting smell. He keeps feeling a prickling sensation in his face: anxiety, he is getting to know it well, *high* anxiety.

High – High – So High So-cie, High So-ci-ety…altogether now…

Fucking Louis Armstrong; keep singing it though, thinking is a fucking bad idea…

Mojito lies on the back seat beside his smelly dough cousin, peering intently as the giant malformed balloon rocks gently with the motions of the car.

Dough-Dog is actually hot to the touch now, and the bottom is clearly darker, some sort of liquid. Captain Morgan is quietly fermenting.

Not surprising really, he's been in a slow pressure cooker here for three fucking days.

Cling film! Who would be so stupid to use that much fucking cling film? It was SO hot in the car, sitting baking in the sun. FUCK.

"Tel, he's doing it again!"

Terry slows a little and glances back over his shoulder at Mojito nuzzling unpleasantly against the mummified Captain.

"Mojito! NO! Leave it ALONE!"

He shouts at the rear-view mirror he has angled downwards to keep an eye on activities on the back seat. Mojito had been paying a completely unhealthy interest in the new Captain Morgan, nuzzling intently against the cling film – *most* unhealthy.

Mojito looks up at Terry in the mirror with his good eye, the other still slightly closed and swollen from battle. Keeping eye contact all the time, he rolls his head sideways and starts gently gnawing with his sharp little teeth at the cling film around Captain's belly: a thin, needy whine coming from his bared teeth.

"NO, MOJITO – NO, YOU LITTLE BASTARD!"

"Why is he doing that? Please stop him Tel!"

Spotting a gap to pull over, Terry slows the car to a crawl and stops. Seat belt released, he turns in his seat to Mojito, tugging now, his teeth digging into the cling film, biting down.

"ENOUGH MOJITO – NO!"

Reaching over to pull Mojito away by his collar, and as Mojito moves away from the reaching hand his teeth finally tear their way through. A fine mist sprays, under pressure, from the cling film, hitting Terry in the face. As he starts to recoil, Mojito's bite hits the jackpot and Captain Morgan's juices jet in the direction of the front of the car.

Becca, who has not really been watching the scene unfolding, screams as "juice" hits her hair; and then something far worse invades her nostrils. Terry is roaring, a deep primal noise, as he wipes frantically at his face. Breathing in deeply, he gags and throws himself out of the car onto the muddy roadside, falling to his knees, retching uncontrollably.

He hears vomiting: Becca is still strapped in, arms over her face, upright in her seat. He drags himself to his feet, slipping in the mud, the rain still battering the ground around him; lurching round to her side of the car, he wrenches open the door.

Becca is heaving deeply, covered in sick, but he reaches through it to unfasten her seat belt and lifts her bodily out of the Range Rover, and falls back into a deep muddy puddle, his arms still clamped around Becca's back.

Releasing her, both covered in sick, dog-juice and mud, they are on their knees scrabbling handfuls of muddy water over their faces, hair, trying to wash off the awful smell, with the rain beating on their backs. Becca is crying hysterically. Terry awkwardly attempts to help her wash, scrub away the mess with puddle water.

Mojito is lying gasping in the rear footwell. Terry grips his back legs and pulls him from the car, landing with a thump. He is clearly very distressed. The smell coming from him is truly awful, having taken the brunt of the Captain Morgan explosion.

Terry rolls him around in the deep muddy puddle he and Becca have been wallowing in, rubbing his face and head around in an attempt to wash out the stench. Mojito starts to come round and also starts heaving. Eventually, he looks up at Terry with a mournful, pained expression. He had loved the Captain, and only wanted to play, but the Captain had turned on him in a most unpleasant fashion; it was all a bit much...

Terry turns away, on his hands and knees, he can't help anyone anymore. He can't help himself – a feeling of total despair wells up inside him, and he too begins to sob, deep, wracking, endless sobs.

Time passes and he feels Becca's hand on the back of his head, comforting him.

"It's all right, it's all right."

It's not all right, but he slowly pulls himself together and they help each other to their feet.

Through the rain and heavy human panting, Terry hears the phone on his hip buzz urgently; he had managed to switch off the fucking klaxon.

Wearily, sliding a muddy thumb over the screen – a text from Mercedes:

Sry Dad, L8 agn – think its no 2 – REELY Sry – can u tell Mum xxxxx M

He sighs; it's always nice to hear from his daughter.

35

MOJITO WATCHES HIS parents "mucking out" the car: foot mats thrown into the ditch, a Millwall scarf used to swab down the juices from the seatbacks, seats, windscreen; repeatedly rinsed out in the muddy puddles.

Captain Dough-Dog is carefully pulled from the seat, Terry applying gentle pressure to the package, pointing the opening carefully away from himself, like expressing milk from a giant leathery tit, firmly pressing down until the stretched cling-film bubble is no longer straining.

The whole soggy, stinking thing now zipped and wrapped in Terry's rolled-up raincoat from the boot, is carefully lowered into the footwell; Mojito laying on the wet-but less-foul back seat, his eyes fixed intently on Terry's offending raincoat contents.

Terry and Becca sit side by side, soaking and muddy, in silence as they continue their journey back to South London.

"Hap-hap-hap-hap happy thoughts…talk about things

*you'd like to dooooo…you've got to have a dream, if you don't
have a dream, how you gonna make a dream come true…"*

Where the fuck did THAT one come from?

He feels calm now, completely fucked, but not anxious.

I've had enough; fucking ENOUGH.

***

Five hours later, the storms long past, fresh air is a blessed
relief as he pulls up at the lock-up. It seems ridiculously big
for Mojito on his own as Terry shuts him into his night-
cage, not shutting the door, just leaving him to curl up on
his blanket.

"Well done mate; we know you didn't mean to make all
that mess – well done boy."

Becca is still asleep, wedged up against the window as
they arrive home. They can decide what to do with Captain
Morgan in the morning…or later in the morning; the car can't
get much worse for leaving him in there a few more hours.

***

God…this is fucking good.

4am, half-asleep, they shower together, the hot water
washing away the awful residues and filth of the journey.
He attempts to help Becca wash her hair, but just gets his
fingers tangled.

"Use the sponge Terry, *don't* just grope me Lamb, we are
going to sleep; just sleep."

Funny how you can fancy a grapple at the most unlikely time.

Terry defers to the sponge, but it *is* still rather nice.

Becca climbs out of the shower, leaving him standing, eyes shut under the hot torrent, almost nodding off in the warm bliss of cleansing.

***

Terry wakes to the penetrating ring of his mobile: it is nearly midday. The caller shows as "Scotch".

He picks up the phone and turns it off. He has been expecting the call. Terry places the phone back on the bedside table and rolls over to hold Becca, her hair still damp inside the towel-turban. She smells clean and rather wonderful. He dozes.

In his shorts and a Cat-in-The-Hat T-shirt, he sits in the kitchen stirring his coffee, two sweeteners; a fresh, as yet untouched cheese and marmalade "doorstep" sits on the plate in front of him, the bread not quite thawed, straight from the freezer. He dwells for a while on the pleasure of sandwich-making with frozen bread – the enforced wait while the whole thing relaxes and warms, in an almost sensual way, sensing its seductive "eat me" vibrations.

Turning his mobile on, he presses the green "answer" button: Scotch's name pops up as the last caller, Terry presses it again, and the phone rings.

***

"Thank God Tel. I need you to talk to these bastards…"
"Terry…"

A new voice, clearly fitting Donald, deliberate, accent softened.

"I'm sitting with your Scots friend Terry. He discharged himself. And now… you've got something I want…that little puppy of yours."

Terry says nothing, listening.

"Your boy here shot one of my men, he shouldn't have done that. So I'll do you a big old favour: just bring the dog, and everyone can get on with their lives."

Nothing still.

"If you don't of course…it will be bad. Very bad, especially for your friend here; he'll just disappear; probably a bit at a time…and of course, we know where you live, we know where your family lives, so be a sensible boy now."

Terry allows the silence to grow.

Nothing wrong with a good silence.

"You done now, Geordie boy? Good. Now fuck off with your threats. You owe me money. Twenty-seven and a half prize money *and* my winnings from the bookies – you *own* all the bookies so let's not fuck about arguing that one. Call me back when you have worked out when and how you are going to pay it."

Terry hangs up the phone and picks up the sandwich.

The secret is the marmalade, strong cheddar and really dark bitter marmalade, darker the better. Brilliant.

The phone vibrates beside him, switched to "silent"; Scotch's name lighting up. He ignores it and sips the coffee and works his way round the sandwich, nibbling wherever the marmalade starts to ease its way out.

The phone rings soundlessly three times.

A decent sandwich always makes you feel good about yourself…hope this fucking works.

Half an hour later, Terry picks up the phone and rings

Scotch's number. It is answered almost immediately, and he just launches.

"So, *you* can fucking listen up this time. I really don't care if you kill the little Scots fucker; in fact, do me a favour and put him out of his misery for me. He shouldn't have been carrying. But your man was right out of fucking order when he touched my missus; NOBODY TOUCHES MY MISSUS; DO YOU FUCKING UNDERSTAND?! NOBODY! So…THIS is what's going to happen…"

Terry hangs up without waiting for an answer.

***

Terry only mentioned the "Millwall firm" once – but he knew, deep inside, with total conviction that the day was HIS. He was in the right. Donald had broken all the rules allowing his man to carry a gun, AND touch his woman. AND Terry had something Donald HAD to have.

***

"I just don't understand. We were hiding away, terrified one minute, and now we get all the money back; probably get Scotch back. And he said he was '*sorry*'! He was going to kill us Tel. I just don't get it!"

"He probably would have Becca; up there, before we got back; before Robbie tapped up his boys in the car. He thinks I have the entire Millwall firm to call on, the nastiest bunch of hard-man hooligans you have ever met, *and* the local fuzz. He *knows* the fight circuit takes a dim view of shooters. His hired help hurt a woman in front of everyone. It's all about '*show*' up there; all that fucking bling Becca. But most of all: he was desperate to have Mojito."

"But he hasn't *got* Mojito Tel."

"No…but he'll borrow him from time to time. No more fighting; he is *absolutely* fucking famous now, and all they want is plenty of little baby Mojitos, which I am sure he will enjoy helping them with. Three weeks, three times a year, for two years. They will treat him like a king Becca. And, at the end of that, a quick snip at the vet, that they witness, so they are the only ones who can *ever* have a little Mojito, and we are all done."

"Mojito…did he do that on purpose, that falling onto his back stuff? Just to get in position? That's horrible Terry."

Sure he did. Scotch says they all keep watching the video of it on an iPhone – convinced themselves it was quite deliberate.

"A salute to 'horrible' Becca; but we'll never know. As long as anyone thinks he did it on purpose…then he did."

Raising a mock toast with his coffee cup, he reaches for Becca, his hand round her waist, pulling her close.

"You smell of marmalade Terry, and cheese…it's not sexy you know, but you are a very clever man; MY clever man!"

Terry glows: a good glow, better than he has felt in a long time. He nuzzles Becca's neck, still hopeful…

Not *all* the money was coming back: the prize money, yes; and the stake money back from the bookies; and even some of the winnings, but Scotch was in such bad shape he wasn't sure what he had bet and with whom. Donald was paying seventy-five grand for *exclusive* "stud services" from Mojito, but only fifteen up front and the rest spread over the two years, assuming he didn't fire blanks.

"Why don't you go and get the Captain out of the car? Dig him a nice hole in the garden, we'll say our goodbyes."

Lovely…just what I had been thinking of doing.

36

BECCA PUTS THE phone down and turns to look at Terry.

"He *actually* sounded like quite a nice man."

"He probably is Doll, under the silly fucking hairdo and the bling; the need to surround himself with showy bouncers; and a temper that could have had us both dead... quite a nice man."

"Alright smart-ass, but at least he *did* apologise!"

The apology had cost him five grand; at least the part where Donald apologised for running over the Captain, quite a stretch considering he had actually watched Becca drive the caravan over him.

That had probably been the trickiest part of the negotiations, and only when Terry had asked him if he was married too had he finally relented; at a price.

"He was genuinely upset about running over the Captain Terry. I think he probably cares more about the dogs than people. I don't feel so bad about Mojito going up there for the 'ladies' now."

It's the mark of a man when he sounds more convincing when he is lying than telling the truth.

***

He was quite short of cash still!

Even with the prize winnings from Newcastle, and his stake money back, they had needed more of those bookies winnings, *and* more up-front for Mojito's stud services; but at least he would have the money for the next couple of repayments in the schedule. It was all staring to feel slightly more manageable

***

"We ARE onto something Dad. I know I SAID I was pregnant again, but it turns out I'm not. I WAS a bit pissed when I did the test! I'm really sorry I scared you. I WILL be really careful; but I have finally found something I want to do with my life Dad. Something I am good at – finally!"

Terry and Becca sit on the sofa opposite their chubby, nineteen-year-old, not-pregnant daughter while she outlines her plans for an "exotic dancing troupe" to tour pubs and clubs in the area and "perhaps beyond".

"We are already bloody famous on YouTube: 120,000 'views'; do you know how many that is?! And…I am going to be an 'influencer', an 'Instagram influencer' – my followers are interested in EVERYTHING, what I say, what I think, what I wear – it's brilliant AND you can make real money from it by wearing Primark things and saying how much you like a nail varnish and everything."

To add insult to injury, Tas, his own sister – *who should know fucking better* – sat on the sofa beside Mercedes, now appears to be the troupe "manager", or maybe she was just their "guru"!

"They are in safe hands with me Terry, I won't let them get exploited. Karma will be there too, taking care of them. He's really looking forward to it. I've made him a special costume and everything. You should trust us; I *know* this will work out well. I've been 'told' Terry."

They had auditioned Karma, introducing them with some sort of soundlessly menacing "mime", standing there in just a loincloth to exaggerate his now-recovered lunchbox.

After everything they have been through in the last few months, this actually feels nearly normal: his teen-mother daughter, with her tit still strapped up from the last accident, describing how the pregnancy-testing kit was "fucked up" by all the booze and "E" she was full of while attempting to collect and test her urine.

His sister sat there, wearing a sort of "cape" made from what appeared to be old squirrels, not just their skins, telling him to trust them, for their sound fucking judgement.

"Say *yes* dad, pleeeeease! We've got two of my other mates involved now, three different acts: *The Poles*, *Weird Hula* and the *Snake Dance*; it's fucking brilliant, Dad…Mum…"

Never seen either of them so excited about anything before – if we say no, they will just do it anyway.

Becca sits beside him, her mouth slightly open in a forced half-smile, hoping Terry will just make this go away.

"And, Mum, Dad, I've got to get rid of that arsehole of a boyfriend. Out of my life. Good bloody riddance. Chloe and I will be *much* better off without him."

I suppose there had to be some good news in there somewhere.

"Well, your mother and I probably need to talk about this. It was really good to tell us about this stuff rather than just going and doing it like last time."

Oh God…I think that means I just said yes.

***

3am. Terry can't sleep. He lies there naked, on his back, beside Becca, one hand resting gently on his crotch as an assortment of events meander through his mind: the surreal burial, as he had tipped the fetid bundle of dog and cling film, still wrapped in his raincoat, into the hole he had dug at the end of the garden. Tas making an elaborate display of dropping in a feathery dream-catcher to "Catch the dreams of The Dog". Becca had said a eulogy, ending with "… and Donald says he is really sorry", which sends a shudder through him even now.

That whole bizarre tableau, as his daughter and sister unfolded their plans; the double-edged sword of finding his daughter wasn't actually expecting number two, tempered with the drugs and alcohol that had interfered with the test.

And then the good bits: the fear had gone away. Becca had been unusually encouraging when he had appeared doing his hip-hop routine in his silkiest black undies, leading to a simply brilliant exploration of the "arrow" and delicious suggestions around where other tattoos might appear; they had only actually made love once, but had rolled around "playing" for ages. Fucking brilliant…

***

He can feel sleep start to descend, but rolls out of bed to take a pee.

Don't want to be waking up when it's taken this long to get off to sleep.

Walking along the landing, yawning, Terry glances out of the window. A figure approaches his car, ghostly in the glow of the streetlamp, and from the roadside leans across the bonnet of the car. And from the small package clutched in its hand, carefully turns out a large turd, stark against the white paintwork, right in the middle.

Terry has stopped breathing, standing rigid as he watches Darren hurry away down the road. He is absolutely still for an age.

He stands in the bathroom, leaning forward, his hand on the wall above the cistern, leaning slightly, peeing into the basin, staring at the disturbed water.

He washes his hands and returns to the bedroom, Becca is asleep, he gets into bed and lays, staring, thinking.

37

A HUGE, OVERDEVELOPED arm extends around Darren's neck from behind as he turns the corner, walking down to the 7:11 to buy a few scratch cards.

The roll-up flies out from between his lips as the burly arm lifts him off the ground, wrapping a hand across his face.

Another arm, from his second assailant, snakes around his legs, just above the knees and he is carried swiftly and efficiently to the waiting white van parked thirty yards back round the corner he had just come from.

The arm round his throat, constricting his windpipe makes crying out impossible.

The rear doors of the van open, duct tape swiftly wound round his mouth, then his eyes, wrists and finally ankles – Darren is dumped unceremoniously into the van, he hears the doors shut, and a few seconds later the van moves away.

***

Terry opens the door to the lock-up as the van pulls up outside, the two heavies move round to the back door, open it up, and carry Darren, as if he were weightless, on his back. One with a hand holding him aloft through the V of his T-shirt, the other holding the duct tape between his ankles.

He opens the lid of the battered chest freezer used to keep the frozen meat for the dogs – which has been stacked in a couple of large crates, it won't thaw in the twenty minutes it will be out.

"We are just going to cool you down a little Darren, you are starting to pong a bit mate."

Darren is gently lowered into the freezer on his back, plenty of room. Terry reaches in and unwraps the tape from his eyes and mouth. Darren gulps deeply, and looks into Terry's eyes as he quietly shuts the lid. Terry hops up backwards into a sitting position on the lid.

There are kicking and struggling noises from inside, and expletives. Now that the contents of the freezer knows that Terry has put him there, he has discovered a new lease of life, and screams threats of appalling, slow retribution.

"Fuckin', fuckin' FUCKER…you FUCKER, I'm SO gonna fuck you – and that fucking bitch daughter of yours. FUCKERRRR – LET ME OUT YOU FUCKERRR"

Terry sits on the freezer smiling. He has been waiting to do this forever. Never mind Darren's mindless, butcher-boy brothers, and his lumbering alcoholic father – this is just a priceless moment, and it is going to get better.

The stream of abuse continues for about five minutes,

and Terry talks loudly and clearly at the freezer, he knows he can be heard inside.

"You should probably stop shouting Darren, the air in there won't last long. We don't want you suffocating before you freeze to death mate, honestly, it will burn your lungs up and you need to just listen for a minute, just listen."

There are a few more plaintive kicks from inside, a few more "fuckers", and a quite incessant use of the C-word – and then it goes quiet.

The freezer is set to minus fifteen degrees. The boys have told Terry that about twenty minutes is the longest you can leave anyone in there before they are in serious trouble, he doesn't ask them how they know this quite so accurately. Darren is a skinny little runt, so he reckons eighteen minutes should be good.

The freezer has been carefully placed right beside the spring pole, and as Terry says "Listen", one of the heavies leads Mojito over and lifts him up onto the pole.

Joyously, noisily, the heavy chain dangling from his collar, just for the additional sound effects, Mojito snarls and shakes away at the rubber ring on the pole.

Inside the freezer this doesn't sound like particularly good news as Darren shivers and tries to stop his teeth chattering.

At fifteen minutes, Mojito is lifted down and pads off for a walk with the big kind chap who lifted him up to play.

***

At eighteen minutes, Terry opens the lid. Darren doesn't look so good.

Should have worn a few more clothes.

"Now, Darren, I am sure you realise that we need a bit of a chat."

The tears have frozen onto Darren's cheeks, the moisture in the air from all that shouting has frozen onto his hair and eyebrows and created a fine white film on his T-shirt. His hands are taped in front of his chest, wrapped round each other.

"You Darren, are going to go away. You are going to go away, and never see or contact my daughter again. Ever again. Is that clear Darren?"

Darren is blinking, trying to defrost his eyes, he is wriggling in an attempt to get to his feet, into the warm, out of the freezer.

"Now Darren, I know that you would like to threaten me with your two scumbag brothers and your vicious old alcy dad. But that is not what is going to happen Darren, because you are going to go away, and go away REALLY quietly Darren."

Darren is starting to thaw a little, the icy base of the chest freezer burning his back as he shifts from side to side, and the hatred is returning to his eyes.

"And now Darren, I am going to show you *why* you are going to do what you are told."

Terry reaches down and pulls Darren upright, onto his feet, facing Terry and the exercise ring on its chain hanging from the garage roof. There are four robust metre square cages along the wall beneath them. Darren takes this all in.

"And now, Darren, you will understand why you are going to do what I tell you."

Terry turns Darren ninety degrees to face the end of the freezer.

***

Karma never really understood why Terry wanted to take him along to the lock-up, he had asked Tas if Karma could help him out with a little chore, said he needed some muscle, and Tas, happy that her brother was starting to get on with Karma, had happily agreed and waved them off.

He had agreed at Terry's insistence to take one of Terry's blue pills, and when offered enough money, had also agreed to pose in his gold lamé loincloth at the end of the lock-up, though the Viagra was making the loincloth quite difficult to keep done up.

***

When Darren turns towards Karma, he blinks a little to focus, then his eyes widen. Terry leans over and says clearly and quietly, "He likes to use the chains, but he is pretty tired now."

Terry slings Darren over his shoulder and carries him easily over to Karma – Darren is fucking cold. Karma, six feet, five inches, smothered in massage oil, holds Darren in his arms like a baby, trussed feet and hands. Terry whips off Karma's loincloth and dashes back to the freezer, picks up his iPad, and begins snapping, gesturing to Karma to move around for the best angles to shoot from. The Viagra is working well, terrifyingly well

Retrieving Darren, he sits him on the floor in front of Karma, who looks down at him with a huge, toothy grin, before pulling up his appendage against his stomach, picking up his loincloth, and walking away to get dressed.

Karma smiles at Terry as he walks away, looking for approval – Terry nods his head grimly and gives a half-smile.

Again, quietly, very controlled:

"It's important you understand what the Beast likes to do to skinny little lads like you, hanging from that chain. He will do it to you in front of your brothers, and then he will do it to them too. I will send you a few photos to remind you. If I ever see you again, the first thing I will do is post these photos on Instagram, I think that's the thing everyone is using these days, and then the boys will come and get you for the real thing rather than just a practice run like tonight."

Terry pulls a strip of tape across Darren's eyes, and calls the boys back in from the van outside, who soundlessly and efficiently pick Darren up, drop him into the van, and reverse their journey.

***

There would be no more shit on the car, and hopefully no more grandchildren for a bit. Terry drives the Range Rover back through the streets of Peckham, Karma sitting beside him – the oil, not properly rubbed off, staining the leather of the car seats. He is smiling, a big black and white grin, and so is Terry.